引領您在銷售與業務上 學會了解客戶需求的必備絕招、
領悟和上司、同事間打好關係、達成團隊合作的關鍵技巧...
跟著本書的**36**堂職場攻略課 + **34**部票房電影
一躍成為**行銷**、**業務**與**國貿高手**

全書有30餘部電影經典台詞、100多句好用延伸句型
外加140餘則公關銷售、餐廳飯店業務、職場人際關係等相關技巧與話術
助你從電影吸收情境對話，練就一身英語好功夫，同時極速掌握職場專業知識！

生意情境 與 對應電影搶先看：
【銷售】**個人電腦之過耳不忘的口號篇**— 看《穿著Prada的惡魔》關鍵台詞怎麼說
【推銷】**最新型手機型號** — 由《全面啟動》了解客戶使用手機的需求
【房仲】**介紹商辦大樓** — 善用《美國心玫瑰情》句型 強調環境與設施的便利性
【飯店業務】**面對客戶不合理的需求** — 讓《女傭變鳳凰》教你化解危機

作者序

正所謂戲如人生，人生如戲，電影雖然虛幻，有時候當中的台詞卻又貼近人生。在英語學習的路上，由於題材多元，電影一直都是很好的練習素材。為了強化情緒張力，電影台詞的句型變化性豐富，經典台詞往往也為人所津津樂道。本書為活用經典台詞，並將之作為語文學習之輔助，特參考收錄 30 餘部電影的經典台詞，並安排數種常用句型，將其應用在行銷公關、業務與國貿三大領域的對話中，輔以相關商學概念的解說，讓學習商用英文不再如此制式且生硬。

邱佳翔

目次 CONTENTS

Part 1 公關行銷篇

Part 2 業務生意篇

3 Part 國際貿易篇

Part 1

行銷公關篇

看《穿著 Prada 的惡魔》（*The Devil Wears Prada*），公司形象要顧好

篇章重點搶先看

1. 本章將從《穿著 Prada 的惡魔》（*The Devil Wears Prada*）耐吉爾與安德莉雅的對話場景切入，強調公司形象（image）與行銷間的關係。
2. 從耐吉爾與安德莉雅說的這句：*"You think this is just a magazine, hmm? This is not just a magazine. This is a shining beacon of hope."*「你以為這只是一本雜誌？這不只是一本雜誌，還是希望的燈塔。」學習本單元核心句型：

   ★You think...? This is not just... This is...「你以為這只是…，但這不只是，還是…」。
3. 搭配學習本單元其他三大重點句型：

   a. Thank you for +Ving（感謝您…）

   b. ... while（…當…）

   c. Since..., we/our...（因為…，我們…）
4. 將四種句型放入實境對話練習，學習四大行銷概念：

   a. 吸引觀眾注意（attention）。

   b. 以重複手法（repeat）加深印象。

   c. 以比較手法（comparison）突顯差異。

   d. 強調產品前景（marketability）。

影片背景介紹

《穿著 Prada 的惡魔》敘述從大學畢業的安德莉雅（Andrea），應徵上時尚雜誌《伸展台》（Runway）總編輯米蘭達（Miranda）的個人助理一職。米蘭達對時尚界有極大的影響力，但也因為個性冷酷，是位讓人敬畏的主管。在片中，安德莉雅由於無法替老闆訂到機票，使得老闆沒能及時返抵紐約，因而遭到米蘭達的斥責語羞辱。受辱的安德莉雅向中階主管耐吉爾（Nigel）訴苦，此場景是說明公司形象很重要的好教材。安德莉雅認為自己跟時尚毫無關聯，但耐吉爾藉此機會告訴她，時尚大師的作品、概念深深影響我們的生活，我們日常服飾的設計都是源自這些先驅的概念，而伸展台就是大師們揮灑想像的空間。

The Devil Wears Prada is a movie that describes a young woman named Andrea who is hired as an assistant to Miranda, the editor-in-chief of *Runway* magazine. Miranda has won the renown for her achievements in fashion, but her icy image also makes her a boss be feared. In this movie, Andrea fails to book a flight for her boss, so Miranda isn't able to get back to New York in time. Miranda is so angry that she blames and insults Andrea. Feeling insulted, Andrea grumbles out her upset to Nigel. The conversation between them shows the importance of the brand image. Andrea thinks fashion is nothing, but Nigel retorts that fashion is around us. The designs of clothes we wear come from the brilliant ideas of fashion designers. And *Runway* is the place passionate fashion designers showcase their works to the public.

看影片怎麼說、怎麼用

At the conference room of ABC Company.

（在 ABC 公司的會議室。）

Jason: Good morning, Ken, (1) thank you for sparing your time. Before starting my presentation today, can I ask you one question?

Jason：早安，Ken，感謝您撥空。在我開始今天的簡報之前，可以先問您一個問題嗎？

Ken: Sure, what is it?

Ken：當然可以，是怎樣的問題呢？

Jason: What's the first **image** about our latest personal computer, TXP-7895?

Jason：請問您對我們的新款個人電腦 TXP-7895 的第一印象如何?

Ken: The first thought that came into my mind is its smaller size.

Ken：我首先想到的是尺寸較小。

Jason: True. (2) You may think it is just a personal computer. This is not just a personal computer. This is a **milestone** in digital devices.

Jason：沒錯。你可能認為這只是一台個人電腦，但它不只是一台電腦，它還是數位裝置的里程碑。

Ken: It sounds this computer is quite different. I am excited to know what makes this computer so special, so please start your briefing now.

Ken：聽起來這台電腦相當與眾不同，我很想知道為何它能如此特別，所以請開始簡報吧！

Jason: Thank you for showing a great interest in our new computer. Now let me show you how capable this computer could

Jason：感謝您對此電腦有興趣，現在讓我像您展示這台電腦有多棒。我們都知道

be. As we know, **efficiency** somehow can't co-exist with **portability**. (3) The one with high efficiency is often bigger in size, while the thinner or smaller one provides lower efficiency. However, we have found the **solution** now.

效能常無法與可攜性並存。高效能的電腦尺寸都較大，而輕薄小型電腦無法具備高效能。但現在我們找出解決方案了。

Ken: It is really a great breakthrough.

Ken：這真的是個重大突破。

Jason: (4) Since we have **minimized** the new chip size and enhanced its efficiency to the **optimization**, our new personal computer now is smaller but more powerful. Now let me make a comparison, the size of the one on your left side is the smallest with the highest efficiency in the market, while the one on the right is quite the contrary. We can tell that ours is much smaller. Though it is small, the efficiency is not sacrificed. The performance is even better than your expectation because you can run several programs at once. This computer will **revolutionize** the high-end PC soon.

Jason：因為我們已研發出尺寸最小，但卻把效能提升至最佳的新晶片，我們的新電腦才能體積輕巧但效能強大。現在讓我們來做個比較，在左手邊的是市面上體積最小的高效能電腦，右邊的是我們新款。我們可以看出右邊的體積明顯較小。雖然它體積小，但並未因此犧牲效能。它的效能甚至比你預期的還更好，因為它可以同時執行多個程式。這台電腦很快就會掀起高階個人電腦的革命。

Ken: Can I try it?

Ken：請問我可以試試看它的性能嗎？

Jason: Sure.

Jason：當然可以。

對話單字說分明

1. **image** *n.* 形象

例：The brand image is way more important than we think.
品牌形象遠比我們想的還重要。

2. **milestone** *n.* 里程碑

例：This portable device is a milestone in the sport industry.
此穿戴裝置是運動產業的一個新里程碑。

3. **efficiency** *n.* 效能

例：Our new chips have high efficiency.
我們公司的新晶片具備高效能。

4. **portability** *n.* 可攜性

例：High portability is the advantage of our new toolkit.
高可攜性是我們新工具組的優點。

5. **solution** *n.* 解決方法

例：The solution we have now is to cut the budget in personnel.
我們現有的解決方法就是削減人事預算。

6. **minimize** *v.* 最小化

例：The case size has been minimized to save the fright.
外盒尺寸已縮至最小以便節省運費。

7. **optimization** *n.* 最優化

例：The efficiency reaches the optimization after adjustment.
調整過後效能達到最佳。

8. **revolutionize** *v.* 徹底改變

例：The system will revolutionize our way of shopping.
此系統將會徹底改變我們的購物方式。

重點句型分析

1. **Thank you for Ving** 意思為「感謝…」，由於 for 是介系詞，其後所接之動作應為動名詞（V+ing）。用來說明感謝對方的事由。

   例：Thank you for participating in our product release.
   感謝您參與我們的新品發表會。

2. **You think this is just... This is not just... This is...** 意思為「你認為這只是…，但這不只…，還是…。」，是 This is…的句型的堆疊，可以用來突顯事物的特別性。

   例：You think this is just a car. This is not just car. This is a castle with unlimited possibility.
   你認為這只是台車。這不只是台車。還是個充滿無限可能的城堡。

3. **... while...** 意思為「…但…」，可用於比較前後兩者的不同之處。

   例：The one on your left side is the normal version, while the one on your right is the flagship version.
   在您左手邊的是普通版，在右手邊的則是旗艦版。

4. **Since..., we/our...** 意思為「因為…，我／我們…」，可用於說明事情的原因。

   例：Since we have solved the problem, our product can be released as scheduled.
   由於我們已解決問題，產品可以如期上市。

職場補給站

行銷是一門非常特別的學問，因為它同時包含多種層面。不論學校的行銷課程內容再怎樣包羅萬象，也只能傳授學生理論上的專業知識與技能，實際踏入職場，還是需要靠經驗的累積，才能真正成為優秀的行銷人員。

行銷，也可說是科學與藝術的巧妙組合，因為行銷需要透過數據與許多科學方法來評估或是擬定策略，但在實際執行時，因為可能遭遇的情況太多，且沒有所謂的正確答案，就如同藝術一般。

在本單元的範例對話中提到四個行銷的常用概念，以下針對每個概念做進一步說明：

1. 如何抓住觀眾注意

- 對應句型：**Thank you for sparing your time.**

  正如上段所述，行銷並無所謂的標準答案，但有一點是所有行銷企劃所一體適用的，那就是必須先抓住觀眾的注意。一旦能夠吸引觀眾的目光，就已邁開銷售的第一步。而吸引注意力的方式有很多種，有的是靠花俏的輔助物來引人注意，有的則是猜測觀眾或消費者的心態來產生認同，抑或是放低姿態讓顧客覺得自己備受尊重。以本範例對話為例，採用的就是第三種手法。**在對話的開頭，Jason 就先對 Ken 願意撥空聆聽產品簡報表示感謝。不論最後 Ken 是否願意購買產品，這樣的行銷操作手法能夠讓對方不論對公司或是產品都能留下好印象。**

2. 以重複手法加深印象：

- 對應句型：**You may think is just a personal computer. This is not just a personal computer. This is a milestone in digital devices.**

  在推銷產品或服務時，其重點之一就是讓對方留下印象。當對方對產品有越深的印象，最後就越可能掏錢購買。加深的印象的方法同樣是五花八門，有的人可能會想出搞笑的廣告詞，讓人一聽難忘。也有人會運用聯想法，透過其他意象來擴大產品或是服務的涵蓋性。而也有人相當直接，就是重複產品或服務的某些特點，讓觀眾或顧客在不知不覺中接收乃至於接受了這些特性。本範例對話中的第二種手法就是重複法。**在對話中，Ken 認為 Jason 所要介紹的電腦不過就是尺寸比小一些而已，因此 Jason 就用堆疊 this is 句型向他說明體積輕巧只是這台電腦的優點之一，公司所推出的新型電腦還有他沒看到的優點。**

3. 以比較手法凸顯差異：

- 對應句型：**The one with high efficiency is often bigger in size while the thinner or smaller one provides lower efficiency.**

在行銷學中，創造差異性是非常重要的一環，若公司所推出的產品或是服務沒有特色，就很容易被相似產品所取代或是瓜分市場。即便產品的市場區隔明顯，也還是需要運用手法來放大這些差異。其中比較法是許多業者所採用的方法。**以本範例對話為例，Jason 舉出目前市面上效能與體積無法有效共存的困境，效能好的電腦體積往往較大，然而輕薄電腦的效能往往較差，最後再點出本公司的新產品以找出解決方法。透過研發新式晶片，這台新電腦雖體積輕巧，但效能強大。**

4. 強調產品前景：

- 對應句型：**Since we have minimized the new chip size and enhanced its efficiency to the optimization, our new personal computer became smaller but powerful.**

運用上述的三種行銷手法後，觀眾或是客戶對於產品已有基本的認識，但對於是否能夠交易成功，可能尚差臨門一腳。由於對方可能已經認同我方所提出部分或是全部的概念，此時要加強的部分就是購買本產品或服務所帶來的效益是具有延續性的。**以本範例對話為例，Jason 就強調本公司的新型電腦成功解決效能與體積的困境，具有良好的市場前景，甚至可能掀起個人電腦的新革命，最後讓 Ken 忍不住想要親自體驗一下，對話至此 Jason 幾乎已抓住 Ken 的心理狀態，成交應是十拿九穩。**

看《全面啟動》（*Inception*），推銷產品有訣竅

篇章重點搶先看

1. 從電影《全面啟動》（*Inception*） 中主角 Cobb 的台詞學習如何運用話術強化公司或產品形象。
2. 以全片的的經典台詞 *"What's the most resilient parasite? An idea. A single idea from the human mind can build cities. An idea can transform the world and rewrite all the rules. Which is why I have to steal it"*「最具有可塑性的寄生生物是什麼？是人的想法。人類一個簡單的念頭可以創造城市。一個念頭可以改變世界重寫一切遊戲規則。這也是為何我要去竊取它」學習本單元核心句型：

   ★ "What is the 最高級+ N. N can... N can... Which is why I..."「什麼是…，N. N 可以…。N 可以…這也是為何我…」。
3. 學習其他重點句型：

   a **As**..., **we**...（做為…，我們…。）

   b **N** is for... who **V**...（**N** 適合…的…。）

   c **Adv** speaking, **N** is-are....（…來說，…是…。）
4. 將核心句型放入實境對話練習，學習四大行銷概念：

   a 以問句（questions）引起注意。

   b 以邏輯（logic）推演論點。

   c 以同義詞（synonym）產生變化性。

   d 以實做（demonstration ）取信客戶。

影片背景介紹

《全面啟動》敘述柯柏（Cobb）與他的搭檔亞瑟（Arthur）利用潛意識夢境盜取別人大腦中的秘密。於一次任務中，為了讓日本國際企業老闆齋藤（Saito）相信他們真的有能力進入夢境，從而用計竊取其商業機密，柯伯便提出人的念頭就像寄生生物般變化萬千，能對這個世界產生巨大影響的論點。而柯伯的這句台詞的句型架構恰巧可以應用在公司或產品形象塑造上。柯伯在此場景的這席話，已成功引起齋藤對這項技術的興趣。

Inspection is a story that describes Cobb and his partner Arthur using technology to infiltrate the subconscious of their targets and get the confidential information by shared dreaming. In the first mission, Saito (the boss of a Japanese International corporate) is the target. To get the business secret, Cobb used some tricks to win Saito's trust. Cobb proposed one theory that a single idea could possibly change the world, showing a good example of image shaping as well as a hook to draw customer's attention.

看影片怎麼說、怎麼用

In the International Conference Room of ABC Hotel.

（在 ABC 飯店的國際會議廳。）

Jason: Good afternoon, ladies and gentlemen. Our product release will begin within 1 minute, please shift your attention to our main stage. Now let's welcome the General Manager of DEF Company Paul.

Jason：各位先生女士午安，產品發表會將於一分鐘後開始，請各位將注意力集中至主舞台。現在讓我們歡迎 DEF 公司總經理 Paul.

Paul: Thank you all for sparing your time to attend this event. (1) As a smart phone manufacturer, it's my honor to show you the milestone we have reached in this industry.

Paul：感謝各位撥空參與本發表會，身為智慧型手機製造商，今天我很榮幸向各位展示我們在此產業所達到的新里程碑。

Audience（applause）

群眾（鼓掌）

Paul: Thank you again. Now let me begin the introduction today. (2) What is the most powerful addiction? A habit. A habit from your childhood can affect your choice of **entertainment** now. A new habit now will challenge your **cognition** and re-shape your life style in the future, which is why I have to introduce our **flagship** smart phone N9 to you. The size of the screen is one of the **concerns** when choosing a smart phone, but N9 gives you more choices. We provide

Paul：再次感謝各位。現在就讓我開始今日的產品介紹。最強大的癮頭是什麼？是習慣。一個你兒時的習慣會影響你現在對娛樂的選擇，一個新習慣會挑戰你的認知並且重塑你未來的生活方式，這也是為何我要向各位介紹我們的 N9 手機。螢幕尺寸是我們選擇手機所在意的項目之一，N9 讓您能

three different sizes to our customers. (3) 4 inches is for users who care about portability. 5.5 inches is for users who value **comfort**. 6.5 inches is for users who concern entertainment. Besides the screen size, the battery of N9 will amaze you. (4) Generally speaking, cables are needed when we recharge the battery and it takes certain time for fully charged. N9 will revolutionize this habit. Solar **cell** and **wireless** recharge functions are added to this phone, indicating that you can recharge your phone anywhere, anytime. And most importantly, it shortens the waiting by 80%. Now let me **demonstrate** these two amazing functions to you. After we select the wireless recharge function and click the start button, the phone will be charged. Through the big screen, we can see the phone is on charging now.

有更多選擇。N9 共有三種規格，4 吋適合強調可攜性的你；5.5 吋適合在意舒適度的你；6.5 吋適合注重娛樂性的你。除了螢幕尺寸外，N9 的電池也會讓你驚豔。一般而言，手機充電都需要使用充電線，而且充飽電需要一定的時間。但 N9 將會徹底改變這個習慣。N9 支援太陽能與無線充電，換言之，N9 隨時隨地都可以進行充電。更重要的是，N9 縮短了百分之八十的充電時間。現在就讓我向各位展示這兩項新功能。當我們選擇無線充電模式並按下開始後，手機就會開始充電。透過大螢幕，各位可以看到手機已經開始充電了。

對話單字說分明

1. **entertainment** *n.* 娛樂

例：Our new smart phone features entertainment functions.
我們的新智慧型手機主打娛樂功能。

2. **cognition** *n.* 認知

例：This smart watch will challenge your cognition of digital device.
這隻智慧型手錶將挑戰你對數位裝置的認知。

3. **flagship** *v.* 旗艦款

例：N9 is our latest flagship smart phone.
N9 我們公司最新推出的旗艦款智慧型手機。

4. **concern** *v.* 在乎

例：What we concern is the unit price.
我們在乎的是單價。

5. **comfort** *n.* 舒適度

例：Our product passes the strictest comfort examination.
本公司產品通過最嚴格的舒適度檢驗。

6. **cell** *n.* 電池

例：Solar cell is widely used in many industries.
太陽能電池已被許多產業廣泛使用。

7. **wireless** *adj.* 無線的

例：Blue tooth is one kind of wireless transmission.
藍芽是無線傳輸的一種。

8. **demonstrate** *v.* 展示

例：Let me demonstrate our latest product to you.
讓我向各位展示本公司最新的產品。

重點句型分析

1. **As..., we...** 意思為「做為…，我們…」，可用於說明該身分所應有之行為或應達到之目標。

   例：As a car manufacturer, we aim to produce cars that combine comfort and safety.

   身為車輛製造商，我們力求生產舒適與安全兼具的車款。

2. **What is the 最高級? N. N can... N can... Which is why I...** 意思為「什麼是…？N。N 可以…。N 可以…。這也是為何我…。」。可先挑起觀眾或客戶的注意，並透過演繹的方式讓對方理解並接受我們所提出的看法。

   例：What is the most durable accessory? Faith. Faith can overcome the challenge we face. It can inspire our potential and make a great breakthrough, which is why I have to show you our new training courses.

   最耐久的配件是什麼？是信念。一個信念能夠讓我們克服所面臨的挑戰。信念可以激發我們的潛能來超越巔峰。這也是為何我要向各位介紹此課程的原因。

3. **N is for... who V...** 意思為「N 適合…的…」，可用於產品所適合的消費者類型為何。

   例：Our flagship smart phone is for the users who value efficiency and design.

   我們的旗艦款智慧型手機適合重視效能與設計的你。

4. **Adv speaking, N is/are...** 意思為「…來說，…是…」，可用於說明現象或是特性。

   例：Generally speaking, portability is considered in the design of digital devices.

   一般來說，可攜性是數位裝置設計的考量項目之一。

職場補給站

本單元以智慧型手機的發表會為場景，發展出一段新品發表之介紹詞，當中提到四個行銷的常用概念，以下針對每個概念做進一步明：

1. 以問句（questions）引起注意：

- 對應句型：What is the most addictive medicine?

  不論是介紹公司產品或是形塑公司形象，其目的都是希望引起消費者的注意。引起注意可以透過圖象、文字、話語等方式。在話語部分，提出問題是常用的方式。當主講人丟出一個問題後，可以讓聽眾或客戶進行思考。**在本範例介紹詞中，總經理 Paul 先讓參與發表會的貴賓想看看哪種藥物最容易讓人上癮，當大家動腦思考藥物的類型後，就會出現各種答案。但事實上，提出這個問題的目的並不是預期聽眾真的給予回答，而是要抓住聽眾的注意力，好讓他們能有效接收接下來的核心訊息。**

2. 以邏輯（logic）推演論點：

- 對應句型：A habit. A habit from your childhood can affect your choice of entertainment now. A new habit now can challenge your cognition and re-shape your life style in the future, which is why I have to introduce our flagship smart phone N9 to you.

  成功抓住聽眾的注意力後，若要成功說服聽眾就需要一定的補充說明。說明可以透過舉例、對比、歸納、演繹等方法。但上述四種方法有一個共通點，也就是邏輯性。主體（公司形象或產品）要與輔助的客體（案例、敘述）具有關聯性，才能發揮相輔相成的功用，讓對方更加理解乃至接受主講人的說法。**在本範例對話中，當 Paul 問完什麼種藥物最讓人上癮後，接下來就點出這種藥就叫作習慣。會將習慣比喻為藥物，所謂「習慣成自然」，當習慣成為自然反應時，就如同藥物上癮般難以戒除。根據此邏輯，Paul 接著提出習慣會造成改變。過去的習慣影響我們對娛樂的選擇，現在開始的**

新習慣會影響我們未來的生活方式。Paul 透過這樣的邏輯推演，鋪陳出 N9 手機的推出會帶動手機使用習慣的變革，也將改變我們未來的生活。

3. 以同義詞（synonym）產生變化性：

- 對應句型：**4 inches is for users who care about portability. 5.5 inches is for users who value comfort. 6.5 inches is for users who concern entertainment.**

在塑造產品或公司形象時，往往需要使用大量的文字或話語進行敘述，當相同的詞語不斷重複出現，容易讓觀眾或讀者產生厭倦感，因而喪失進一部了解的意願。**在本範例中，當 Paul 要介紹 N9 的三種規格時，分別使用 care、value、concern 來表達重視之意，讓原本具高度重複性的字句，產生一定的變化性。**

4. 以實做取信（demonstration）客戶：

- 對應句型：**Now let me demonstrate these two amazing functions to you. After we select the wireless recharge function and click start button, the phone will start to be charged.**

完成上述的三種行銷手法後，聽眾或客戶對於我方所提出的想法已大致上理解。在此階段，可能已有部分人完全接受我方論點，但也有人仍抱持懷疑。若要消除他們的疑慮，最好的方是直接進行操作。當客戶親自看過功能的展示後，便可自己比較我方的說法與實際的功能是否相符。**在本範例中，Paul 提到 N9 可以進行無線充電，因此在介紹完此功能後，便透過大螢幕向與會貴賓展示此功能的實際操作。**

看《X 戰警：未來昔日》（*X-Men: Days of Future Past*），學會塑造公司形象並向客戶介紹產品

篇章重點搶先看

1. 以《X 戰警：未來昔日》（*X-Men: Days of Future Pas*）當中史崔克博士向各國軍事領袖介紹哨兵機器人的台詞學習如何塑造公司形象，並向客戶介紹產品。
2. 以片中反派腳色史崔克博士（Dr. Bolivar Trask）的經典台詞：*"There is a new enemy out there: Mutants. You need a new weapon for this war. I call them Sentinel."*「我們現在有新的敵人：變種人，你需要新武器來應付這場戰爭，這個武器叫做哨兵機器人。」學習本單元的核心句型：

   ★There is... You need... for... I called them...「現在有…，你需要…來…，它叫…。」
3. 搭配學習本單元其他三大重點句型：
   a. Thanks to..., the... is/are 比較級 compared to that of...（感謝…，…比…。）
   b. To V..., we...（為了…，我們…。）
   c. Through..., you can...（透過…，你能…。）
4. 將四種句型放入實境對話練習，學習四大行銷概念：
   a. 依趨勢（trend）創造需求。
   b. 找缺點（weakness）突顯需要。
   c. 提優點（strength）解決問題。
   d. 講價值（value）尋求認同。

影片背景介紹

《X 戰警：未來昔日》（*X-Men: Days of Future Past*）敘述變種人與人類歷經激烈戰爭過後，雙方皆傷亡慘重。變種人在哨兵機器人的追殺之下，幾近滅亡。為避免走向滅絕一途，倖存的變種人透過其中成員可讓意識回到過去的能力，將讓主角之一的金鋼狼回到過去來扭轉當前困境。在戰爭發生之前，反派角色史崔克博士（Dr. Bolivar Trask）為了說服各國政府支持哨兵機器人計畫，在簡報的開頭就點名當前的各種武器無法有效嚇阻變種人，因此該種族絕對會是潛在的國安威脅，而他所研發的哨兵機器人是針對變種人的弱點所設計，可以有效克敵。博士的這一段台詞，剛好可以作為塑造公司形象與說服客戶購買的良好教材。

X-Men: Days of Future Past describes the war between human and mutants. After the fierce battle, the casualties of both sides are great. The mutants are almost wiped out by the robot named Sentinels. To overturn their fate, one of mutants uses special talent to send Wolverine's consciousness back to his body in the past. Before the war, Dr. Trask firstly indicates that the serving weapons actually fail to deter the mutants in his presentation to the military leaders from each nation. Thus, this race turns out to be the potential threat to the national security. To seek support in the development of Sentinels from each national, Trask points out that this robot is designed to attack the weakness of mutants. The words Trask said in the presentation can be a good material to reveal the importance of brand image shaping and product marketing.

看影片怎麼說、怎麼用

At 302 Meeting Room in the Headquarters of ABC Group.

（在 ABC 集團總部的 302 會議室。）

Jason: Good afternoon, Mr. Huang and Mr. Li. Thank you for giving me the opportunity to have the briefing about the **cooperation** between two companies.

Jason：黃經理、李專員午安。感謝您給我此機會針對公司合作一事進行簡報。

Huang: You are welcome. You can begin the briefing now.

黃經理：不客氣，你可以開始簡報了。

Jason: OK. (1) There is a trend out there: smart devices. You will need new technology to gain certain market **share.** I call it high speed recharge. (2) Thanks to the development in **chip** design, the size of digital devices become smaller compared to that of old devices 10 years ago. However, users still need to wait 30 minutes or longer for recharging. (3) To solve this problem, we **re-design** the recharger. The new product can **shorten** 80% waiting time; **namely** your smart device can be fully recharged within 5 to 6 minutes.

Jason：好的。我們現在市場有個新趨勢：智慧裝置。你需要新科技來獲得市佔率。這個技術叫高速充電。由於晶片設計技術的進步，數位裝置的尺寸與十年前相比，已縮小許多。但使用者仍需花 30 分鐘甚至更長的時間來充電。為了解決此問題，我們重新設計充電器。新款產品可以節省百分之八十的充電時間，換言之只要五到六分鐘就能讓你的智慧裝置充飽電。

Li: It sounds great. Can you demonstrate how to recharge it?

李專員：似乎很不錯，可以實際展示給我們看嗎？

Jason: Of course. To show the difference, today I prepare two N9 phones. Now I'm connecting one phone with the traditional recharger, while the other with our product. Let's wait for one minute and check the **volume** recharged in both cells.

Jason：當然可以。為了展現差異，今天我準備了兩隻 N9 手機。一隻連接傳統充電器，一隻連接我們的新產品。充電一分鐘後我們來看看兩者的電量差異。

（One minutes passes.）

一分鐘過去。

Jason: Now let's check the outcome of this **experiment**. The one with the old type is only recharged by 3%, but the volume of the one with ours has reached 20%. (4) Through this comparison, you can tell which one works better.

Jason：現在讓我們看看實驗的結果。連接舊型充電器的手機的電量只有 3%，而連接新款的以充電 20%。透過此比較，你可清楚看出何者功能較好。

Huang: Your new recharger is awesome. What's the unit price?

黃經理：你們公司的新款充電器很棒。單價多少呢？

Jason: It depends on the amount you order. One for 20 USD.

Jason：單價會依訂購而有差異。一個 20 元美金。

Huang: It is more expensive than most rechargers in the market. I need to report this price to my boss.

黃經理：這比市面上大部分充電器的價格都高，我需要向老闆呈報此價格。

Jason: Although the cost is higher, if you use our product, time-saving is the niche of this product. When consumers actually are satisfied with its convenience, they are willing to buy more. The value of this product is greater than you think.

Jason：雖然使用我們的充電器會讓你的成本提高，但省時是本產品的市場優勢，當消費者體驗過其便利性，它們會願意購買更多產品。本產品所能產生的價值是超乎你的想像的。

對話單字說分明

1. **cooperation** *n.* 合作

例：We are seeking the cooperation with the local brands.

我們正尋求與當地品牌之合作。

2. **share** *n.* 部分

例：The market share has made a great progress this year.

今年市佔率有大幅的進步。

3. **chip** *n.* 晶片

例：The efficiency of the chip determines the overall performance of the computer.

晶片的效能影響電腦的整體效能。

4. **re-design** *v.* 重新設計

例：To solve the leaking problem, we re-design the drain system.

為了解決漏水問題，我們重新設計排水系統。

5. **shorten** *v.* 縮短

例：To shorten the shipping time, we use express.

為了縮短運送時間，我們使用快遞。

6. **namely** *adv.* 換句話說

例：The revenue decreases 8 percent, namely 80,000 USD.

收入下跌百分之八，換句話說，減少八萬美金。

7. **volume** *n.* 容量

例：The volume of the new battery is greater than that of its previous type.

新款電池的容量比舊款的大。

8. **experiment** *n.* 實驗

例：Through this experiment, we can find the machine with the best performance.

透過此實驗，我們可以找出效能最好的機器。

重點句型分析

1. **There is... You need... for... I called them...** 意思為「有…，你將需要…來…，它叫…。」，可以說明某種情況下所需要的某種要素為何，並說明該要素的名稱。

   例：There is a new competitor out there: EFG Company. You will need a new product for this competition. I call it a smart watch.
   現在我們新的競爭對手：EFG 公司。你將需要新產品來面對競爭。這個產品叫做智慧錶。

2. **Thanks to..., the... is/are 比較級 compared to that of sth** 意思為「由於…，…的…比（比較級）…。」，可用說明造成兩個時期差異性的關鍵原因。

   例：Thanks to the breakthrough in the chip design, the performance of the phone is much better compared to that of previous phones 5 years ago.
   由於晶片設計的技術有所突破，現在手機的效能比五年前好很多。

3. **To V..., we...** 意思為「為了…，我們…」，可用於說明為了達到某種目的，可使用的方法為何。

   例：To gain a market share in this region, we release the jointed products with one local brand。
   為了要在此區域取得市佔率，我們與當地品牌合作推出聯名商品。

4. **Through..., you can...** 意思為「透過…，你可以…」，可用使用某種方法後所能帶來的效果。

   例：Through this mechanism, all the data can be collected in time.
   透過此機制，所有資訊都可及時收集。

在向客戶介紹產品，若其內容有清楚脈絡，可讓對方更快理解產品特性並接受我方提出的論點與看法。本範例對話中提到四個可相互連結行銷的概念，以下針對每個概念做進一步說明：

1. 依趨勢（trend）創造需求：

- 對應句型：You will need a new technology to gain certain market share. I call it high speed recharge.

  在行銷學中，了解市場趨勢是非常重要的一環。趨勢的變化也牽動著需求的方向，因此理解產品的未來性可使你的推銷更具說服力。**在本範例中，Jason 在簡報開頭就直接點明智慧裝置是當前趨勢。在此趨勢下，其公司所推出的技術可讓合作夥伴的產品更具市場競爭力。**

2. 找缺點（weakness）突顯需要：

- 對應句型：However, users still need to wait 30 minutes or longer for recharging.

  要讓客戶願意花錢購買公司產品，其種一種行銷手法就是點出其他產品的缺點。此處的點出缺點並不要去批評其他產品有多不好，而是要強調這些缺點所帶來的不便利性，然後提出自家產品針對這些缺失所做出的修正。**在本範例中，Jason 先提出傳統的充電需要花三十分鐘甚至更久的時間，替之後介紹公司產品預留了伏筆。**

3. 提優點（strength）解決問題：

- 對應句型：The new product can shorten 80% waiting time, namely your smart device can be fully recharged within 5 to 6 minutes.

  說明其他產品的缺點後，接下來就是針對自家產品的優點加以著墨。敘述的方式可以是數據輔助、兩相對照等等。**本範例採用的是兩相比較。**

Jason 透過實驗，讓對方比較經過一分鐘的充電後，兩種充電器所能讓手機回復的電量有多少。傳統型的只有 3%而新型卻能到 20%。透過這樣的比較，讓對方相信公司產品確實能夠高速充電。

4. 講價值（value）尋求認同：

- 對應句型：**Though cost is higher if you use our product, but time-saving is the niche of this product. When consumers actually are satisfied with its convenience, they are willing to buy more. The value of this product is greater than you think.**

　　運用上述行銷技巧向客戶推銷產品後，若客戶已經接受我方想法，距離成交僅剩一步之遙。倘若此時仍對產品有所疑慮，其考量因素之一往往是價格。若在我方價格上已無法讓步，此時應強調產品價值，說明成本雖然增加，但因為可銷售數量也提高，整體效益是更好的。**在本範例中，由於黃經理認為 20 元美金的單價太高，Jason 便從價值的角度進行分析。Jason 強調省時是本產品的最大優勢，一但消費者體驗過這樣的便利性，購買意願一定會提升。當消費者願意花錢購買，即使成本提高，只要銷售達到一定數量，利潤仍可為持相同，甚至可以更高。**

看《白日夢冒險王》（*The Secret Life of Walter Mitty*），學會塑造公司形象

篇章重點搶先看

1. 以《白日夢冒險王》（*The Secret Life of Walter Mitty*）主角任職的生活雜誌的座右銘為範例，學習如何塑造公司形象。
2. 以片中生活雜誌公司的座右銘 *"To see the world, things dangerous to come to. To see behind walls, to draw closer, to find each other and to feel. That is the purpose of life."*「開拓視野，衝破艱險，看見世界，身臨其境，貼近彼此，感受生活，這就是生活的目的。」學習本單元核心句型：
   ★To V..., To V... That is...（做…，做…，這就是…）。
3. 搭配學習本單元其他三大重點句型：
   a. **Before**..., let me/us...（在…之前，讓我（們）…。）
   b. **When it comes to**..., **N** is...（一談到…，…是…。）
   c. **If**..., **N** is...（如果…，N 是…。）
4. 將四種句型放入實境對話練習，學習四大行銷概念：
   a. 以詮釋（interpretation）創造話題。
   b. 以簡潔（neatness）強化印象。
   c. 給方向（direction）引導思考。
   d. 用創意衝擊認知（perception）。

影片背景介紹

《白日夢冒險王》（*The Secret Life of Walter Mitty*）的主角華特・米堤（Walter Mitty）是《生活雜誌》的員工，但常常有各式各樣的白日夢。與他共事的知名攝影師尚恩·歐康諾（Sean O'Connell）有一天送了一捲特別的底片作品，並說明希望當中的 25 號相片能夠成為紙本「生活雜誌」最後一期的封面。華特在相片部門工作，而過去從未弄丟過任何相片，然而這次卻找不到這張所謂的 25 號相片。為了尋找尚恩與找回照片，愛作夢的華特這次決定出門探險。片中生活雜誌的座右銘，明確點出哪些生活中該做的事，而華特的旅程就像是這段話語的實踐，兩者相互印證下，該座右銘實為形塑公司形象之教材。

In *the Secret Life of Walter Mitty*, the protagonist Walter Mitty is an employee of Life Magazine who likes daydreaming. One day his co-worker, a famous photographer, Sean O'Connell sends him a roll of negative film and tells Walter that he hopes the No. 25 photo could be used as the cover of the final print issue. Working in a Negative Department, Mitty never misses any photo, but he fails to find No. 25 this time. To find Sean to get the photo, Mittty starts the adventure instead of daydreaming. The motto of Life Magazine clearly points out some things we should do in our life, and Mitty's journey is like the realization of these words. Meanwhile, this motto is also a good material to learn how to shape the brand image.

看影片怎麼說、怎麼用

At the conference room of ABC Company.

（在 ABC 公司的會議室。）

Jason: Good morning, everyone. Thank you for coming today. The topic we will cover in the meeting today is about our new **slogan**. (1) Before we start the discussion, let me recap the conclusion we have made in the meet last Friday. Currently, we have two directions. One is the word with new interpretation. The other is the explanation of our **spirit**. Please provide as many suggestions as possible.

Jason：各位早安。感謝與會。今天的會議主題是新標語。在進行討論之前，讓我們先回顧一下上次會議所達成的結論。目前我們有兩個思考方向：一是賦予單字新的詮釋。二是公司精神的解釋。請各位盡量給予建議。

Ken: C-A-M-E-R-A, catch a moment ever ran along.

Ken：C-A-M-E-R-A，抓住曾溜走的瞬間。

Jason: What a creative an idea. You re-define the word “camera”. Can you share how you **come up with** this to us?

Jason：真有創意的想法。你的重新定義了「相機」這個字。可以分享一下是如何想出來的嗎？

Ken: Of course. (2) When it comes to the function of camera, recording the important moment is the first thing that came into our mind. The first three **letters** of camera are “c”, “a” and “m” happened to be the same as the **initials** of “catch”, “a” and “moment”. Besides, the last three letters “e”, “r” and “a” can also be interpreted as the abbreviated

Ken：當然可以。談到相機的功能，我第一個想到的是記錄重要時刻。相機的前三個字母 C、A、M 恰巧又與「抓住」（catch）、「一個」（a）、「瞬間」（moment）相同。另外後三個字母又可詮釋為「曾溜

"ever ran away". I combine these two to form this slogan.

走」的縮寫字。我結合兩者成為本標語。

Jason: Thank you for your impressive explanation.

Jason：謝謝你令人印象深刻的解釋。

Alice: As a professional camera manufacturer, I think "(3) To see world, to catch the world, to save the world. That is the purpose of photography." is a suitable **option**.

Alice：本公司身為專業相機製造商，我認為「看見世界，抓住世界，紀錄世界。這就是攝影的目的。」會是個適合的標語。

Jason: It sounds catchy, too. Please tell us how you develop it.

Jason：聽起來也很棒，請告訴我們是如何發想的嗎？

Alice: (4) If we standardize the procedure of photo taking, making, seeing, catching, and saving are definitely needed. When we see something worth being recorded, we will use camera to catch it and save this image in the memory card. This slogan does point out the key element of photography.

Alice：如果把拍照的步驟標準化，看見、捕捉、儲存都是必須的程序。當我們看到值得紀錄的瞬間，會用相機將其捕捉並儲存該影像，這個標語的確點出拍照的重要元素。

Jason: Thank you. Any other suggestions? If none, let's vote. If you favor Ken's suggestion, please raise your hand. Five. If you like Alice's idea, please raise your hand. Four. As the chairman of this meeting, now I announce our new slogan is "c-a-m-e-r-a, catch a moment ever ran along."

Jason：謝謝。還有其他建議嗎？沒有的話，就進行投票。支持 Ken 的提議，請舉手。共五位。支持 Alice 的想法，請舉手。共四位。身為本次會議主席，本席於此宣布新的標語為：「c-a-m-e-r-a，抓住曾溜走的瞬間。」

對話單字說分明

1. **slogan** *n.* **標語**

例：Slogan is an important element in marketing.

標語是行銷的重要環節。

2. **spirit** *n.* **精神**

例：This video clips successfully conveys the spirit of our product.

此短片成功傳達產品精神。

3. **come up with** *ph.* **想出**

例：It takes me one day to come up with the suitable slogan of this activity.

我花了一天才想出適合本活動的標語。

4. **letters** *n.* **字母**

例：The first letter T in T/T means telegraphic.

電匯這個單字中的第一字母 T 代表電信的。

5. **initial** *n.* **首字母**

例：The initial of the abbreviation of our company name is T.

本公司名稱縮寫的首字母是 T。

6. **option** *n.* **選項**

例：We have many options to choose in main dish. .

在主餐部份我們有多個選項可供挑選。

7. **catchy** *adj.* **容易記住的**

例：Your new slogan is catchy.

您們的新標語非常好記。

8. **element** *n.* **要素**

例：Sharing the risk is one of key elements in investing.

分散風險是投資的要素之一。

重點句型分析

1. **Before..., let us/me...** 意思為「在…之前，讓我（們）…」，可用於說明事情的先後順序。

   例：Before we finish the meeting today, let's decide the date of our next meeting.

   在結束本次會議之前，讓我們先決定好下次開會日期。

2. **When it comes to..., N is...** 意思為「一談到…，N 是…。」，可用於說明優先想到的事物為何。

   例：When it comes to the leading brand in sport shoes, Nike is the one firstly coming into my mind.

   一談到運動鞋的領導品牌，我第一個想到 Nike。

3. **To V..., To V....That is....** 意思為「做…，做…，這就是…」，可用於說明某事物所應包含的面向。

   例：To analyze the world. To explore the world. That is the purpose of science.

   分析世界。探索世界。這就是科學的目的。

4. **If..., N is...** 意思為「如果…，N 是…」，可用於說明某事物在某條件的特性為何。

   例：If we rank the emergent level of these three projects, project A is definitely the priority.

   如果要排列出這三個專案的緊急程度，專案 A 絕對是最優先。

本單元以公司內部開會為場景，以新標語為討論主題。發展一段實際對話。對話內容提到四個行銷的常用概念，以下針對每個概念做進一步說明：

1. 以詮釋（interpretation）創造話題：

● 對應句型：c-a-m-e-r-a, catch a moment ever ran along.

在行銷學中，創造話題性是相當動重要的一環。一旦能夠引起消費者的熱烈討論，產品的曝光度肯定大增。能創造話題的方式有很多，奇裝異服、顛覆傳統是常見的方法。所謂的顛覆傳統，其中的一種做法就是以新想法解釋既有物件或是概念。**在本範例中，Ken 的標語就是以此模式發想。Ken 將 camera 的六個字母視為六個獨立概念，分別賦予其意涵，而這六個意涵又可再組合成一個具有意義之短句。**

2. 以簡潔（neatness）強化印象：

● 對應句型：To see world, to catch the world, to save the world. That is the purpose of photography.

在消費市場中，消費者一天之內所接觸的訊息可能多到不計其數，當訊息的內容不具吸引力時，該訊息可能就會被直接忽略。從廠商的立場來看，當然不希望此種情況發生。若要吸引消費者，容易記憶是很好的切入點，因為消費者不需要耗費太多心力便可理解並記住訊息內容。**在本範例中，Alice 標語的發想就是循此模式。她先針對攝影的重要元素進行分類，然後以祈使句的方式進行敘述，簡單明瞭地說明攝影的三要素是看見、捕捉與儲存。**

3. 給方向（direction）引導思考：

● 對應句型：When it comes to the function of camera, recording the important moment is the first thing that came into our mind.

在消費市場中，有時消費者本身對於自身需求也不甚了解。這樣的情況對廠商而言，是危機也是轉機。若將其視為危機，其切入點是認為市場動態不明，就生產方來說，較難評估產品可能的市場反應為何。若視為轉機，則是從可引導消費者接受我方思維的角度切入。在本範例中，**Alice 對如何發想標語所提出的解釋就是運用此模式。她認為當提到相機功能時，首先想到的是要拿來記錄重要時刻。這樣的說法可以讓對方由此面向開始思考自己的看法是否相同。**

Lesson 01
Lesson 02
Lesson 03
Lesson 04
Lesson 05
Lesson 06

4. 用創意衝擊認知（perception）：

- 對應句型：**The first three letters of camera are "c", "a" and "m" happened to be the same as the initials of "catch", "a" and "moment". Besides, the last three letters "e", "r" and "a" can also be interpreted as the abbreviated "ever ran away."**

在消費市場中，不論是對公司形象或產品往往都會存有一個既定印象。這樣的印象同時包含正面與負面效益。若從正面角度看，代表消費者對我方有基本認識。從負面角度切入，則是認為這樣的認知同時也限縮可能性，一旦市場趨勢改變，消費者也跟著流失。為避免負面情況產生，許多公司（特別是歷史悠久的）會運用創意來扭轉公司形象，讓消費者有耳目一新的感覺。**在本範例中，Ken 依序解釋自己是如何賦予 camera 這個單字新的解釋方式。傳統上，這個單字可能被解釋為能夠紀錄影像的裝置。但 Ken 是將每個字母視為一個單字的縮寫，將這六個單字還原後，其意涵是「捕捉曾溜走的瞬間」，正好就是人們購買相機的目的。**

看《鋼鐵人 1》（*Iron Man, 2008*），學習產品推銷的技巧

篇章重點搶先看

1. 以鋼鐵人電影中主角東尼史塔克推銷飛彈時的台詞學習如何推銷公司產品。
2. 以電影史塔克的經典台詞 *"They say the best weapon is you never have to fire it. I respectfully disagree. I prefer the weapon you only have to fire once. That's how Dad did it! That how American does it! And it works out pretty well so far."*

   「有人說最好的武器根本不必發射，但我不同意，我認為發射一次就能殲滅對手的武器才是最好。我爸這樣做，美國這樣做，到現在這套也很行的通。」學習本單元核心句型：

   ★They say... I prefer... That's how... That's how... And it...「有人說…，我覺得…。…這樣做…。…這樣做，且…。」
3. 搭配學習本單元其他三大重點句型：

   a What make... is...（讓…是因為…）

   b Once..., N...（一旦…，N 會…）

   c According to..., the... of...（根據…，N 的…）
4. 將四種句型放入實境對話練習，學習四大行銷概念：

   a 以案例（case）證明效果。

   b 以數據（data）分析表現。

   c 以術語（term）展現專業。

   d 以互動（interaction）炒熱氣氛。

影片背景介紹

鋼鐵人第一集敘述主角史塔克前往阿富汗進行耶利哥飛彈測試後，在搭車返回機場的路上遭遇伏擊並被恐怖分子組織綁架，因為心臟受損而被安裝機械心臟，也在囚禁途中發明了用來逃離的鋼鐵盔甲。成功返美後，史塔克發現其合作夥伴奧比戴爾竟整個事件背後的藏鏡人。為阻止其野心，史塔克先是摧毀他所建立的秘密工廠，並在殊死戰中成功將其殲滅。片中史塔克向各國推銷飛彈的介紹詞，也是學習推銷並塑造公司產品形象的良好教材。

On the way back to the airport after the presentation and testing of Jericho Missiles, the protagonist of *Iran Man* Stark is being attacked and kidnapped by terrorists. After being injured, Stark's chest was implanted a mechanical heart. To have the freedom again, Stark invents an iron armor. When Stark goes back to the States, he finds his partner Obadiah is the man behind this accident, and he plans to sell missiles to the terrorists. To stop his evil plan, Stark firstly destroys Obadiah's secret factory and kills him after a fierce battle. The line that Stark uses to introduce Jericho Missiles is a good material to learn how to promote and shape the brand image and products of a company.

看影片怎麼說、怎麼用

In the booth of ABC Company in 2015 New York Software **Expo**.

（在 2015 紐約軟體展 ABC 公司的攤位。）

Jason: Good afternoon, I am Jason, the host of our product release today. Now let's welcome the Software Department Manager of ABC Company, Mr. Anderson.

Jason：各位午安，我是本日產品發表會的主持人 Jason。讓我們有請 ABC 公司軟體部經理 Anderson 先生。

Anderson: Good afternoon. I am Anderson. Before I start my presentation, I have few words that I want to share with you. (1) "They say the best software is you never have to set it. I disagree. I prefer the software you only have to set once. That is how Bdobe did it. That is how Nicrosoft did it. And it works out pretty well so far." Now let me officially introduce our latest machining software DIZ to you!

Anderson：各位午安，我是 Anderson。在開始介紹前。有些話想跟各位分享。「有人說最好的軟體不需要設定，我不同意，我認為最好的軟體是只須設定一次。Bdobe 這樣做，Nicrosoft 這樣做，到現在這套也很行的通。」現在就讓我向各位正式介紹我們最新的加工軟體 DIZ。

Anderson: DIZ is the one that modifies the flaws we have in our prevision version. (2) What makes it **distinguish** from that of the competitor in the market is its smart **alignment** and adjustment. For many machine operators, **parameter** key-in is their nightmare. Those figures are usually long and complicated, so mistakes could be

Anderson：DIZ 修正我們上一代軟體的缺點，而讓此軟體不同於坊間其他軟體的是其智慧校正與調整功能。對許多機器操作員而言，輸入參數就像惡夢。這些數字經常是冗長且複雜，操作員一旦失去專注力，就

made once the operator lost their **concentration**. More importantly, the price of those mistakes are high because the tool of the CNC machine could be damaged. (3) Once the tool is broken, the production will be shut down and the maintenance fee is a fiscal burden. (4) According to the statistics, the average repair fee of a slight damage is 1,000 USD and the loss of downtime is hard to calculate. Now you find the solution! DIZ will provide users a hint when some errors are **detected**. To see is to believe. Can I invite the man with blue T-shirt to do me a favor?

會有錯誤產生。更重要的是，為這些錯誤所需付出的代價很高，因為加工機的刀具可能因此而損壞。一旦刀具損壞，會導致停工且維修費也是財務上的負擔。根據統計，輕微損壞的平均維修費用是 1000 美金，而停工所造成的損失更是難以計算。但現在我們替您找到解決方案了！當系統偵測到錯誤，DIZ 會對使用者發出提醒。所謂眼見為憑。我可以請穿藍色 T 恤的男士幫我一個忙嗎？

The man: Sure. What do I need to do now?

男士：當然可以，我該怎麼幫您呢？

Anderson: Randomly key in some figures in each blank and press enter.

Anderson：隨意在空格內鍵入數字並按確認。

The man: OK.

男士：好的。

Anderson: Thank you for your help. Time for us be the **witnesses** the convenience. As we can see on the big screen, a window has been shown to remind users that the parameter in blank 2 is too big. The tool will be damaged, if users run this program. Want to save your money! Our software is your best choice!

Anderson：感謝您的協助。現在讓我們見證本軟體的便利性。從大螢幕上可以看到，有跳出個視窗提醒使用者空格二的參數值過大，如執行此程式恐導致刀具損壞。各位，如果想省下維修費，DIZ 是您的最佳選擇！

對話單字說分明

1. **expo** *n.* **會展**

例：There will be three to four machinery expos in Taiwan this year.
本年度台灣將有三到四場的機械展。

2. **distinguish** *v.* **區別**

例：What makes our product to distinguish from that of the competitors is its material.
材質使我們的產品不同於市面上的競爭者。

3. **alignment** *n.* **校正**

例：Alignment should be made before each operation.
使用前請先進行校正。

4. **parameter** *n.* **參數**

例：If you want to switch to mode 2, please reset the parameter.
如需切換至模式 2，請重設參數。

5. **concentration** *n.* **集中力**

例：Since the operation of this machine is complicated, you need to keep the concentration all the time.
由於此機器操作複雜，你需要隨時保持專注。

6. **detect** *v.* **偵測**

例：The system will automatically shut down when some errors are detected. 當發現錯誤時，系統會自動停止。

7. **randomly** *adv.* **隨機地**

例：The inspector will randomly select one sample to check the quality.
稽查人員將隨機挑選樣本檢驗品質。

8. **witness** *v./n.* **見證；見證人**

例：We are so lucky to be the witnesses of/to witness the great breakthrough in this industry. 我們幸運地見證業界的重大突破。

重點句型分析

1. **They say... I prefer... That's how... That's how... And it...** 意思為「有人說…，我覺得…。…這樣做…。…這樣做，且…。」，可用於說明自己不同的見解，並以其他成功案例加以輔助。

   例：They say the best shoes are the ones with all functions. I prefer the shoes can change the function with time and environment. That is how Nike did it. That is how Adidas did it. And it works well so far.
   有人說最好的鞋子要能包含所有功能。我覺得最好的鞋應該是要能隨時間與環境變換更能。Nike 這樣做。Adidas 這樣做。這套目前也還行得通。

2. **What makes... is...** 意思為「讓…的是…。」，可用於說形成某特性的原因為何。

   例：What makes our product special is its high efficiency.
   高效能讓我們的產品與眾不同。

3. **Once..., N...** 意思為「一旦…，N 就…」，可用於說明某種情況所帶來的後果。

   例：Once the inspection can't be finished today, the shipment will be delayed。
   一旦今日無法完成稽核，出貨就會延遲。

4. **According to..., the... of...** 意思為「根據…，…的…。」，可用於說明論點所詢之依據。

   例：According the 2014 balance sheet of ABC Company, PC ranks number one in the sales。
   根據 2014 年 ABC 之損益平衡表，PC 的銷售名列第一。

本單元以商展中的產品發表為背景，發展出一段實用對話。對話當中共提到四個行銷的常用概念，以下針對每個概念做進一步說明：

1. 以案例（case）證明效果：

- 對應句型：**That is Bdobe did it. That is how Nicrosoft did it. And it works out pretty well so far.**

  在商場上，消費者對於未知的產品或服務容易抱持觀望的態度，若要消除這樣的遲疑，最有效的方法就是提出當前成功的案例與我方的相似之處。透過這樣的並列，可提升消費者對我方產品的信心。**在本範例中，作為公司軟體部門的主管 Anderson 在介紹產品時，就提出現在公司新軟體所依循的開發理念跟 Bdobe、Nicrosoft 這些大廠相同，因此消費者對於公司產品的品質與功效大可放心。**

2. 以數據（data）分析表現：

- 對應句型：**According to the statistics, the average repair fee of a slight damage is 1,000 USD and the loss of downtime is hard to calculate.**

  正所謂數字會說話。對消費者而言，有時再多的敘述都不如上述具有說服力。針對這樣的消費族群，統計數字就是說服他們的最好武器。倘若資料的來源是來自權威機構，更可提高其可信度，使消費者對產品放心。**在本範例中，Anderson 為了要讓消費者了解到底刀具損壞會造成多大的財務損失，提出輕微損壞的平均維修費金額就已高達 1000 美金，且尚未把停工的損失算入，替之後公司軟體能替消費者省下這筆費用的論點預先做好鋪陳。**

3. 以術語（term）展現專業：

- 對應句型：**More importantly, the price of those mistakes are high because the tool of the CNC machine could be damaged.**

在消費市場中不乏具備相關專業背景之消費者，若要說服這個族群，單靠一般的行銷話術可能行不通，此時有最有效的輔助工具就是專業術語與行話（jargon）。當我方在介紹產品時，若能做出專業的解釋，方可取信這些具備專業素養的族群。**在本範例中，為了展現我方是專業的加工軟體製造商，Anderson 特別出 tool 這個專業詞彙。該詞彙在加工領域內指的是「刀具」而非平常所指稱的工具，可讓相關加工業者願意多加留意這個加工軟體。**

4. 以互動（interaction）炒熱氣氛：

- 對應句型：**Can I invite the man with blue T-shirt to do me a favor?**

在行銷學中，除了理性的客觀因素外，有時帶有非理性的行為也會左右最後的成交與否。舉例來說，當兩種產品的價格與性能都相差無幾，但由於兩個行銷場域的氣氛有所差異時，消費者可能就會依其偏好做出選擇。而炒熱氣氛的方式之一就是與消費者互動。透過互動，消費者的購買意願會有相當程度的提升。**在本範例中，Anderson 為了讓所有觀看發表的觀眾更清楚看到產品的優點，於是邀請一位男士隨機鍵入數字並確認執行該程式，讓群眾有參與感，並對軟體的偵錯功能留下印象，提高之後成交的可能性。**

從《蝙蝠俠：黑暗騎士》（*The Dark Knight*），掌握消費者心態來塑造公司及產品形象

篇章重點搶先看

1. 以《蝙蝠俠：黑暗騎士》（*The Dark Knight*）中布魯斯韋恩的台詞學習如何以掌握消費者心態來塑造公司及產品形象。
2. 以主角布魯斯韋恩台詞 "Sometime the truth isn't good enough. Sometimes people deserve more. Sometimes people deserve to have their faith rewarded."「有時候真話並不夠好，人們須要的更多，人們需要他們的信仰被證實。」學習本單元核心句型：

   ★Sometimes N... is... Sometimes...+比較級. Sometimes N...「有時…，有時…。有時…。」。
3. 搭配學習本單元其他三大重點句型：

   a Not to V..., I will...（為了不…，我將…。）

   b If..., ... can turn out to be...（如果…，…可以轉變為…。）

   c For most..., N is/are...（就…來說，N 是…。）
4. 將四種句型放入實境對話練習，學習四大行銷概念：

   a 以同理心（empathy）引起共鳴。

   b 以比較（comparison）突顯價值。

   c 以贈品（free gift）吸引消費。

   d 以主動（activeness）促使成交。

影片背景介紹

電影《蝙蝠俠：黑暗騎士》（*The Dark Knight*）（是主角蝙蝠俠與反派小丑對抗的故事。片中高譚市的黑幫選擇雇用小丑對抗象徵正義勢力的蝙蝠俠與檢察官哈維丹特（Harvey Dent）。小丑揚言除非蝙蝠俠自曝身分，否則將每天殺害市民。善於操縱人心的小丑除讓市民生活於恐懼之中外，更讓丹特淪為罪犯。片尾警方雖然成功抓到小丑，為避免丹特的醜聞公諸於世，世人會對正義失去信心，蝙蝠俠選擇一肩擔起丹特的所有罪行，成為警方追緝的對象。片中蝙蝠俠用來鼓舞人心的經典台詞，若從心理學的角度切入，其實不失為學習行銷的良好教材。

The Dark Knight is the story about the battle between Batman and Joker. The gangsters in Gotham City hire Joker to rebel against the symbol of justice represented by Dent and Batman. Joker announces that he will kill one citizen a day until Batman reveals who he really is. Knowing how to manipulate the dark side of people's mind, Joker successfully makes people live under worries and even makes Dent commit a crime in the long run. Though Joker is captured by the police, Batman decides to shoulder all the scandals that Dent have made to keep Dent's positive image in case people lose the faith in justice. If the lines that Batman uses to encourage people from the psychological aspect are carefully examined, they turn out to be a material to explain the importance of brand or product image shaping.

看影片怎麼說、怎麼用

You meet a customer in ABC **Automobile** Exhibition Center.

（你與客戶相約在 ABC 汽車展示中心。）

Jason: (1) Not to waste you precious time, I will directly get to the point. From your point of view, what makes a good CAR?

Jason：從您的觀點來看，怎樣稱的上一部好車呢？

Sam: Safe and comfortable.

Sam：安全且舒適。

Jason: True. Without this **premise**, even the most **luxurious** sedan can't be regarded as a good car. This is our latest SUV WILD. We often say "(2) Sometimes in-time protection is not good enough. Sometimes people deserve more than that. Sometime people deserve the protection before they notice it."

Jason：缺乏這兩個前提的話，再豪華的轎車都稱不上好車。這是我們最新款的 SUV WILD。我們常說：「有時及時保護還不夠好。有時人們值得更好的保護。有時人們值得在甚至他們都沒留意到的保護。」

Sam: It seems that safety is your **priority**. Can you tell me more about this car?

Sam：看來 ABC 公司把安全放在第一位。可以多說一點嗎？

Jason: Of course. GPS has become the necessity of a car, so we definitely have the one in WILD. However, (3) if we combine this equipment with distance sensor, this combination turns out to be the best **reminder** when drivers lose their concentration. Regarding all customers as

Jason：當然。因為 GPS 已經是必備項目，WILD 當然也有裝配。但如果將 GPS 結合距離感知器，這樣的搭配可成為駕駛人喪失專注力時的最佳提醒。我們視每位客戶為家人，提供您

our family, we provide you the best protection.

最佳的保護。

Sam: I like this innovation. Here I want to ask few questions concerning the airbag. How many airbags does WILD have and its **arrangement**?

Sam：我喜歡這樣的創新。現在我想問幾個關於安全氣囊的問題。WILD 一共有幾顆安全氣囊？是怎樣的配置？

Jason: WILD has nine in total. Five in the front of each seat. Four on the both sides of car doors. Here I need to introduce the one in front of the middle of the back seats to you. (4) For most SUV, eight is maximum. But in many cases, the passenger who sits in the middle of the back seat tends to be seriously injured in the accident due to the lack of comprehensive protection. The ninth airbag is added to keep the passenger free from getting hurt.

Jason：WIID 共配有九科安全氣囊。五顆在每個座位之前。四顆在兩邊的車門。這邊我要向您特別介紹後座中央位置的這顆氣囊。多數的 SUV 氣囊的最大配製數量就是八顆。但在許多意外中，坐在後座中央位置的乘客常因為缺乏全面性的保護而重傷。這增加的第九顆氣囊就是要避此位置免乘客受傷。

Sam: This additional protection is awesome!

Sam：此一額外保護真是太棒了！

Jason: Currently we have a special sale in all series of our cars. Once you place an order today, you can have 24 interest-free monthly **installment** and get a free dashcam. 24999 NTD a month is really an **affordable** figure.

Jason：我們全車系目前皆有特惠。若今日下訂，除享 24 期零利率分期外，更可免費獲得一台行車紀錄器。月付 24999 絕對是個負擔得起的數字。

對話單字說分明

1. **automobile** *n.* 汽車

例：Automobile industry used to be the pillar of Detroit's economy.

汽車工業曾是底特律的經濟命脈。

2. **premise** *n.* 前提

例：The project is approved with several premises.

此專案在符合數個前提之下通過。

3. **luxurious** *adj.* 奢華的

例：The case of this phone is made of luxurious materials such as platinum and diamond.

此手機的外殼是以奢華材質如白金與鑽石所打造。

4. **priority** *n.* 優先考量

例：Considering the urgency level, this project will be put as the top priority.

考量到其緊急程度，此專案將被優先處理。

5. **reminder** *n.* 提醒

例：E-calendar is a good reminder for us to check the schedule.

電子日曆是用來提醒行程的好幫手。

6. **arrangement** *n.* 安排

例：Please check the seat arrangement before the meeting.

開會前請確認座位的安排。

7. **installment** *n.* 分期付款

例：The monthly installment is a good way to reduce the burden of payment after the purchase of expensive products.

每月分期付款的方式很好，可減輕購買昂貴商品的付費負擔。

8. **affordable** *adj.* 負擔的起的

例：2000 NTD a month is really an affordable investment amount. .

一個月兩千元是個負擔得起的投資額。

重點句型分析

1. **Sometimes N... is... Sometimes...+比較級. Sometimes N...** 意思為「有時…，有時…。有時…」，是相似句型的堆疊，可用於比較數種情況的層遞性。

   例：Sometimes fast is not good enough. Sometimes deserved more than that. Sometimes people need a fast, but stable car.
   有時快還不夠好。有時人們值得更多。有時人們需要一台快但平穩的車。

2. **Not to V..., I will...** 意思為「為了不…，我將…。」，可用於說明如何避免某些負面情況的發生。

   例：Not to waste our time in meaningless discussion, I will list some possible directions that we can follow.
   為了避免浪費時間在無意義的討論上，我將列出幾個可行的方向。

3. **If..., ...can turn out to be...** 意思為「如果…，…可以變為…」，可用於如何讓事物產生變化。

   例：If we can improve the efficiency in energy converting, this machine will turn out to be the milestone in this industry.
   如能提升能源轉換之效能，此機器將會成為本產業的新里程碑。

4. **For most..., N is/are...** 意思為「對多數…，N 是…」，可用於敘述某一群體所共有之特性。

   例：For most investors, risk is the top concern.
   對多數投資者而言，風險是最大的考量。

職場補給站

本單元以汽車銷售為背景，發展一篇客戶與推銷人員之對話。對話當中一共提到四個行銷的常用概念，以下針對每個概念做進一步說明：

1. 以同理心（empathy）引起共鳴：

- 對應句型：**Regarding all customers as our family, we provide you the best protection.**

  在消費市場中，消費者對於行銷人員的話語往往抱持懷疑態度。若要取信於消費者，使其願意購買產品，將其視為朋友家人一般，改從他們的角度來分析產品優劣是個有效的方法。**在本範例中，為了表現出 ABC 汽車重視客戶，Jason 表示 ABC 汽車視每位客戶為自己的家人，所生產的車輛以能保障客戶的安全為最高指導原則。**

2. 以比較（comparison）突顯價值：

- 對應句型：**But in many cases, the passenger who sits in the middle of the back seat tends to be seriously injured in the accident due to the lack of comprehensive protection. The ninth airbag is added to keep passenger free from getting hurt.**

  當客戶質疑產品是否真的如同銷售人員所述那樣優良時，疑惑可以比較的方式來加以消除。行銷人員可以舉出統計數字或實際案例做為輔助。在兩相比較後，方可證明公司產品確有其功效。**在本範例中，為了強調 ABC 公司在安全性上做出的努力，Jason 針對第九顆安全氣囊的設計做進一步說明。根據統計發現，做在後座中央位置的乘客，因為缺乏完善的保護，車禍發生時受傷程度往往較為嚴重。這顆額外增加的安全氣囊就是要避免此種情況發生在 WILD 上。**

3. 以贈品（free gift）吸引消費：

- 對應句型：**Once you place an order today, you can have 24 interest-free installment and get a free dashcam.**

當多數銷售話數都無法打動消費者時，除給予折扣外，贈品是可用運用的一項工具。而在贈品的選擇上，價值並非時唯一考量，話題性與實用性也須一併納容。話題性可能源自贈品本身的稀有性或獨特性，例如本贈品只送不賣或是本贈品數量有限。而實用性指的則是消費者之後可以如何使用，若贈品本身價值很高，消費者卻難以使用，形成消費誘因的相對大大降低。**在本範例中，Jason 特別提出現在下訂購車，還可以免費獲得一台行車紀錄器。由於消費者 Sam 相當注重車輛安全性，此一裝置足以形成吸引他的誘因。**

4. 以主動（activeness）促使成交：

- 對應句型：**Currently we have a special sale in all series of our cars.**

當銷售人員發現消費者已對產品動心，但因某些因素尚在猶豫不決時，此時銷售人員應掌握先機，率先提出誘因讓消費者下定決心。此處提到的誘因可以是折扣、贈品、分期付款等，而至於採用的順序則端看相關人員的觀察能力。不論選擇何種，記住主動出擊就有機會成交。**在本範例中，Sam 明顯已經被 Jason 的銷售術所打動，此使 Jason 在 Sam 尚未詢問價格之前就先提出目前有優惠活動，成功掌握先機，讓 Sam 下單的意願大增。**

看《賈柏斯傳》（*Jobs*），學習如何塑造公司與產品的形象

篇章重點搶先看

1. 以傳記電影《賈柏斯傳》（*Jobs*）中賈伯斯的經典台詞學習如何塑造公司與產品的形象。
2. 以片中賈伯斯的台詞 *“How does people know what they want if they haven't seen it?”*

   「如果人們還沒看到他們想要的東西，他們怎麼會知道自己想要什麼呢？」學習本單元核心句型：

   ★How do sb..., if sb have pp...「如果…還沒…，…怎麼會…。」
3. 搭配學習本單元其他三大重點句型：

   a The fact is that...（事實上…。）

   b S might be..., but... also indicate...（…也許…，但這也意味…。）

   c You as..., I strongly...（你/們身為…，我強烈地…。）
4. 將四種句型放入實境對話練習，學習四大行銷概念：

   a 以呼籲（appeal）集中焦點。

   b 以反問（rhetorical question）引導思維。

   c 以時效（effectiveness）調整策略。

   d 以稱讚（praise）拉近距離。

影片背景介紹

《賈柏斯傳》是已故蘋果公司創辦人賈伯斯之傳記電影，但值得注意的是本片並非改編自賈伯斯所授權自傳，而是針對其 1971 年到 2000 年間生活與工作的部分加以著墨。在這將近三十年的光陰中，賈伯斯歷經其一生重要的兩個時期，一是 21 歲時創立蘋果公司，二是在 31 歲時離開蘋果成立皮克斯動畫公司（Pixar Animation Studios）。由於取材的限制，無法對我們所熟知的 iPhone 與 iPad 加以描述，但片中賈伯斯諸多台詞，都是作為學習塑造公司形象與產品行銷的良好教材。

Jobs is the biographical film of the deceased founder of Apple, Steve Jobs. However, one thing worthy of noticing here is that this film is not the adaption of the autobiography that received the authorization from Steve Jobs, but a film that focuses on his life and work from 1971 to 2000. During those years, Steve Jobs encountered two turning points in his life: the founding of Apple when he was 21; the founding of Pixar Animation Studios when he was 31. Due to the restriction in material choosing, the detailed description concerning iPhone and iPad can't be found in this film. Though this movie fails to represent some important moments of this great person, but many lines that Jobs have said in the movie are good materials for brand image shaping and product marketing.

看影片怎麼說、怎麼用

At the conference room of ABC Company.

（在 ABC 公司的會議室。）

Jason: Good afternoon, Leo. Thank you for coming today. To save your precious time, I will skip the **lip service**. As a member of the e-generation, what makes our daily lives different is the Internet, right?

Jason：午安，Leo。感謝你今天撥空前來。為了節省你寶貴的時間，應酬話我就不講了。身為 E 世代的一員，網路使我們的日常生活大大不同，對吧？

Leo: True.

Leo：沒錯。

Jason: The power of the Internet is even greater nowadays. The growth in online shopping is **tremendous** as well and that is the reason why I have to introduce our service to you. I often say (1) "How does people know the convenience of the **cross-platform** if they are not aware of the change in the shopping habits?"

Jason：今日網路的力量又更加強大。線上購物的成長相當驚人，而這也是我為何要向你介紹本公司服務的原因。我常說：「如果人沒有意識到消費習慣的改變，他們怎麼會知道跨平台的便利性在哪呢?」

Leo: Indeed. The rising of online shopping does challenge **brick and mortar** businesses.

Leo：沒錯。線上購物的崛起對於實體店面來說確實是一大挑戰。

Jason: (2) The fact is that online shopping breaks the limitation in business hours, so consumers can purchase the items they need at anytime and anywhere as long as they are able to **access** the Internet. If your

Jason：事實上線上購物突破了營業時間的限制，只要能夠連接上網，消費者可以在任何時間任何地點購買所需的物品。如果你的產品能

products can be seen in several main entrance websites, the publicity of your products will become higher and higher.

夠在各大入口網站曝光，產品的知名度會越來越高。

Leo: In my opinion, shooting a creative or **controversial** video clip and put it on Youtube can serve the same function. Why do I have to use your service?

Leo：就我看來。拍一個有創意或是具爭議性的短片放上 Youtube 也能有相同效果。為何我需要使用你的服務？

Jason: Yeah! A video with eye-catching plots or images do attract consumer's attention in a very short time, but the fever will gradually fade out. To keep the **publicity** and visibility to certain level, making your product to be seen by the consumer **periodically** is crucial. Our service can help you to make it easily.

Jason：是的！搶眼的情節或畫面確實可以在短時間內吸引消費者目光，但這樣的熱潮終究會慢慢散去。若要維持一定知名度與能見度，定期讓消費者看到公司產品是必要的。而我們的服務能讓你輕鬆做到這點。

Leo: (3) You might be right, but using your service also indicates that I have to make a budget for this. How much money should I pay per month?

Leo：也許你是對的，但使用貴公司的服務也意味要編列預算。請問每月所需的費用是多少？

Jason: 30 USD per month. If you purchase this service one year at once, you can have free extension for two months. (4) You as a company with a promising future, I strongly recommend that you purchase one-year service. Our service won't disappoint you.

Jason：每月 30 美金。但如果你一次購買一年，可以享受兩個月的免費延長服務。你們是一間有前景的公司，所以我強烈建議你至少購買一年的服務。本公司的服務不會讓你失望。

對話單字說分明

1. **lip service idiom 空口的社交話**

   例：Lip service sometimes is needed in business occasions.

   許多商業場合有時會需要社交話。

2. **tremendous** *adj.* **極大的**

   例：The growth in the sales figure of smart phones is tremendous.

   智慧型手機的銷售數字的成長相當驚人。

3. **cross-platform 跨平台**

   例：Cross-platform marketing can make the whole industry more profitable.

   跨平台行銷能替整個產業增加更多利潤。

4. **brick and mortar business** *ph.* **實體店面**

   例：The rise in online shopping greatly affects bricks and mortar businesses.

   線上購物的崛起大幅影響實體店面的生意。

5. **access** *v.* **連接**

   例：As long as consumers can access the Internet, they can purchase our products in the online shop.

   只要連的上網路，消費者可在線上商店購買我們的產品。

6. **publicity** *n.* **知名度**

   例：The publicity of a product can affect its sales figure.

   產品知名度會影響其銷售數字。

7. **controversial** *adj.* **有爭議性的**

   例：The controversial issue always can raise a heated discussion.

   爭議性話題總是可已引起熱烈討論。

8. **periodically** *adv.* **定期地**

   例：This machine will be maintained periodically.

   此機器會定期進行保養。

重點句型分析

1. **How do sb..., if sb have/haven't pp...** 意思為「如果…還沒…，…怎麼會…」，可用於說明產品的未來性或解釋某現象的形成因素。

   例：How do people know the convenience of smart devices, if they haven't experienced it?

   如果人們還沒體驗過智慧型裝置，他們怎麼會知道其便利性在哪呢？

2. **The fact is that...** 意思為「事實上…。」，可用於釐清消費者的迷思或重申某事物的重要性。

   例：The fact is that the sales figures of e-shopping grow year after year.

   事實上線上購物的銷售數字年年成長。

3. **S might be..., but... also indicate...** 意思為「…也許…但也意味…」，可用於說明某現象所帶來某些後果或是影響。

   例：You might be right, but cost down also indicates that we have to stop some projects temporarily.

   或許你是對的，但節省成本代表有些專案必須暫停。

4. **You as..., I strongly...** 意思為「你做為…，我強烈地…」，可用來稱讚對方，而後陳述我方的立場或是欲推薦的產品或服務。

   例：You as the leading company in this industry, I strongly recommend you to develop the European market in the coming year.

   身為此產業的佼佼者，我強烈建議你於明年進軍歐洲市場。

職場補給站

本單元以推銷跨平台銷售為主軸，發展一段完整對話，其對話內容共提到四個行銷的常用概念，以下針對每個概念做進一步說明：

1. 以呼籲（appeal）集中焦點：

- 對應句型：**How does people know the convenience of cross-platform if they are not aware of the change in shopping habits?**

  當消費者在接收賣方給予的訊息時，會針對訊息的對自身的重要性加以篩選，因此若要有效引起消費者的注意，以呼籲的方式開頭會是不錯的選擇。此手法的優點在於能夠快速聚焦，有利於後續的產品介紹。**在本範例中，為了要讓 Leo 了解跨平台的便利性，Jason 先從網路的重要性開始鋪陳，之後便以問問題的方式來切入主題，讓 Leo 去思考跨平台銷售與傳統銷售的差異性為何。**

2. 以反問（rhetorical question）引導思維：

- 對應句型：**As a member of e-generation, what makes our daily life different is the Internet, right?**

  在銷售產品時，若銷售人員是主動的一方，對於最後的成交是有利的，但此處的主動並不是要咄咄逼人，要消費者趕快掏錢買單，而是採循序漸進的方式，讓消費者接受我方的看法。若要達到這樣的效果，以反問法開頭是可行的策略。透過反問，消費者會去思考我方所提出的論點是否與其認知相同。若相同，則可進行詳細解釋。若不同，可向其詢問想法原因，重新擬定說法或是解釋有疑問之處。**以本範例為例，Jason 先透鋪陳網路的重要性，反問 Leo 是否認為網路改變了我們的日常生活，替之後介紹跨平台銷售預做伏筆。**

3. 以時效（effectiveness）調整策略：

- 對應句型：**A video with eye-catching plots or images do attract consumer's attention in a very short time, but the fever will gradually fade out. To keep the publicity and visibility to certain level, making your products to be seen by the consumer periodically is crucial.**

  若要消費者花錢買單，產品或服務的效益是其關心重點。而影響效益的因素有二，一次本身的品質，二是搭配的場域、設備等等。兩者搭配良好方可產生最大效益。若就廣告行銷面向來看，訴求的時效長短如有不同，其搭配的策略也不同。如要短時間引起話題，特殊性或爭議性為主要考量。若要保持一定曝光度，穩定性是重點。**以本範例為利，Jason 表示有吸引力的情節或影像確實可以引起討論熱潮，但熱潮一過注目度就大減。若要保持一定知名度，就需要穩定的曝光。**

4. 以稱讚（praise）拉近距離：

- 對應句型：**You as a company with promising future, I strongly recommend that you purchase one-year service.**

  在行銷學中，掌握消費者心態是非常重要的一環，若在銷售過程中能讓消費者保持心情愉快，最後成交的可能性也大增。要達到這樣的效果，最直接的方法就是適度的稱讚。雖然說好話人人愛聽，但如果話語太過虛華，其實會形成反效果。**以本範例為利，Jason 稱讚 Leo 所在的公司是間有前景的公司，由於業績會蒸蒸日上，更需要輔助工具來提升產品曝光度。**

看《沒問題先生》（*Yes Man*），學習行銷產品

篇章重點搶先看

1. 以電影沒問題先生中主角卡爾艾倫的經典台詞學習如何行銷產品。
2. 以電影中主角卡爾艾倫台詞 *"When you say yes to things, you embrace the possible."*「當你對一件事情說好的時候你就擁抱了可能性」，學習本單元核心句型：

   ★When you say yes/no to..., you...「當你對…說好／不，你就…。」
3. 搭配學習本單元其他三大重點句型：

   a Considering..., N is/are...（考量到…，N 是…。）

   b The focus of... will be put on...（…的焦點將放在…。）

   c ... or I should say... here has become...（…或在這邊該說是…已經成為…。）
4. 將四種句型放入實境對話練習，學習四大行銷概念：

   a 以假設（presumption）推演後續。

   b 以二分法（dichotomy）強調差異。

   c 按趨勢（trend）提出計畫。

   d 以回饋（feedback）活化討論。

影片背景介紹

沒問題先生（*Yes Man*）的主角卡爾艾倫是名銀行放款員，他愛找藉口，愛拒絕別人。與妻子離婚後，在朋友的介紹下，因緣際會地參加「YES」講座，演講的內容切中卡爾內心的痛處，且講師預言他必須對接下來所遭遇的所有事情說 Yes，若說 No 則會惹禍上身。卡爾的人生自此出現巨大變化，開始學習許多過去不曾嘗試的事物，最後還與美女樂手陷入熱戀。片中主角對所有所奉為圭臬的話語，若應用在行銷上，正好可以做為說明突顯重要元素對公司形象塑造的重要性。

The protagonist of *Yes Man,* Carl Allen, is a bank loan officer who likes finding excuses for himself and rejecting other's request. After he gets divorced with his wife, his friends encourage him to attend "The Yes Session". This session touches Carl's heart, and the lecturer even predicts that Carl should always say yes to everything from now on; otherwise, he will be in a big trouble. Carl's life has encountered a great change ever since. He starts to learn things he refuses to try in the past and falls in love with a beautiful young women. If we analyze the words that Carl views as the guidelines after the session from the perspective of marketing, they can be good materials which illustrate the importance of highlighting the key elements in marketing.

看影片怎麼說、怎麼用

At the conference room of ABC Company.

（在 ABC 公司的會議室。）

Jason: Morning Mr. Lin. Thank you for coming today. Hope we can reach the **consensus** and begin the cooperation this year.

Jason：林經理早。感謝您今日前來，希望我們今日達成共識，於本年度進行合作。

Lin: I think so, too.

Lin：我也這樣認為。

Jason: Now let me briefly illustrate few key points in our proposal.

Jason：現在讓我向您簡單說明提案中的幾個要點。

Lin: OK. Please start it.

Lin：好的，請開始吧！

Jason: As we know the population engaged in sports grows year after year. And more importantly, the taste of this group has changed. Functional **apparels** and accessories can't fully meet their needs because the fashionable style has become one of their concerns. Although we are sport goods manufacturer with 40 years of history, we need to change. I would say (1) "When you say no to the trend, you will lose the market." To remain our feet stand firm in the market, finding a partner with **expertise** in fashion industry to **overturn** the fixed image is needed. (2) Considering the above mentioned reason, you are definitely our first

Jason：我們都知道運動人口逐年成長，且更重要的是，這個族群的喜好已經有所改變。由於時尚度成為消費者購買與否的考量之一，機能性服飾與配件已無法完全滿足他們的需求。雖然敝公司已在運動用品界耕耘四十年，但我們仍須有所改變。我會說：「當你對趨勢說不，你將失去市場。」，若要在市場中佔有一席之地，找尋具備時尚專業的夥伴來扭轉既有形象是必要的。考量上述因素，您絕對

choice.

是我們的優先選擇。

Lin: Thank you for recognizing our profession.

Lin：謝謝您認可我們的專業。

Jason: The way we would like to use in the project as the first step is to release **crossover** running shoes. If the market response is good, we can develop a series of collections.

Jason：本專案所可採用的初步做法是發行跨界聯名慢跑鞋。如果市場反應良好，可再擴大推出系列產品。

Lin: Can you give a more **specific** explanation about the "series" you just mentioned?

Lin：能針對「系列」這部分做更詳細的說明嗎？

Jason: Of course. (3) The focus of the series will be put on the runner's apparels and accessories.

Jason：當然可以。剛剛所提到的系列指的是推出慢跑服飾與配件。

Lin: Good. (4) Running or I should say jogging here has become one of the most popular sports in this **region**. Getting a share in the growing market first is a good strategy.

Lin：很好。跑步，或是這邊該說慢跑已經變成此區域最受歡迎的運動。在這個持續發展的市場先佔有一席之地是非常好的策略。

Jason: Since the talk almost can be closed as we scheduled and I have a meeting 30 minutes later, let's **wrap it up** here.

Jason：因為現在也差不多到我們預計結束的時間，且我半小時後還有另一個會議，今天就先討論到這邊吧！

對話單字說分明

1. **consensus** *n.* 共識

例：We need to reach consensus in the direction of our annual marketing strategy first.
我們必須先就年度行銷策略的大方向達成共識。

2. **apparel** *n.* 服飾

例：The target consumer of this apparel is teenagers.
這個服飾系列的目標客層是青少年。

3. **expertise** *n.* 專業

例：The expertise in machining is our strength in this industry.
加工技術上的專業是我們在業界的最大優勢。

4. **overturn** *v.* 扭轉

例：This smart phone successfully overturns the old-school image of the ABC Company.
這隻智慧型手機的推出成功扭轉 ABC 公司老派的形象。

5. **crossover** *adj.* 跨界的

例：The release of crossover products can stimulate the sales.
推出跨界商品可以刺激銷售。

6. **specific** *adj.* 明確的

例：To make sure the project feasible, we want to hear a more specific explanation from you.
為了確保此專案可行，希望您可以給我們更明確的說明。

7. **region** *n.* 區域

例：Consumers' taste can be different from region to region.
各區域消費者的喜好都不盡相同。

8. **wrap up** *ph.* 結束

例：Since we have run out of time, let's wrap up the meeting today.
由於時間已經不夠了，今天的會議就先到這邊結束。

重點句型分析

1. **When you say yes/no to..., you...** 意思為「當你對…說好／不，你就…。」，可用於說明選擇所帶來的結果。

   例：When you say no to the digitalization, you will fall far behind your competitors.

   當你向數位化說不時，你將遠遠落後於你的競爭對手。

2. **Considering..., N is/are...** 意思為「考量到…，N 是…。」，可用於說明在某條件下，某事物的適切性。

   例：Considering the feasibility, project A is our best choice.

   若考量到可行性，A 專案是我們的首選。

3. **The focus of... will be put on...** 意思為「…的核心將放在…上」，可用於說明事物最重要的部分為何。

   例：The focus of the promotion campaign will be put on the discount of our best sellers.

   本次促銷活動的重點將放在明星商品的折扣上。

4. **... or I should say... here has become...** 意思為「…或是在這邊該說…，已經變成…」，可用於說明某種事物的變化情況。

   例：Smart devices or I should say smart watches have become a necessity for many runners.

   智慧裝置，或是這邊我該說智慧腕表已經變成許多跑者的必備品。

職場補給站

本單元以商討合作案為背景，發展一段完整之對話，在其內容中共提到四個行銷的常用概念，以下針對每個概念做進一步說明：

1. 以假設（presumption）推演後續：

- 對應句型：**The way we would like to use in the project as the first step is to release crossover running shoes. If the market response is good, we can develop a series of collections.**

  行銷學可以解釋為以科學方法分析市場要素，再對此做出因應對策，在這樣思維模式下，使用假設的機會非常多。透過假設，行銷人員可以先行推測策略所帶來的效果為何，以及擬定備案。**在本範例中，Jason 表示本次合作案會先透過推出聯名跑鞋來試水溫，假設市場反應很好，方可考慮將合作擴大為一整個系列，推出各類相關產品。**

2. 以二分法（dichotomy）強調差異：

- 對應句型：**When you say no to the trend, you will lose the market.**

  在行銷學中，清楚傳達訊息給消費者是相當重要的，為了達到此目的，將訊息簡單化是很實用的策略。簡單化可以透二分法來達到。二分法可以是接受與拒絕；對與錯等等相對的概念。行銷人員可以透過二分法將所欲傳達的訊息包裝於其中，使其更加容易理解。**在本範例中，Jason 提到：「若你對趨勢說不，你將失去市場」。這段話就是運用接受與拒絕的二分法。雖然並未說出接受趨勢的結果為何，但消費者應該都能推測出 Jason 是要表達接受趨勢才能擁有市場。**

3. 按趨勢（trend）提出計畫：

- 對應句型：**To remain our foot stand firm in the market, finding a partner with expertise in fashion industry to overturn the fixed image is needed. Considering the above mentioned reason, you are definitely our first choice.**

若要成為一名優秀的行銷人員，在掌握市場趨勢後，接下來就是依照當中的要素發展出適合的策略。在此分析過程中，公司的形象為須考量的重要因素。舉例來說，若一間歷史悠久的公司希望透過新產品來改變消費者的印象，就需要先清楚認知自己的既有定位，以及訴求的新定位為何。**在本範例中，Jason 提到自家公司雖然在運動用品界歷史悠久，但因為缺乏時尚專業，因此希望透過合作案來改變品牌形象。**

4. 以回饋（feedback）活化討論：

- 對應句型：**Good. Running or I should say jogging here has become one of the most popular sports in this region. Getting a share in the growing market first is a good strategy.**

不論是一般的閒話家常或是商務上的協商討論，若參與者彼此都能給予適切的回應，整個談話效率會大大提升。此處回饋可並不侷限在一定得認同對方，若覺得有疑問或是有其他看法，可以明確表達，縮短達成共識或做出結論的時間。**在本範例中，林經理聽完 Jason 的闡述後，對於他所提出的看法表示認同，也覺得慢跑用品是很有市場潛力的，搶先佔有一席之地是正確的選擇。**

看《鐵娘子：堅固柔情》（*The Iron Lady*），學習掌握群眾心態

篇章重點搶先看

1. 以傳記電影《鐵娘子：堅固柔情》（*The Iron Lady*）中柴契爾夫人的經典台詞學習如何掌握群眾心態，使其對我方保有信心。
2. 以片中主角柴契爾夫人的經典台詞 *"It used to be about trying to do something. Now it's about trying to be someone."*「過去人們在乎做了些什麼事，現在人們在乎自己變成什麼人。」學習本單元核心句型：

   ★N used to be... Now is about...「過去…現在…。」
3. 搭配學習本單元其他三大重點句型：

   a If we compare the... of A and B, we can find.....（如果我們比 A 和 B 的…，會發現…。）

   b When... reach..., the... can...（當…達到，…會…。）

   c The... can be changed in accordance with...（…可以根據…去修改。）
4. 將四種句型放入實境對話練習，學習四大行銷概念：

   a 以今昔（before-after）對照差異。

   b 以規模經濟（economies of scale）提高購買數量。

   c 以使用習慣（habit）區隔客層。

   d 以客製（customization）滿足需求。

影片背景介紹

本片透過柴契爾夫人在整理亡夫遺物時所產生的幻覺與勾起的回憶為開端，由此開展其人生重要片段的回顧。受到擔任市議員父親的影響，柴契爾夫人在就讀牛津大學期間就已決定未來將踏上政治一途，她堅忍不拔的性格讓她成為英國第一位女性首相，更帶領英國打贏福克蘭戰爭。戰爭的勝利使柴契爾夫人的聲望達到頂峰，但也因此使其慢慢走向獨斷之路。雖然柴契爾夫人的政治生涯末段飽受批評，但她對英國所做出的諸多貢獻仍為多數人讚揚。在戰亂時，柴契爾夫人鼓勵人心的諸多演講詞，若套用在行銷學上，也可以用來塑造並且穩定消費者對於公司形象與產品的信心。

The movie *Iran Lady* begins with Margaret Thatcher's sorting out the goods of her dead husband and recalling the good time. Affected by his father as a city councilman, Thatcher decides to participate in politics when she was studying in Oxford University. Her perseverance makes her the first female Prime Minister in Britain and leads Britain to win the Falklands War. The victory of the war makes Thatcher's reputation reach the zenith, but it is also the beginning of her dictatorship. Though the Thatcher is greatly criticized in the last few years of her political life, the contribution she had made for Britain is still highly recognized. If we apply the speeches she had made to encourage the people of Britain during the war time to marketing, those words turn out to be good materials to learn how to shape the brand image and establish consumers confidence in our products.

看影片怎麼說、怎麼用

At the conference room of ABC Company. Jason is going to introduce cycling accessories to Mark.

（在 ABC 公司的會議室 Jason 將介紹自行車配件給 Mark。）

Mark: You are the leading company in this field, so we really want to know more details about your products.

Mark：貴公司在此領域，所以我們想進一步了解你們的產品。

Jason: Thank you for your **compliment**. Let me begin with the changes of cycling in the past ten year. (1) If we compare the cycling population of one decade ago to that of nowadays, we can find a great growth. (2) Cycling used be only regarded as one way of transportation. Now it is regarded as one way of exercise. Such a change makes cycling accessories a market with a great potential.

Jason：感謝您的稱讚。讓我先從過去十年間自行車運動的變化來開始說起。如果比較十年前與十年後自行車運動人口數，我們可以明顯看出成長。過去騎自行車被當成一種通勤方式。現在則被當成一種運動。這樣的變化使自行車配件深具市場潛力。

Mark: Indeed.

Mark：的確是。

Jason: To gain more shares in this **booming** market, currently we put the focus on the manufacturing of bicycle saddles. For riders, the comfort of the seat is their main concern. Our seats can meet the needs of the beginner and the professional riders. Today I would like to show you the saddle which is designed for advanced riders. As

Jason：為了要在這個具發展性的市場佔有一席之地，目前我們將產品主力放在座墊。對車友來說，座墊舒適度很很重要。我們的座墊可以滿足從初學者到專業人士的需求。今天我準備了一個為進階車友設計的的座墊。

you can see, the seat is in the streamline shape. Such design can reduce the wind **resistance**.

我們可以看到這個座墊成流線型，在騎車時可以降低風阻。

Mark: It sounds great. But I have few questions here. All the models you just mentioned are in a **standard** size, right? What if the size I need is special, can you **customize** it for me?

Mark：聽起來很不錯。但這邊我有個問題。你剛所提到的型號應該都是標準尺寸對吧？如果我需要特殊尺寸，能夠客製嗎？

Jason: The answer of the first question is yes. About the customization, (3) the design can be totally changed or slightly **modified** in accordance with consumers' needs, and the cost charged will be based on the complexity of modification. The maximum of the extra charge will be 60 percent.

Jason：第一個問題的答案：是的，都是標準尺寸。關於客製部分，我們能夠依照客戶需求去整體變更或是些微修改設計，加收的費用則是依照複雜度決定。最多加收 60%。

Mark: I see. Do you have the minimum purchase amount?

Mark：我了解了。有最低購買數量的限制嗎？

Jason: Yes, we do. For the standard ones, 100 is the minimum. (4) When the purchase amount of customized products reaches 500 pieces, the scale of economy of **mold** can be reached and therefore we will accept this order.

Jason：有。標準品的最低數量是 100 件。當客製品的採購數量達 500 件，便可達到新開模具的規模經濟，我們也才會接受此訂單。

對話單字說分明

1. **compliment** *n.* **稱讚**

例：This is the kindest compliment I have ever had.

這是我聽過最好的稱讚。

2. **booming** *adj.* **急速發展的**

例：The market of organic food is booming.

有機食物的市場正急速發展。

3. **resistance** *n.* **阻力**

例：To reduce the wind resistance, most sport cars are designed with streamline shape.

為降低風阻，多數的跑車都成流線型。

4. **standard** *n.* **標準的**

例：The standard cleaning service fee we charge is 15USD.

標準清潔服務我們收費 15 美金。

5. **customize** *v.* **客製化**

例：The parts can be customized according to buyers' needs.

零件可以根據買方需求加以客製。

6. **modify** *v.* **修改**

例：The plan needs to be modified to meet the company policy.

此計畫需要修改，以便符合公司政策。

7. **mold** *n.* **模具**

例：The cost of the new mold is included in the budget of the project.

新模具的成本已包含在次專案的預算之內。

8. **quotation** *n.* **報價單**

例：Please send us your quotation by fax within two days .

請於兩日內傳真您的報價單給我們。

重點句型分析

1. **N used to be... Now sth is...** 意思為「過去…，現在…」，可用於比較過去與現在的差異。

   例：Taxi used to be the top choice for many commuters. Now it is almost replaced by the MRT.
   過去許多通勤者搭計程車，現在幾乎改搭捷運。

2. **If we compare the... of A and B, we can find...** 意思為「如果我們比 A 和 B 的…，會發現…。」

   例：If we compare the thickness of the computer screen five years ago and that of now, we can find the new model is thinner.
   如果我們比較五年前與現在電腦螢幕的厚度，現在的型號較薄。

3. **When...reach..., the... can...** 意思為「當…達到，…能…」，可用於說達到某項指標時所會產生的變化。

   例：When the purchase amount reaches 100 sets, the shipping fee can be deducted to 80 percent。
   當購買數量達到一百組時，運費能夠打八折。

4. **The... can be changed in accordance with...** 意思為「…可以根據…修改」，可用於說明某某部分可以按照怎樣的方式修改。

   例：The size of the parts can changed in accordance with you needs.
   零件尺寸可以根據您的需求修改。

本單元以推銷自行車配件為場景，發展一段完整的的範例對話，其內容中共提到四個行銷的常用概念，以下針對每個概念做進一步說明：

1. 以今昔（before-after）對照差異：

- 對應句型：**Cycling used to be only regarded as one way of transportation. Now it is regarded as one way of exercise.**

  在行銷產品或是塑造公司形象時，讓消費者感受差異性是非常重要的，差異性可以透過比較過去與現在來顯現。這邊的差異性可以是使用習慣、精良程度、尺寸等等，因此在使用時並不會有侷限性。**在本範例中，Jason 提到過去大家把騎單車當成通勤方式，現在則當成一種運動，將比較的重點著眼於使用習慣的變化。**

2. 以規模經濟（economy of scale）提高購買數量：

- 對應句型：**When the purchase amount of customized products reaches 500 pieces, the scale of economy of mold can be reached and therefore we will accept this order.**

  在經濟學上，當生產數量達到一定程度，其生產成本會因為操作人員的熟練度提高等因素而得以降低。基於上述因素，銷售人員在推銷產品時，應善加利用此點，鼓吹客戶一次購買較多數量，已獲得價格上的優惠。**在本範例中，Jason 就提到客製品因為需要重新開模，因此一次需購買 500 件才會接下訂單，讓可能需要客製品的 Mark 先去思考最後實際下單的可能數量。**

3. 以使用習慣（habit）區隔客層：

- 對應句型：**Today I would like to show you the saddle which is designed for advanced riders. As you can see, the seat is in streamline shape. Such design can reducing the wind resistance.**

  在行銷學中，清楚的市場區隔是很重要的，因為不同的消費族群會有不同的偏好，針對其喜好推出商品，才容易有好的銷售成績。舉例來說，青少年的產品可能會訴求新潮，但中年人的會講求穩重。**在本範例中，Jason 準備了專業級的單車座墊給 Mark 看，透過實際展示的方式讓他了解自家公司能根據客層需求生產適合的商品。**

4. 以客製（customization）滿足需求：

- 對應句型：**About the customization, the design can be totally changed or slightly modified in accordance with consumers' needs and the cost will be based on the complexity of modification.**

  不論市場上的產品怎樣多元，總是會出現無法滿足消費者需求的時候，這時候就需要透過客製化來彌補。客製的範圍可能包括顏色、尺寸或是整個設計上的大變革，因此相較一般標準品，會需要額外收費。**在本範例中，Jason 提到自家公司可以根據客戶需求小幅或是大幅修改產品，增加的費用則是依照修改的難度來決定。**

看《美國隊長》（*Captain America: The First Avenger*），了解塑造產品形象的重要性

篇章重點搶先看

1. 以電影《美國隊長》（*Captain America: The First Avenger*）主角史提夫羅傑斯的經典台詞學習塑造產品形象的重要性。
2. 以電影主角史提夫羅傑斯的經典台詞 *"The price of freedom is high... and it's a price I'm willing to pay!"*「自由的代價很高，但是這是我願意付的代價。」學習本單元的核心句型：

   ★The...of... is... and it is the... I am willing to...「…的…是…，但這是我願意…的…。」
3. 搭配學習本單元其他三大重點句型：

   a Once... is Ved, ... will...（一旦…被…，…將…。）

   b To keep..., N is...（為保持…，N 是…。）

   c No N is..., so we...（沒有…是…，所以我們…。）
4. 將四種句型放入實境對話練習，學習四大行銷概念：

   a 以價值創造品牌忠誠度（brand loyalty）。

   b 以當前技術瓶頸（bottleneck）突顯產品優勢。

   c 以售後服務（after-sale service）提高購買意願。

   d 以即時性（Immediacy）滿足客戶需求。

影片背景介紹

《美國隊長》（*Captain America*）一片是關於主角史提夫羅傑思如何從一名瘦弱矮小的男性，之後變成一位帶領美軍於二戰時期擊退九頭蛇軍團的英雄人物的故事。在電影的開頭，羅傑斯因為體格太差，始終無法如願從軍報效國家，但他後來得到軍方科學家艾斯金的協助，成為超級士兵。不過羅傑斯一開始的工作並非上戰場殺敵，而是擔任像是募款大使的角色。不甘於位居後勤，史提夫決定前往歐洲剿滅九頭蛇。電影中，羅傑斯的經典台詞，除可以表現愛國之外，若將其句型架構應用應用於公關行銷上，恰可作為說明形塑產品核心概念的重要性。

Captain America: The First Avenger is a story about how the protagonist, Steve Rogers, transforms from a weak and short guy and later becomes a super hero to lead US army to defeat Hydra in the WWII. In the beginning of the movie, Steve is too weak to join the US army. Receiving the help from the military scientist Erskine, Steve reborns as a super soldier. However, Steve is not assigned to kill the enemy in the war field at the very beginning, but works like a fundraising ambassador. Feeling unsatisfied with his duty, Steve decides to go to Europe to fight with Hydra. The classic line of Steve not only shows the patriotism, but also can be used as a good material to show the importance of faith shaping to products.

看影片怎麼說、怎麼用

At the Briefing Room of ABC Company. Jason is going to introduce the latest security system of his company to Peter.

（在 ABC 公司的簡報室 Jason 將介紹公司最新的資訊系統給 Peter。）

Jason: Now let me officially introduce our new information security system SHEALD to you. In the age of information **explosion**, we get and receive a great amount data each day. When people convey important messages, checking the safety level of the net is their priority. (1) Once the **confidential** information leaks out, the consequence could be serious. After using our system, we promise you will never have to worry about this problem.

Jason：現在讓我正式向您介紹我們最新推出的資訊安全系統 SHEALD。身處資訊爆炸世代，我們每天都發送與接受大量的資訊。當人們傳送重要資訊時，首先會去注意網路的安全層級。一但這些機密資訊外洩，其結果可能非常嚴重。而我們的系統可以讓您不再為此擔憂。

Peter: Indeed. (2) The price of the information security is high and it is a price I am willing to pay. Compared with the great price we have to pay after leakage, the price of buying a system is relatively low.

Peter：的確是。資安的代價很高，但這是我願意支付的代價。與發生資訊洩漏的代價相比，購買一套系統的價錢是相對便宜的。

Jason: True. Now let me show you the strength of this system. Password does serve as the function of delaying the **abnormal** data accessing, but it will be broken if the **hacker** uses programs to key in the combination of figures and letters for a certain period of time. Our system makes

Jason：的確是。現在讓我向您展示本系統的優點。密碼確實可以延後不正常的資料存取，但只要駭客運用程式不斷輸入數字與字母的組合，一段時間後一定會被破解。我們的系統讓這種入侵

their method useless. Why I say so is because this system will randomly add 1 or 2 digits when the user keys in the wrong password for ten times. In other words, the more the **invader** tries, the more complicate the password will become.

方式無用武之地。我會這樣說是因為當輸入錯誤密碼超過十次後，本系統會隨機增加一個到兩個數字密碼。換言之，錯誤越多次，密碼就越複雜。

Peter: This protection seems comprehensive. However, the hacker will find the new way to **decode** this program one day. How do you deal with this?

Peter：這樣的防護似乎很全面，但駭客總有一天能夠對程式進行解碼，你們會如何因應呢？

Jason: (3) To keep the security level stable to a certain extent, the coding of password is the key. This system will change the coding at least two times a week.

Jason：為了保持一定的安全等級，密碼的編碼方式是關鍵。本系統一週至少會變更編碼兩次。

Peter: I see. What can I do if the system crashes?

Peter：我了解了。還有一點要問的是萬一系統故障，我該怎麼做？

Jason:(4) No system is **flawless**, so we have established a back stage to receive abnormal signals sent from our customers. The system will firstly detect the source of problem, and we will contact our customers and send **technicians** soon if the problem cannot be fixed by the system itself.

Jason：沒有系統是完美的，所以我們設計了後台系統來接收客戶所發出的異常訊號。系統首先會偵測問題來源，若系統無法自行修復，我們會派出技術人員。

Peter: I got it. I think we will place an order soon. Thank you for your presentation.

Peter：了解。我想我們很快就會下單。謝謝你的簡報。

對話單字說分明

1. **explosion** *n.* 爆炸

例：As a secretary, I face the message explosion every day.
身為一名秘書，我每天面對訊息轟炸。

2. **confidential** *adj.* 機密的

例：Please keep this document confidential until the meeting tomorrow morning. 明天早上開會前請先對此文件保密。

3. **abnormal** *adj.* 不正常的

例：The system will send a warming message to the user, if any abnormal data accessing is found.
如果有任何不正常的資訊存取，系統會發送警告訊息給使用者。

4. **hacker** *n.* 駭客

例：The system is designed to prevent the attack from hackers.
這套系統是設計來防堵駭客的攻擊的。

5. **invader** *n.* 入侵者

例：The sensor of security system will make sounds, if any invader is found. 如發現入侵者，保全系統的偵測器會發出聲響。

6. **decode** *v.* 解碼

例：The complicate password is the way we use to keep this message from decoding. 這串複雜的密碼是我們用來防止訊息被解碼的方法。

7. **flawless** *adj.* 完美的

例：No system is flawless, and that is why it needs an upgrade.
沒有一個系統是完美的，而這也是為何需要進行升級。

8. **technician** *n.* 技術人員

例：We will send one technician to check the machine for you this afternoon. 我會派一名技術人員今天下午幫你檢查機器。

重點句型分析

1. **The... of... is... and it is the... I am willing to...** 意思為「…的…是…，但這是我願意…的…」，可用於說明我方所願意進行的動作或是認可的概念。

   例：The cost of the imported goods is high, and it is the cost I am willing to pay.

   進口品的成本高，但這是我所願意支付的成本。

2. **Once... is Ved, ...will...** 意思為「一旦…，N 將…」，可用於說明在某種情況下，所可能發生的狀況為何。

   例：Once the machine is broken, the shipment will be delayed.

   一旦機器壞掉，出貨將會延遲。

3. **To keep..., N is...** 意思為「為保持…N 是…」，可用來說明達到某項指標所需的要素為何。

   例：To keep the efficiency, periodical maintenance is needed.

   為保持效能，定期保養是必要的。

4. **No N is..., so we...** 意思為「沒有…是…，所以我們…」，可用於說明某事物所無法去除或避免的面相，以及其可行的彌補方式。

   例：No plan is prefect, so we accept any practical suggestions.

   沒有一個計畫是完美的，所以我們接受任何有建設性的建議。

本單元以行銷資訊安全系統為背景，發展一段範例對話，其內容共提到四個行銷的常用概念，以下針對每個概念做進一步說明：

1. 以價值創造品牌忠誠度（brand loyalty）：

- 對應句型：**Once the confidential information leaks out, the consequence could be serious. After using our system, we promise you will never have to worry about this problem.**

  在行銷產品時，讓客戶看見產品價值是非常重要的，其原因在於當客戶認同這樣的價值時，對於價格相對就不會如此執著，雙方最後成交的可能性隨之提高。**在本範例中，Jason 提到機密資料外洩可能會造成嚴重的後果，而使用本公司的資安系統可以避免這樣的情況發生，借此希望讓客戶產生品牌忠誠度。**

2. 以當前技術瓶頸（bottleneck）突顯產品優勢：

- 對應句型：**Password does serve the function of delaying the abnormal data accessing, but it will be broken if the hacker uses programs to key in the combination of figures and letters for certain period of time. Our system makes their method useless.**

  若突顯自家產品的優點，先敘述當前技術上的限制是很好的引言。透過這樣的資訊傳達，客戶會先接受到一個負面的訊息，而後我方再提出自家產品能夠克服此問題，故與其他產品有所不同。**在本範例中，Jason 提到密碼確是可以暫緩不正常的資料存取，但只要駭客多花點時間用程式暴力破解，最後還是能夠取得資料。而本公司的系統可讓這種入侵方式失效。**

3. 以售後服務（after-sale service ）提高購買意願：

- 對應句型：No system is flawless, so we have established a back stage to receive abnormal signals sent from our customers. The system will firstly detect the source of problem and we will contact our customers and send technicians soon if the problem cannot be fixed by the system itself.

在行銷產品時，各客層所在乎的面向可能有所不同，但售後服務這塊絕對是不容忽視的。不論產品再精良，服務再週到，總是可能出現預期之外的狀況，此時唯有透過售後服務幫客戶解決問題，才能是維持長久的買賣關係。**在本範例中，Jason 提到沒有系統是完美的，所以本公司有預設後台系統來偵測異常狀況，若系統無法即時修復，就會派出技術人員協助處理。**

4. 以即時性（Immediacy）滿足客戶需求：

- 對應句型：Why I say so is because this system will randomly add 1 or 2 digits when the user keys in the wrong password for ten times. In other words, the more the invader tries, the more complicate the password will become.

在消費市場中，客戶的需求不可能一成不變，因此當需求變更時，特別是臨時性的調整時，銷售方應當有足夠的應變能力。當銷售方能夠應付各種突發狀況，購買方對產品的信心也會相對提高。**在本範例中，Jason 提到本系統會在輸入錯誤密碼後自動加高密碼複雜度，以及時處理的方式讓駭客可能因此知難而退，從而提高 Peter 對此系統的信心。**

看《購物狂的異想世界》（*Confessions of a Shopaholic*），學習進行差異性行銷

篇章重點搶先看

1. 以《購物狂的異想世界》（*Confessions of a Shopaholic*）主角的經典台詞學習如何進行差異性行銷。
2. 以購物狂的異想世界主角 Rebecca 的經典台詞 *"You want your scarf, I want my hot dog. Cost and worth are very different things."*
「你要你的圍巾，我要我的熱狗。價錢和價值並非一回事兒」。學習本單元核心句型：
★You want your N 1, I want my N2. N1 and N2 are...「你要你的 N1，我要我的 N2。N1 和 N2 是…。」
3. 搭配學習本單元其他三大重點句型：
a To show our..., we provide...（為表示我們的…，我們提供…。）
b ... features..., making it the... for...（…主打…，使其成為…的…。）
c Holding the faith of..., we...（秉持…的信念，我們…。）
4. 將四種句型放入實境對話練習，學習四大行銷概念：
i. 以價格（price）吸引一般消費者。
ii. 以價值（value）吸引頂端消費者。
iii. 以通路（channel）創造更多營收。
iv. 以限量（limit edition）創造話題性。

影片背景介紹

《購物狂的異想世界》(*Confessions of a Shopaholic*)的主角 Rebecca 是名購物狂，她與好友 Suze 住在一起，由於熱愛購買名牌，導致 Rebecca 大學畢業許久仍無法有太多存款。Rebecca 一直夢想進入時尚雜誌工作，但卻陰錯陽差的成為一名財經專欄作家。Rebecca 特殊的理財觀點使她深受讀者喜愛，但在她撰文教導別人理財的同時，仍不斷地購物。揮霍無度讓她面臨巨額債務；「價格」與「價值」的比較是本片所描繪的的重點之一，價格的高低並不等同其價值的高低。Rebecca 在電影開端所比較圍巾與熱狗的台詞恰巧為這論點下了最好註解，也說明行銷策略需要因目標客群的不同而有所調整。

The protagonist of *Confessions of a Shopaholic* Rebecca is a shopaholic who lives with her best friend Suze. Because Rebecca likes to buy luxury goods, she doesn't have much saving after the graduation from the university. Rebecca's dream job is to become an employee in a fashion magazine publishing company, but she turns out to be a financial management column writer. Her special viewpoints make her beloved by readers. However, she ironically continues her shopaholic behaviors when she writes articles to teach people how to manage their money. Such a bad habit makes Rebecca in debt. The comparison of "price" and "value" is one focus of this movie. The lines about scarf and hot dog is the best denotation of this concept and it also illustrates that that the marketing strategies shall be changed with the needs of target groups.

看影片怎麼說、怎麼用

At the conference room of ABC Company.

（在 ABC 公司的會議室。）

Jason: Good morning General Manager and Chief **Executive** Officer. Today I represent the Home Video Game **Console** Department to report our 2015 marketing campaigns to you.

Jason：早安，總經理與執行長。今天我代表電玩主機部門向您報告本部門 2015 年行銷活動。

General Manager: Morning Jason. You can start the briefing now.

總經理：Jason 早安。可以開始簡報了。

Jason: Sure. Let me begin with the spirit of our company - Make a game console for all. (1) Holding the faith of serving more players, we develop the following campaigns. People may say (2) "You love your Toyota, I love my Ferrari. Toyota and Ferrari are different things." From those words, we can tell that the preference can be different from group to group. To develop the clear market **segmentation**, directions of the marketing strategy are polarized. We release the original edition and flagship edition. (3) The original model features its economical price, making it the best choice of the player with limited budget for the new console. The price of this model costs 199 USD. The flagship model features the high definition, Dolby **surround,** and 1 TB memory, making

Jason：好。讓我先從公司的信念：打造一台適合所有人的主機。秉持此信來服務更多玩家，我們策畫了以下的行銷活動。人們會說「你喜歡你的豐田，而我喜歡我的法拉利。豐田和法拉利是完全不同的東西。」從這句話我們可以得知各消費族群的偏好有所不同。為做出清楚的市場區隔，我們制定兩極化的策略。我們同時推出一般版與旗艦版主機。一般版主機主打實惠的價格，讓預算有限的玩家可以購買新主機。訂價是 199 美金。旗艦版主打高畫質、杜比音效與 1TB 儲存空間。雖然

it the favorite of high-end players. Though the listed price 399 USD is double, its power will make your investment worth. To generate more revenue and shorten the waiting time, two models are both available in our retailers and online stores. Players choose the either way to buy the edition they want by cash or credit card. Lastly, (4) to show our **appreciation** to the consumers, we provide 100 limited free key chains and T-shirts only available in this campaign for the first one hundred consumers who buy our new consoles.

訂價來到一般版兩倍的 399 美金，但它的效果絕對讓你大呼值得。為了要增加收益與縮短消費者的等待時間，兩種版本皆可在零售商與線上商店購得。玩家可選擇其一以現金或是信用卡支付款項。最後，為了表達我們對消費者的感謝，我們將贈送前一百名購買的消費者本活動免費的專屬限量鑰匙圈與 T 恤。

CEO: The campaign you propose sounds practical, but I am in a state of **confusion**. Since we have two distribution channels, how do you define who are the first one hundred consumers?

執行長：你剛所提出的活動很實際，但我有一點讓我很疑惑。因為我們有兩種銷售管道，請問你是怎樣定義前一百名購買者？

Jason: Sorry for confusing you. To make sure all the shoppers share the same right, we provide 100 gifts for retailers and another 100 for online stores.

Jason：抱歉讓您產生疑惑。為確保所有購買人都享有相同權利，我們提供一百份的贈品給零售商，一百份給線上商店。

CEO: I see. Any **comments**, General Manager?

執行長：我了解了。總經理有任何意見嗎？

General Manager: No. Please send me the **proposal** through e-mail and I will approve it when I get back to my office.

總經理：沒有，但請將提案寄到我的信箱。我回辦公室後會批准此案。

Lesson 07
Lesson 08
Lesson 09
Lesson 10
Lesson 11
Lesson 12

對話單字說分明

1. **executive** *adj.* **執行的**

   例：Tom is our new Chief Executive Officer.

   Tom 是本公司新首席任執行長。

2. **console** *n.* **控制器**

   例：Home video game consoles are products with potential.

   家用電玩主機是個具有市場潛力的產品。

3. **segmentation** *n.* **區分**

   例：Clear market segmentation can help us gain a share in the market.

   清楚的市場區分有助於在新市場取得市佔率。

4. **surround** *n.* **環繞音效**

   例：7.1 surround is the feature of this set of speakers.

   這組喇叭主打 7.1 聲道環繞音效。

5. **appreciation** *n.* **感謝**

   例：To show our appreciation, we will deduct the freight.

   為表達感謝之意，我們將減免運費。

6. **confusion** *n.* **疑惑**

   例：To avoid confusion, please use a marker to highlight the total amount.

   為避免產生疑惑，請使用馬克筆標註總數。

7. **comment** *n.* **評論**

   例：Do you have any comments on this project?

   你對此專案有任何評論嗎。

8. **proposal** *n.* **提案**

   例：Please submit the proposal before this Friday.

   請於本週五前呈報提案。

重點句型分析

1. **You want your N 1, I want my N2. N1 and N2 are...** 意思為「你想要你 N1，我想要我的 N2，N1 和 N2 是...」，可用於說明個人的偏好，以及各偏好間的差異為何。

   例：You want your Jordan shoes, and I want my Chanel perfume. Jordan shoes and Chanel perfume are totally different things.
   你想要你的喬丹鞋，而我想要我的香奈兒香水。喬丹鞋跟香奈兒香水是完全不同的一回事。

2. **To show our..., we provide...** 意思為「為表示我們的…，我們提供…。」，可用於說明我方表達

   例：To show our gratitude, we provide you a 15% discount coupon for the next purchase.
   為表達我們的感激之意，我們提供您下次購買時享八五折的優惠券。

3. **... features..., making it the... for...** 意思為「…主打…，使其成為…的…」，可用於說明產品的特色，以及其所適合的族群。

   例：The shoes features the cushion, making it the best choice for runners.
   這雙鞋主打避震性，使其成為跑者的最佳選擇。

4. **Holding the faith of..., we...** 意思為「秉持…的信念，我們…」，可用於說明公司的信念與該信念具體化之行為。

   例：Holding the faith of meeting the needs of all consumers, we provide a customized service.
   秉持滿足所有客戶需求的信念，我們提供客製服務。

本單元以員工向總經理與執行長報告行銷策略為場景，發展一段完整對話，其內容中一共提到四個行銷的常用概念，以下針對每個概念做進一步說明：

1. 以價格（price）吸引一般消費者：

- 對應句型：**The original model features its economical price, making it the best choice of the players with limited budget for the new console. The price of this model is 199 USD.**

  在制定行銷策略時，在經濟金字塔中段的一般消費者是不可忽略的一群。這個族群雖然無法像頂端消費者一次進行大額消費，但加總該族群所有中小額消費，其總額依舊驚人。若要吸引該族群，價格絕對是重點之一，只要產品的基本功能齊全並搭配上實惠的價格，一般消費者多願意買單。**在本範例中，Jason 提到一般版的主機就是主打價格戰，199 美金的低售價足以成為吸引預算有限的玩家換新機的誘因。**

2. 以價值（value）吸引頂端消費者：

- 對應句型：**The flagship model features the high definition, Dolby surround, and 1 TB memory, making it the favorite of high-end players. Though the listed price 399 USD is double, its power will make your investment worthy.**

  針對金字塔頂端的消費者會是追求頂級產品的消費者，產品價格對其重要性相對較低，左右該族群購買與否的關鍵因素在於產品所呈現出的價值。舉例來說，當某一產品能夠完全滿足其需求，即便價格偏高，這類型的消費這仍願意買單。**在本範例中，Jason 提出旗艦版主機主打高解析度、環繞音效與大記憶體，這些功能正是高階玩家所需。因此即便售價是一般版的兩倍，還是會讓該族群玩家感到值得。**

3. 以通路（channel）創造更多營收：

- 對應句型：**To generate more revenue and shorten the waiting time, the two models are both available in our retailers and online stores.**

當公司製造出產品後，接下來就是要透過通路加以行銷，在網路發達的現在，虛擬通路是相當值得耕耘的一塊。實體通路的優點在於消費者可以親眼看到與體驗產品功能，虛擬通路則只需支付倉租，可將節省下的成本反映在售價的降低上。由於各通路都有其優點，多方使用可產生更大的效益。**在本範例中，Jason 提到，此主機可在零售商店面與線上商店購得，讓消費者可依其需求選擇購買方式。**

4. 以限定商品（limit edition）創造話題性：

- 對應句型：**...to show our appreciation to the consumers, we provide 100 limited free key chains and T-shirts only available in this campaign for the first one hundred consumers who buy our new consoles.**

正所謂物以稀為貴，當一項產品具備稀有性時，就可能吸引消費者的注意，進而產生搶購或是引起熱烈討論。此處的稀有性可以是限點販售、活動限定或是數量限定。透過推出這類的限量商品，可讓產品的曝光度大增。**在本範例中，為了回饋消費者與引起話題性，Jason 表示說將贈送免費的限量鑰匙圈與 T 恤給實體店與網路商店的前一百名購買者，藉此強化玩家購買新機的動機。**

看《雙面情人》（*Sliding Doors*），學習漸進式塑造產品或公司形象

篇章重點搶先看

1. 以《雙面情人》（*Sliding Doors*）電影男主角 James Hammerton 的經典台詞學如何漸進的方式塑造產品或公司形象。
2. 以本片的台詞之一 *"Everything happens for the best; you'll never know if you don't try."*「每件事都有好的一面，放棄就看不到了」，學習本單元核心句型：

   ★… happen for…, you will never… if you…「…都有…的一面，如果…就…。」
3. 搭配學習本單元其他三大重點句型：

   a When you… in a… way, you will…（當你以…的方式…，你將…。）

   b With…, you can…（有了…，你可以…。）

   c Though…, the N can…（雖然…，但 N 可以…。）
4. 將四種句型放入實境對話練習，學習四大行銷概念：

   a 以吸引力法則（law of attraction）強調正面思考。

   b 說明現況（current status）來展現產品優勢。

   c 讓需要（need）成為必需（necessity）。

   d 以優惠套餐（combo）增加銷售。

影片背景介紹

《雙面情人》（*Sliding Doors*）是一部以平行時空來敘述故事女主角海倫不同命運的電影。海倫在某個星期三遭到所任職的公關公司解雇，難過的她決定搭地鐵回家，到站時列車剛好進站，故事自此展開成兩線。片中詹姆士鼓勵海倫的台詞恰可用來作為漸進塑造公司產品或是服務的良好教材。

Sliding Doors is the story of Helen in two parallel universes. On one Wednesday, Helen is laid off by the public relations company she works for. Feeling sad, she decides to take Subway home. When she steps into the station, the train is about to arrive. The plot is divided into two parts from this scene. The lines that James says in the movie to encourage Helen turn out to be the good materials for us to learn how to shape the product image in a progressive way.

看影片怎麼說、怎麼用

At the **counter** of the ABC Training center. Jason, the sales of ABC Training Center, is helping Kevin know more about the design courses Kevin is interested in.

（在 ABC 訓練中心櫃檯。ABC 訓練中心的業務 Jason 正在協助 Kevin 了解 Kevin 有興趣的設計課程。）

Jason: I see. (1) Everything goes for a reason; You will never know if you don't try. To give you the best suggestion, could you let me know your **motive**?

Jason：我了解了。事出必有因，如果沒去找就不知到底是為什麼。為了給您最佳的建議，可以跟我說明一下上課的動機嗎？

Kevin: Of course. I like trendy things, and I hope I am able to design something creative one day. However, I don't know what kind of design software I should learn first. Can you give me some recommendations?

Kevin：當然。我喜歡潮流的東西，而且我希望自己有天能夠設計一些有創意的東西。但我不知道我該從哪種設計軟體開始學起，可以給我一些建議嗎？

Jason: In the current job market, Illustrator and Photoshop are the two popular software in the market.(2) With the **proficiency** in the abovementioned software, you can meet the basic **qualification** of many design companies. As a result, I suggest you choose the either one as your first design course.

Jason：在目前就業市場中，Illustrator 和 Photoshop 是兩個熱門的軟體。若熟悉上述兩種軟體的操作，您就符合許多設計公司職缺的基本要求了。所以我建議您擇一做為入門。

Kevin: I got it. I think I will choose Illustrator. One more question here is how long could I

Kevin：我想我會選擇 Illustrator。另外想問的就

become an experienced user?

是需要多久才能對此軟體上手呢？

Jason: (3) When you learn something in an **aggressive** way, you will learn it better and quickly. Since there is a strong motivation supporting your learning, I would say a three-month intensive course is enough.

Jason：當你以積極的態度學習，你就會學得更快更好。因為你有強烈的動機支持你的學習，所以我想三個月的密集課程就足夠了。

Kevin: Three months? How many courses do I need to take in a week?

Kevin：只要三個月！一星期需要上幾次課呢？

Jason: Twice a week, three hours for each. (4) Though the time is not very long, the assignment after class can help you **integrate** the knowledge you have learned and **sharpen** the skills through practice.

Jason：一週兩次，每次三小時。雖然上課的時間並不長，但課後作業可以你整合課堂所學並透過實作琢磨技巧。

Kevin: What a solid training. Last one but also the most important question, how much is the **tuition**?

Kevin：好紮實的訓練。最後也是最重要的一個問題，請問學費是多少錢？

Jason: For the new student, a 3 month intensive course costs 1500USD. But we have a special combo project. If you buy two beginner classes a time, we only charge you 500USD. It is really a great deal.

Jason：新學員三個月密集課程收費 1500 美金。但現在我們有一個特別的套餐專案。如果一次購買兩堂初學者課程，只收 500 美金，非常划算。

Kevin: Great. I will take both Illustrator and Photoshop classes.

Kevin：太棒了。我要買 Illustrator 和 Photoshop 課程。

對話單字說分明

1. **counter** *n.* **櫃檯**

例：If you have any question, please contact our information counter.

如果你有任何問題，請洽服務櫃台。

2. **motive** *n.* **動機**

例：The sales figure could be raised, if we can create the motive for the purchase of our product.

如果能夠創造購買我們產品的動機，銷售數字就會上升。

3. **proficiency** *n.* **能力**

例：Operation proficiency determines the efficiency of production.

操作熟悉度影響生產效率。

4. **qualification** *n.* **資格**

例：Please modify the content of project to meet the qualification of the public bidding.

請修改專案內容以符合公開招標的資格。

5. **aggressive** *adj.* **進取的**

例：An aggressive attitude can help a sales to sell more products.

進取的態度能讓業務售出更多產品。

6. **integrate** *v.* **整合**

例：It takes us one day to integrate the data of our system.

整合系統資料花了我們一天的時間。

7. **sharpen** *v.* **精進**

例：This training course can sharpen your sales skills.

這個訓練課程可以精進你的銷售技巧。

8. **tuition** *n.* **學費**

例：The tuition of this course is 150USD.

這堂課的學費是 150 美金。

重點句型分析

1. **... happen for...; you will never... if you...** 意思為「凡事都有…的一面，如果…就…」，可以說明如何做才不會錯過事物的一些面向。

   例：Everything happened for the bright side; you will never know if you give up early.

   凡事都有好的一面，如果太早放棄就看不到了。

2. **When you... in a... way, you will...** 意思為「當你以…的方式…，你將…」，可用於引導對方按照我們預設的方式思考。

   例：When you think in a creative way, you will develop some ideas that you will never think about in the past.

   當你進行創意思考，你會發展出一些你過去從不曾想到的想法。

3. **With..., you can...** 意思為「有了…，你就可以…」，可用於說明具備某種條件後所能帶來的好處。

   例：With English proficiency, you can communicate with our foreign customers.

   當你英文流利，就能跟外國客戶溝通。

4. **Though..., the N can...** 意思為「雖然…，但…可以…」，可用於說明如何補強產品或服務的不足之處。

   例：Though our business hours are shorter, the online customer service can help solve the technical problems during night time。

   雖然我們的營業時間較短，但線上客服可以於夜間協助您解決技術問題。

本單元以推銷課程為場景，發展一段範例對話，當中提到四個行銷的常用概念，以下針對每個概念做進一步說明：

1. 以吸引力法則（law of attraction）強調正面思考：

- 對應句型：**When you learn something in an aggressive way, you will learn it better and quickly. Since there is a strong motivation support your learning, I would say three month intensive courses is enough.**

 若以白話的方式來解釋吸引力法則，指的就是當你正面思考，就可能帶來正面的結果。反之，負面思考就可能帶來負面結果。雖然此法則源自哲學領域，但若套用在行銷上，也相當適切。當銷售人員不斷向客戶介紹產品優點，最後客戶就有可能會買單。**在本範例中，Jason 問出 Kevin 為何想上課的動機後，便善用此點加以推銷。稱讚 Kevin 是有心想學習設計軟體，然後推薦他上三個月的密集課程。**

2. 說明現況（current status）來展現產品優勢：

- 對應句型：**In the current job market, Illustrator and Photoshop are the two popular software in the market.**

 在行銷產品時，說明現況是很重要的一環，其原因在於並非所有消費者都對市場趨勢有所掌握。這樣的解釋除了可以給予基本資訊外，更重要的是能夠藉此突顯自家產品可以解決當前所遭遇的一些問題。**在本範例中，Jason 提到 Illustrator and Photoshop 是目前職場上熱門的軟體，藉此向 Kevin 訓練中心所推出的相關課程。**

3. 讓需要（need）成為必需（necessity）：

- 對應句型：**With the proficiency in the abovementioned software, you can meet the basic qualification of many design companies.**

當消費者猶豫不決時，就代表其選購的服務或產品還只在「需求」階段，需求代表可能有需要，並不是非買不可。此時銷售人員應想辦法增加其購買動機，使其成為「必需」。動機可以著眼於購買後所帶來的差異，舉例來說，當消費者因為冰箱耗電而想換新，一直強調自家冰箱的節能效果，就有機會說服他們這冰箱是非買不可。**在本範例中，Jason 強調 Illustrator and Photoshop 是目前許多設計公司徵人時所設定的條件，希望藉此說服 Kevin 這兩種課程是必選課程。**

4. 以優惠套餐（combo）增加銷售：

- 對應句型：**For the new student, 3 month intensive course costs 1500USD. But we have a special combo project. If you buy two beginner classes a time, we only charge you 500USD. It is really a great deal.**

在銷售產品，優惠套組是許多公司會使用的手法。這樣的產品組可能會是幾樣主力商品相互搭配，或是熱門商品搭配冷門商品。然後以特惠價買給消費者。此種行銷手法是利用消費者想撿便宜的心態，讓其以折扣價買到多個商品，每一商品的利潤降低，但總消費額增加。**在本範例中，Jason 告訴 Kevin 現在有特惠方案，原本一次三個月的密集課程要 1500 美金，現在一次買兩堂初級課只要 500 美金，要他別錯過此機會。**

Part 2

業務生意篇

看《大亨遊戲》（*Glengarry Glen Ross*），用創意口號推銷地產

篇章重點搶先看

1. 以《大亨遊戲》（*Glengarry Glen Ross*）中 Blake 經典台詞學習如何以創意口號向客戶推銷地產或是房屋。
2. 以大亨遊戲中 Blake 的經典台詞 *"A-I-D-A. Attention, Interest, Decision, Action. Attention -..."*「A-I-D-A，注意，興趣，決定，行動」。學習本單元核心句型：

   ★capitalized letter-capitalized letter capitalized letter- capitalized letter. N1+N2+N3+N4-...「（字母首字），（定義），（定義），（定義）…。」
3. 搭配學習本單元其他三大重點句型：

   a N is about to, making it...（N 將要…，使其…。）

   b The chance is high that（…的機率很大。）

   c It is not easy to..., so I suggest you...（要…不容易，所以我建議…。）
4. 將四種句型放入實境對話練習，學習四大行銷概念：

   a 以口號（slogan）吸引注意。

   b 以未來性（futurity）增加吸引度。

   c 以升值（appreciation）提高價值性。

   d 以稀有性（scarcity）增加搶手度。

影片背景介紹

《大亨遊戲》(*Glengarry Glen Ross*)是部關於四位地產仲介人員 Levene、Roma、Moss、Aaronow 與其主管 Williamson 的故事。這個團隊常使用小技倆來假造銷售,因此績效越來越差。為了刺激銷售,公司的老闆 Mitch 和 Murray 派了 Blake 來教導這些仲介如何銷售房屋與土地,並宣布接下來將有一場業績競賽。業績表現最好的將會獲得一台凱迪拉克轎車,最差的兩位就會被裁員。為避免失業,不論本來的業績如何,所有的仲介都開始思考如何提升績效。Blake 一進公司所說的開場白恰巧可作為學習如何以創意口號來吸引觀眾注意的良好教材。

Glengarry Glen Ross is the story of four Chicago real estate salesmen - Levene, Roma, Moss, and Aaronow - and their supervisor, Williamson. This team tends to use tricks to make sales, making the their sales performance worse and worse. To trigger the sale, the owner of this company, Mitch and Murray, one day send Blake to teach all agents how to sell houses and lands and announce there will be a sales contest: The one who has the best performance will win a Cadillac, and the two salesmen who perform the worst will be fired. Not to be fired, all agents start to think about how to generate more sales. The words that Blake uses at the opening when he enters the real estate office turn out to be good materials for us to learn how use a slogan to attract the audience's attention.

看影片怎麼說、怎麼用

Jason: Good morning Emily. This is a house you **appoint** to see. Now I will briefly introduce its **condition** to you. This is a 10-year apartment with an elevator. The total is 148.5 square meters with 16.5 as the public **utility**.

Jason：Emily，早安。這間就是指定要看的房子，現在讓我向您簡單介紹屋況。這棟公寓有十年之久，配有電梯，這戶總面積為 148.5 平方公尺，16.5 平方公尺為公設。

Emily: In other words, the remaining room space belonging to the owner is 132 square meters left. This size is a little bit too small for me.

Emily：換句話說，屬於屋主的坪數剩 132 平方公尺，這對我說有點太小。

Jason: May I ask how many people you plan to live in this apartment?

Jason：方便請問您是多少人要住呢？

Emily: My husband and I and my two children.

Emily：我跟我先生與我們的兩個孩子。

Jason: If the children both want to have their own rooms, this apartment is not big enough. However, this apartment is a good investment you should not miss. Now let me tell you the reasons. A dream item in real estate should have (1) F-A-C-T: futurity, **appreciation**, convenience, and taste. This apartment happens to have the first three out of four. Futurity means the future of this item, namely its development. (2) This

Jason：如果小孩都想要有他們自己的房間，這個公寓可能略小了一點。但這真的是個不應錯過的物件。現在就讓我來跟您說明原因。一個夢幻的地產物件要有 F-A-C-T，未來性、增值性、便利性與品味性。這間公寓剛好具備了前三項。未來性指的是此物件的發展。

apartment is located in the community which is about to have a new shopping mall, making it a good location for a family to live. Appreciation is the value that can be added to this property. With this shopping mall, the price will get higher. Convenience is about the transportation. There're several bus stops in the community and (3) the chance is high to have an MRT station next year. It is really the good news for the **habitants**.

這間公寓位在即將興建新購物中心的社區，使其成為家庭居住的好地點。增值指的是該物件可增加的價值，因為這裡未來有購物中心，地價一定會變高。便利性指的是交通。這個社區有數個公車站牌，且明年還可能有捷運站，對居民來說是項好消息。

Emily: What you just said is attractive, but the price is still my major concern. As I know, the 2,000 USD per square meter is the best price now. That is to say the lowest price is 90,000USD. It will be a heavy financial burden, even if I pay with a monthly installment.

Emily：你剛所說得很吸引我。但價格還是我最主要的考量。就我所知，目前每平方公尺的最低價是 2000 美金。也就是說最低價來到 9 萬美金。即使是分期繳款，對我一樣是沉重的經濟負擔。

Jason: Believe me, (4) It is not easy to find a good location like this place, so I suggest that you should **reconsider** it. If you fail to grasp it now, it is not possible to buy an apartment with this affordable price one or two years later.

Jason：相信我，要找到如此好的地點並不容易，所以我建議您三思。如果現在沒買，一兩年後就不可能以現在這樣還負擔的起的價格買到這間房子了。

Emily: I see. I will give you the reply. Thank you today.

Emily：我了解了。我會回覆您，謝謝您今天的介紹。

對話單字說分明

1. **appoint** *v.* 指定

例：This is the model you appoint, please pay the down payment after checking.

這是你所指定的型號，請於檢查過後支付尾款。

2. **utility** *n.* 設施

例：This utility is made for the emergency.

此設施是為緊急狀況所設。

3. **appreciation** *n.* 增值

例：Currency appreciation can greatly affect the national economy.

貨幣升值對國家經濟影響甚鉅。

4. **located** *adj.* 位於…

例：Our company is located in the A-3 zone of the Park.

本公司位於園區的 A-3 區。

5. **habitant** *n.* 居民

例：This factory is built with the permission of habitants.

此工廠是獲得居民許可後才興建的。

6. **burden** *n.* 負擔

例：The rent will be a financial burden, if the sales is getting worse.

如果銷售情況變糟的話，店租就會是個很大的經濟負擔。

7. **reconsider** *v.* 重新考慮

例：The quotation is too high, please reconsider it.

此報價過高，請重新考慮。

8. **grasp** *v.* 抓住

例：This is really a favorable, so I suggest that you grasp the opportunity to buy it today.

這個價格真的很優惠，所以我建議趁此機會購買。

重點句型分析

1. **Capitalized letter-capitalized letter capitalized letter- capitalized letter. N1+N2+N3+N4-...** 是口號或標語的一種格式，以四個名詞的首字母組合出一個具有意思（無意義亦可）的新字來吸引觀眾獲讀者的注意。

   例：The new slogan we have this year is T-A-G-S---target, alignment, glory, and success.

   本年度的新口號是 T-A-G-S，目標、合作、榮耀與成功。

2. **N is about to, making it...** 意思為「N 將要…使其…。」，可用於說明即將產生之變化。

   例：The community is about to have the urban renewal, making it a popular property in the real estate market.

   此社區將要進行都更，使其成為房仲業的熱門物件。

3. **The chance is high that...** 意思為「…機會很高」，可用於某事很可能會發生。

   例：The chance is high that the raw material price will get higher next month.

   下個月原物料很可能又漲價。

4. **It is not easy to..., so I suggest you...** 意思為「要…不容易，所以我建議你…」，可用於說明某事物的困難性，並提出我方之建議。

   例：It is not easy to get a limited edition sport car, so I suggest you to place an order soon.

   要買到限量版跑車並不容易，所以我建議你盡快下單。

職場補給站

本單元以房仲帶客戶看房為場景，發展一段完整對話，其內容中一共提到四個行銷的常用概念，以下針對每個概念做進一步說明：

1. 以創意口號（slogan）吸引注意：

- 對應句型：**A dream item in real estate should have F-A-C-T: futurity, appreciation, convenience, taste.**

  為吸引消費者的注意，銷售人員有時會運用想像力創造出一些特別的話語來吸引消費者。此類口號常以縮寫的方式出現，例如將取出數個單字的首字母，將其組合成新的詞語。新詞語若有意義最好，若無法產生新意，則要容易記憶。**在本範例中，Jason 所使用的口號是 F-A-C-T。F 代表未來性，A 代表增值性，C 代表便利性，T 代表品味。而 FACT 本身又具備事實之意，引伸出這四個要素都是真實不虛華的意涵。**

2. 以未來性（futurity）增加吸引度：

- 對應句型：**Futurity means the future of this item, namely its development. This apartment is located in the community which is about to have a new shopping mall, making it a good location for a family to live.**

  銷售地產時，若客戶是打算買來當作投資，未來性的重要程度自然不言可喻，即使是用來自住，房仲也應懂得著墨此區塊。當一個物件的週邊有良好的發展性，該物件所能吸引到潛在客戶自然不在少數。**在本範例中，Jason 先仔細定義何謂物件的未來性，然後提出該社區未來會有新的購物中心，其便利性符合家庭的需求。**

3. 以升值（appreciation）提高價值性：

- 對應句型：**Appreciation is the value that can be added to this property. With this shopping mall, the price will get higher.**

　　在銷售房地產時，即便客戶是要自住，該物件是否有增值空間仍是其關注重點。撇除房屋的折舊，若其週邊的客觀因素無法使其保持或是提高一定價值，甚至造成下跌，消費者可就會因此而卻步。**在本範例中，Jason 以購物中心將進駐來強調該物件的價值性。由於購物中心可使採買各類用品更加方便，對房價絕對有正面效益。**

4. 以稀有性（scarcity）增加搶手度：

- 對應句型：**It is not easy to find a good location like this place, so I suggest that you should reconsider it. If you fail to grasp it now, it is not possible to buy an apartment with this affordable price one or two years later.**

　　一件商品若數量眾多，消費者要買到就很容易，其特殊性自然就降低。這樣的情況若發生在地產銷售上，就容易被消費者殺價。此時房仲若要保持其利潤，就需要懂得利用話術來包裝物件，使其客觀條件聽來都是不可多得。**在本範例中，Jason 先是強調這間公寓的地點絕佳，未來又有購物中心與捷運站，現在不搶先入手，未來的價格肯定更高，藉此鼓吹 Emily 盡快與其簽約。**

看《大亨遊戲》（*Glengarry Glen Ross*），學習用解析法來銷售地產

篇章重點搶先看

1. 以《大亨遊戲》（*Glengarry Glen Ross*）中四位房仲之一的 Dave Moss 台詞學習如何以解析法來銷售地產。
2. 以 Moss 的台詞 “The rich getting richer, that's the law of the land.”「富者更富，這就是土地的法則」。學習本單元核心句型：
   ★The adj getting adj 比較級, that is the law of...「…更…，這就是…的…。」
3. 搭配學習本單元其他三大重點句型：
   a The... of... will be reflected in..., so you can（…的…會反映在…上，所以你可以…。）
   b Viewing you as..., here I...（視您為…，於此我…。）
   c If you decide to..., please...（如果您決定…，請…。）
4. 將四種句型放入實境對話練習，學習四大行銷概念：
   a 以定律（law）穩固論點。
   b 按需求給予解決方案（solution）。
   c 以應酬語（social words）塑造愉快氣氛。
   d 以異業結盟（cross-industry alliance）創造更多商機。

影片背景介紹

延續上一堂課的介紹，當所有房仲得知有此競賽後，便各自努力。Ricky 業績原本就還不錯，所以面對這樣的比賽相對從容。Levene 因為女兒生病，因此十分擔心工作不保。Aaronow 因為年紀最長，選擇聽天由命。Dave 為了要贏得競賽，不惜盜用同事 Ricky 所想出的方案。Dave 自認只要花點錢來疏通，就能神不知鬼不覺，但殊不知一切並非像他想的那樣容易。這場業績比賽忠實呈現了職場上的爭權鬥力，有人為了生計不斷掙扎，有人為了獎金不擇手段，這一切的一切都再再說明人性的黑暗面往往因為職場的現實而被揭開。片中 Moss 關於土地價值的台詞，恰可作為我們學習如何善用定律、名言這類具代表性的話語來穩固自己銷售話術的良好教材。

Following the introduction of the previous lesson, all agents try some ways to win this contest. Ricky's performance has been acceptable for long, so he can face the competition at ease. Levene's daughter is sick, so he is worried about losing this job. Aronnow is the oldest agent, so he chooses to be resigned to his fate. Dave is eager to win the contest, so he tries to plagiarize Ricky's idea. Though Dave regards that money can keep his trick in secret, the thing doesn't go in the way he expects. This contest vividly shows the competition in a workplace. Someone struggles for the living rightly, while the others use trick to get the reward. The dark side of the humanity is revealed due to the cruel reality of the workplace. The words that Moss says illustrate the importance of using proverbs or famous theories to support the viewpoint in product sale.

看影片怎麼說、怎麼用

In one apartment that is included in a new project. Jason is showing Brown around inside the apartment.

（在某個新建案的公寓內。Jason 帶 Brown 先去看看公寓的內部環境。）

Brown: It looks nice. How many sizes do this plan have?

Brown：看起來很不錯，此建案共有幾種坪數呢？

Jason: It has three: 25, 30, and 35 square meters. The one I am going to show you is 30 square meters.

Jason：有三種選擇，分別是 25、30、35 平方公尺。我要帶您去看的是 30 平方公尺的。

Brown: Its size is much smaller compared to that of many projects, does it **target** at any specific groups?

Brown：與其他建案相比，這個案子的坪數明顯較小，是有特別針對任何族群嗎？

Jason: Yes, it does. This project is mainly for young **generation** like you. (1) "The weak getting weaker, that is the law of economy." These words point out the **dilemma** of this group. The **recession** in economy makes the young hard to buy their own house, making small apartments their good choices. (2) The result of the size reducing will be reflected in the total price, so you can have a home with a more affordable budget.

Jason：確實有。本建案主要是針對向您這樣的年輕人。「窮者更窮，這就是經濟的定律」，這句話點出了這個族群的困境。經濟的衰退讓年輕人很難買下一間屬於自己的房子，但這也讓我們的小公寓成為他們的好選擇。縮小坪數的效果會顯現在總價上，所以你可以以更負擔的起的預算來擁有一個家。

Brown: True. According to your advertisement, the price per square is 5000 USD. Is there any room for negotiation?

Brown：的確是。根據貴公司的廣告，每平方公尺的價格是 5000 美金。還有議價的空間嗎？

Jason: (3) Viewing you as our **distinguished** guest, here I provide you a favorable price for 4800 USD. This **better** price is provided to the first ten consumers, and you will be one of them if you make the decision this week. (4) If you decide to sign the contract, please inform me through this number-0911123456. I will prepare the document for you.

Jason：我們將您視為貴賓，於此我提供您每平方公尺 4800 美金的優惠價。僅前十位購屋的消費者可享此優惠，若您於本週內決定，您就是那十位之一。如果您決定簽約，請撥打 0911123456 這個號碼聯絡我，我將為您準備文件。

Brown: I see. I will inform you my decision as soon as possible.

Brown：了解。我會盡快告知您我的決定為何。

Jason: To make having a home much easier, we also form an **alliance** with a furniture company, Kitchenware Companies. Our customer can have the **exclusive** discount from it. If you want to know the details, I can send you the document later.

Jason：為了要讓擁有個家變得更容易，我們與家具商和廚具商結盟，本公司客戶可以享有獨家優惠。預知詳情，我可以將檔案寄給您。

Brown: I am interested in this discount, please send the document to my e-mail address: 123@abc.com.

Brown：我對此折扣有興趣，請將檔案寄到我的電子信箱：123@abc.com。

對話單字說分明

1. **target** *v.* 鎖定

　例：Does this product target at the teenage group?
　此商品是鎖定青少年族群嗎？

2. **generation** *n.* 世代

　例：The taste of clothing is different from generation to generation.
　各世代對於服裝的品味各有不同。

3. **dilemma** *n.* 困境

　例：The dilemma we are facing now is that we have the need of expansion, but find no proper place.
　我們現在所遭遇的困境是有擴張需求但苦無適合地點。

4. **recession** *n.* 衰退

　例：The economy recession greatly affects the performance of our company this year. 經濟衰退對本公司今年度的績效影響甚鉅。

5. **distinguished** *adj.* 重要的

　例：Viewing you as our distinguished guest, we arrange the best accommodation for you. 視您為貴賓，我們為您安派最好的飯店。

6. **better** *adj.* 較低的

　例：We can give you a better price if you order 1000 sets at once.
　如果一次購買一千組，我們可以給你更低廉的價格。

7. **alliance** *n.* 結盟

　例：We form a cross industry alliance to provide a more comprehensive service to our consumers.
　我們透過異業結盟來提供更全面的服務給消費者。

8. **exclusive** *adj.* 獨有的

　例：Our members can have the exclusive discount in the new items.
　我們的會員可獨享新品優惠。

重點句型分析

1. **The adj getting adj 比較級, that is the law of...** 意思為「…更…，這就是…的…」，可用於說明某些現象背後的原則。

   例：The stronger getting stronger, that is the law of competition.
   強者更強，這就是競爭的鐵則。

2. **The... of... will be reflected in..., so you can...** 意思為「…的…會反映在其…上，所以你可以…。」，可用於說明所呈現的意涵，以及我們所能進行的後續動作為何。

   例：The cost of the modification will be reflected in the listed price, so you can reconsider its necessity.
   修正所花費的成本會反映在售價上，所以你可以重新考慮其必要性。

3. **Viewing you as..., here I...** 意思為「視您為…，於此我…」，可用於說明。

   例：Viewing you as our important partner, here I would like to invite you to attend our 30th anniversary party.
   視您為我們重要的夥伴，於此我想邀請您參加我們的 30 週年慶祝派對。

4. **If you decide to..., please...** 意思為「如果您決定…，請…」，可用於說明進行某動作後，下一步驟為何。

   例：If you decide to place an order this week, please contact me through 046985235.
   如果您決定於本週下單，請透過 046985235 這個號碼聯絡我。

職場補給站

本單元以房仲向前來看屋的客戶推銷新建案為場景，發展一段完整對話，其內容中一共提到四個行銷的常用概念，以下針對每個概念做進一步說明：

1. 以定律（law）穩固論點：

- 對應句型：**"The weak getting weaker, that is the law of economy" These words point out the dilemma of this group.**

  由於房地產的價格高昂，消費者往往需要相當的思考時間，才能決定是否購買。此時若要縮短這樣的等待時間，可以利用大家普遍認可的定律做為引言，由此帶出所銷售物件的優點。**在本範例中，Jason 就利用「貧者更貧，這就是經濟的定律」做為引言，點出當前年輕人所遭遇的困境，為之後鋪陳小型公寓的優點預做伏筆。**

2. 按需求給予解決方案（solution）：

- 對應句型：**The result of the size reducing will be reflected in the total price, so you can have a home with a more affordable budget.**

  消費者在購屋時，其需求導向可能差異甚大，預算寬裕的消費者可能會考量大坪數，相反地，若預算有限，小坪數才不會造成沉重的經濟負擔。地產從業人員若能根據這樣需求給予最適當的推薦，成交的機會就會大增。**在本範例中，Jason 強調本建案就是針對預算有限的年輕族群，因此所小坪數能讓該族群更有購屋的可能性。**

Lesson 13
Lesson 14
Lesson 15
Lesson 16
Lesson 17
Lesson 18

3. 以應酬語（social words）塑造愉快氣氛：

- 對應句型：**Viewing you as our distinguished guest, here I provide you a favorable price for 4800 USD. This better price is provided to the first ten consumers, and you will be one of them if you make the decision this week.**

在接待每位客戶時，雖然從業人員都知道其重要性有別，但在態度不應有所差別，都應將其視為貴賓。為保持與客戶的良好溝通，應酬語就是個很實用的工具。客戶其實也知道很多稱讚的話語都只是場面話，但我方願意說出，還是會讓人覺得愉悅。**在本範例中，Jason 提到他可以提供 4800 美金的優惠價給 Brown，而且還是只有 10 個名額的限量特惠。也許 Jason 對下一位看屋的客戶也會說同樣的話，但 Brown 在這當下會覺得自己是很受重視的。**

4. 以異業結盟（cross-industry alliance）創造更多商機：

- 對應句型：**To make having a home much easy, we also form an alliance with a furniture company, Kitchenware Companies. Our customer can have the exclusive discount from it.**

在瞬息萬變的消費市場中，一間公司不可能生產所有類型的產品，因此異業結盟的概念就應運而生。不同行業形成同盟之後，彼此可以支援需求，進而共享更大的市場。**在本範例中，Jason 提到本公司有裝潢公司與廚具公司結盟，當消費者有意購屋時，可就會產生裝潢與廚具的需求，而同盟廠商所給與的獨家優惠就成為購買的誘因。**

看《美國心玫瑰情》（*American Beauty*），替房仲業務加分

篇章重點搶先看

1. 以《美國心玫瑰情》（*American Beauty*）男主角妻子 Carolyn 的經典台詞學習讓房仲的身分更加分。
2. 以本部電影的台詞 *"As you know, my business is to selling an image. And part of my job is to live that image."*「如同你所知，這個事業就是在銷售一個形象，而我的工作的其中一環就是去維持它。學習本單元核心句型：
   ★ As you know, my business is Ving. And part of my job is to...「如同你所知，這個事業就是在…，而我工作的其中一環就是…。」
3. 搭配學習本單元其他三大重點句型：
   a How can you say... is/are...（為何能說…是…。）
   b Located in..., N is the... of...（位在…，N 是…的…。）
   c What you just... is..., N is...（你剛所…是…，N 是…。）
4. 將四種句型放入實境對話練習，學習四大行銷概念：
   a 以便利設施（amenities）提高搶手度。
   b 以安全性（security）增加滿意度。
   c 以比較利益原則（comparative Advantage）說明實惠度。
   d 以認可（recognition）做為開端。

影片背景介紹

《美國心玫瑰情》（*American Beauty*）以諷刺的手法呈現中產階級的自我滿足。片中角色的人生際遇都不太順遂，男主角萊斯特是位失意的雜誌作家，他的妻子是位有野心但始終業績不太好的房仲，他們的女兒珍，是個缺乏自信的少女。在看過珍的好友安喬拉的舞蹈表演後，萊斯特竟對其產生迷戀。卡洛琳因工作的關係認識了巴迪，最後與之有染。他們的鄰居費茲無法對自己同性戀的身分坦白，兒子里奇吸食並販賣大麻。本片的重點雖然放在各角色不順遂的人生上，但當中卡洛琳對於房仲事業的一番定義，恰可作為我們學習定義自身職業特性，並將之介紹給客戶的良好教材。

American Beauty uses a sarcastic way to describe the self-gratification of the middle class. The life of the leading characters is somehow not that smooth. Lester is a frustrated magazine writer. His wife Carolyn is an ambitious real estate agent with bad working performance.Their daughter Jane is a teenager who is lack of self-confidence. After watching Jane's friend Angela's dance, Lester has sexual fantasies about her. Carolyn knows Buddy in her work and has an love affair with him. Lester's neighbor Fitts refuses to accept himself as a gay. His son Ricky uses and sells marijuana. Though the focus of this movie puts on the unhappy life, the words that Carolyn uses to describe the image of real estate industry turn out to be good materials for us to learn how to define the features of our job and introduce them to our customers.

看影片怎麼說、怎麼用

In the **lobby** of an office building. Jason is taking Sam to take the elevator to 26F.

（在辦公大樓的大廳。Jason 正帶著 Sam 搭電梯到 26 樓。）

Jason: Here we are. This is the office I mentioned on the phone yesterday. It looks nice, right.

Jason：到了，這就是我昨天在電話中跟您提到的辦公室。看起來很不錯對吧！

Sam: Yeah. My major concerns are safety and convenience, so can you explain why you recommend this place?

Sam：是啊！我主要考量安全性與便利性，可以跟我說明為何推薦這個物件嗎？

Jason: Sure. (1) As you know, my business is selling a sense of security. And part of my job is to keep that sense. That is the reason I recommend this place. This building has the most comprehensive security system, making invasion a mission impossible.

Jason：當然。如你所知，這個事業就是在銷售一個安全感，而我工作的一環就是去維持它。這也是推薦這個地方的原因。這棟建築物有最完善的保全系統，讓入侵如同不可能的任務般困難。

Sam: (2) How can you say it is convenient?

Sam：為何能說是方便呢？

Jason: Let's **oversee** from the window of the office. What do you see?

Jason：讓我們從辦公室的窗戶往下俯瞰，請問你看到什麼呢？

Sam: The City Hall, banks, restaurants, and few coffee shops, and so on.

Sam：市政府、銀行、餐廳、咖啡廳等等。

Jason: That's right. (3) Located in

Jason：沒錯。位居市中

downtown, this place is the top choice of your **headquarters**. Since the City Hall is few **blocks** away from here, you can easily send sales **representatives** to submit a hard copy to the related departments. With banks nearby, you'll find it awesome when you have capital needs. Coffee shops are the good places for you to have a general discussion with customers.

心，此地點是貴公司總部的最佳選擇。由於市府僅在數街區之遙，你可以派業務走路過去提交紙本文件給相關單位。當你有緊急的資金需求，會發現附近有銀行是很棒的一件事。咖啡廳是你和客戶初步洽談的好地方。

Sam：You words almost convince me, but I have one more concern here-the rental. Acting as the **hub** in this commercial zone, the rental per month could be sky high. Can you tell me the market price now?

Sam：你快說服我了，但這邊我還有一個考量，就是租金。做為商業區的樞紐，其租金應該是天價，可以透露一下行情價嗎？

Jason: Of course. (4) What you just said is right, 10,000 USD monthly rental here is relatively higher compared to that of other office buildings. But here let me use Comparative Advantage to prove it is worthy. With well-developed facilities surrounded, the great transportation expenses can be saved. Though you pay more rent, you save more if you **relocate** here.

Jason：當然可以。你說得沒錯，10,000 美金的月租確實比鄰近的其他辦公大樓都高，但這邊讓我用比較利益原則來證明這樣的花費是值得的。由於其周遭機能完善，可省下龐大的交通費用。雖然多付租金，但事實上你省了更多。

Sam: I think you are right. I will consider this place and give you the answer this Friday. Thank you.

Sam：我想你是對的。我會仔細考慮並於週五給你答覆。謝謝。

對話單字說分明

1. **lobby** *n.* 大廳

例：Let's meet in the lobby of ABC Hotel before the meeting.
開會前我們先在 ABC 飯店大廳碰面。

2. **oversee** *v.* 俯瞰

例：Why this place becomes famous is because you can oversee the whole city here.
這邊因為能夠俯瞰整個城市而聲名大噪。

3. **downtown** *n.* 市中心

例：Located in downtown, your company has the convenient transportation.
位居市中心，貴公司的享有便利的交通。

4. **headquarters** *n.* 總部

例：Many companies establish their headquarters in this city.
許多公司把總部設在這個城市。

5. **block** *n.* 街區

例：Citi Bank is two blocks away from here. 再兩個街區就到花旗銀行了。

6. **representative** *n.* 代表

例：Please send at least one representative to attend the meeting tomorrow. 請至少派一名代表參加明日的會議。

7. **hub** *n.* 樞紐

例：As a hub of finance, many international companies set its Asian headquarters in Taipei.
身為一個金融樞紐，許多跨國公司將亞洲總部設在台北。

8. **relocate** *v.* 搬遷

例：To reduce the labor cost, many companies choose to relocate their factories to Southeast Asia.
為降低人力成本，許多公司選擇將工廠遷至東南亞。

重點句型分析

1. **As you know, my business is Ving... And part of my job is to...** 意思為「如你所知，這個事業是在…，而我工作的一環就是…」，可用於說明某種工作的特形，以及簡述自己的業務職掌。

   例：As you know, my business is selling a feeling of belongingness. And part of my job is to keep that feeling.
   如你所知，這個事業就是在販賣一種歸屬感，而我工作的一環就是維持它。

2. **Located in..., N is the... of...** 意思為「位在…N 是…的…。」，可用於說明建物或是土地的地理位置與其發展的優缺點。

   例：Located in the rural area, the land is the best choice for the new shopping mall.
   位在郊區，這塊土地是新購物中心的最佳選址。

3. **How can you say... is/are...?** 意思為「為何能說…是…？」，可用要求對方給予更進一步的解釋。

   例：How can you say this project is feasible?
   為何能說此專案是可行的呢？

4. **What you just... is..., N is...** 意思為「你剛剛…是…，N 是…」，可用於認同或否定對方的動作或論點。

   例：What you just said is right, and the rent is really too high.
   你剛剛所說是對的，而租金實在是太高了。

職場補給站

本單元以房仲向客戶介紹商辦為場景，發展一段完整對話，其內容中一共提到四個行銷的常用概念，以下針對每個概念做進一步說明：

1. 以便利設施（amenities）提高搶手度：

- 對應句型：**Since the City Hall is few blocks away from here, you can easily send one sales representative to submit to hard copies to the related departments.**

  在推銷地產時，除物件本身的地理位置外，相關設施也是消費者考量的重點。所謂的便利設施，包含建物內部的設備、附近的交通與機能，甚至整體的生活氛圍。**在本範例中，Jason 說明本商業大樓離市政府很近，提交文件非常方便，所強調的就是週邊機能的部分。**

2. 以安全性（security）增加滿意度：

- 對應句型：**This building has the most comprehensive security system, making invasion a mission impossible.**

  不論是商辦或是住家，消費者對於安全性都會有一定的要求。由於商業大樓會存放各家公司的一些機密資料，因此保全與門禁系統會是其關注的重點。**在本範例中，Jason 提到這棟商辦有最完善的保全系統就是希望客戶能先對這個物件的安全性有信心，以利後續的介紹。**

3. 以比較利益原則（Comparative Advantage）說明實惠度：

- 對應句型：**With well-developed facilities surrounded, many transportation expenses can be saved. The money you saved is greater if you relocate your office here.**

  在進行地產銷售時，客戶不見得會完全認可我方的論述，此時若要說服對方，善用比較利益原則是非常有效的方法。從最終效果的面向去比較我方與客戶的想法，可讓客戶了解何者的效益最大。**在本範例中，Jason 提到這棟商辦週邊機能良好，因此無須再花額外的交通費，比較搬來與不搬，將總部搬來其實是幫公司省下更多錢。**

4. 以認可（recognition）做為開端：

- 對應句型：**What you just said is right, 10,000 USD monthly rental here is relatively higher compared to that of other office buildings. But here let me use the concept of Comparative Advantage to prove it is worthy.**

從心理學的角度來看，多數人在雙方溝通時都會希望自己的看法獲得認可。同理可證，客戶也希望自己的觀點為銷售人員所接受。但萬一我方的看法就是與客戶相左呢？此時可以透過先認可再補充的方式來說服客戶。此處的認可指的是點出當中合理的部分，補充則是挑出當中有疑義的部分再與之討論。**以本範例為例，Jason 先是對 Sam 的觀點表示認同，也覺得 10000 美金的租金比較高，然後才透過解析的方式說明雖然租金變高，但因為其他花費降低，整體而言是替公司省錢。**

看《美國心玫瑰情》（*American Beauty*），學會了解客戶需求

篇章重點搶先看

1. 以《美國心玫瑰情》（*American Beauty*）片中女主角 Carolyn 經典台詞學習如何按照客戶需求提供最適推薦。
2. 以美國心玫瑰情片中女主角 Carolyn 的台詞 *"It is a dream come true for any cook. Just filled with positive energy. Huh?"*「這是個讓廚師美夢成真的地方，感覺到正面能量對吧！」學習本單元核心句型：

   ★It is a... for... Just filled with...「這是個讓…的地方。感覺到…對吧？」
3. 搭配學習本單元其他三大重點句型：

   a Situated in..., N is just... away from...（坐落於…，N 僅離…之遙。）

   b With the view of..., N is suitable for...（擁有…景緻，N 適合…。）

   c The... in... allow you to...（在…裡的…讓你可以…。）
4. 將四種句型放入實境對話練習，學習四大行銷概念：

   a 以公共設施（public facility）說明便利性。

   b 以景觀（view）創造討論度。

   c 從回應中追加誘因（incentive）。

   d 以格局（pattern）引起注意。

影片背景介紹

承接上一堂課之介紹，卡洛琳的銷售態度很積極，但卻總是無法成交，導致其業績表現不佳。在工作場合上，她遇到了巴迪。巴迪是名銷售手腕高明的房仲，嚴格說來算是卡洛琳的競爭對手。由於卡洛琳與其丈夫的關係幾乎降至冰點，她與巴迪越走越近，最後終於出軌。片中卡洛琳仔細向前來看屋的客戶介紹每項設施，但他們似乎不太領情，甚至認為公司的廣告有欺騙之嫌。雖然卡洛琳在銷售過程中處處碰壁，但當中她介紹的廚房的台詞，恰可用來做為學習如何按照客戶需求給予最佳推薦的教材。

Following the introduction of the previous lesson, Carolyn works aggressively, but fails to finalize the deals all the time. As a result, her working performance is always bad. In the workplace, she meets Buddy, a real estate agent with great sales tricks. Frankly speaking, he is the rival of Carolyn. However, their relationship becomes closer day by day because Carolyn's marriage is about to end. Finally, Carolyn betrays her husband and has an extramarital affair with Buddy. Meanwhile, though Carolyn introduces the utilities in details, the customers are reluctant to give her a positive reply and think they are fooled by the advertisement. Although Carolyn fails to sell the house, the lines she uses to introduce the kitchen turn out to be good materials for us to learn how to provide the best recommendation to the customer in accordance with their needs.

看影片怎麼說、怎麼用

At the car lane of a **villa**.

（在某個別墅的車道。）

Jason: Good afternoon, Lance and Amy. This is the villa I recommend to you. (1) Situated in the rim of the city, this villa is one mile away from the downtown. Here, you can enjoy the convenience of **modernization** and the relaxed **atmosphere** of the nature at the same time.

Jason：午安，Lance 和 Amy，這就是我跟你們推薦的別墅，雖然位在郊區，但離市區只有一英里。在這您可同時享受現代化的便利，還有大自然輕鬆的氛圍。

Lance: What do you mean by saying the house owner can enjoy the nature?

Lance：享受自然指的是什麼意思呢？

Jason: If we look out from the yard of the villa, the mountain and forest are just few miles away. You can simply sit on the grass to watch the sun rise or sunset during the daytime as well as stars during the night time. (2) With the view of open **horizon**, the place is suitable for people who want to relax after work.

Jason：如果從別墅的院子往外看，高山與森林就僅在數英里之外。你可就坐在草皮上白天看日出日落，晚上看星星。擁有開闊的景致，這個地方適合下班後想放鬆的人居住。

Lance: I got it. The view is nice indeed.

Lance：我了解了。整個風景的確很棒。

Jason: Let's enter to see its **interior** design.

Jason：讓我們進去看看內部格局吧！

Lance/Amy: Ok.

Lance/Amy：好的。

Jason：When you step into this villa, a spacious living room is revealing in front of you. (3) It is a dream come true for **audiovisual** lovers. Full of excitement, Huh? (4) The 100-inch projector screen and surround speakers allow you to watch a film with the greatest satisfaction.

Jason：一進到屋內，映入眼簾的就是寬敞的客廳。這是個讓影音愛好者美夢成真的地方，感覺到興奮感對吧！一百吋的投影螢幕與環繞喇叭讓你看影片時能得到最大的滿足。

Lance: Fantastic. I think I will rent movie DVDs very often, if I live here.

Lance：太棒了。如果我住這，我想我會很常去租DVD。

Jason: Moving few steps forward, we will see a kitchen with a series of kitchenware. For people who love cooking, they will stay here for the whole day.

Jason：再往前幾步。我們會看到一個充滿各式廚具的廚房。對於愛煮菜的人，他們可以在這待上一整天。

Amy: I am the one you just mentioned. I could cook like a chef, if I live here.

Amy：我就是你說的那種人，住在這我的廚藝可以像大廚一樣好。

Jason: The environment around this villa also worth being mentioned. Half mile away is the public complex gym, so we can walk there for fitness or ball games.

Jason：別墅四周的環境也很值得一提。半英里外就有公共複合型體育館，你可以去那健身或是看球賽。

Lance/Amy: This villa really looks great. We will make our decision by this Thursday. Thank you.

Lance/Amy：這間別墅真的很不錯，我們會在本週四前做決定，謝謝你。

對話單字說分明

1. **villa** *n.* 別墅

例：This villa is sold in a sky high price.
此別墅以天價售出。

2. **modernization** *n.* 現代化

例：If you live in the city, you can enjoy the convenience of modernization.
住在城市可以享受現代化所帶來的便利。

3. **atmosphere** *n.* 氣氛

例：The interior atmosphere can affect the consumers' purchase intention.
內部氣氛會影響消費者的消費意願。

4. **horizon** *n.* 視野

例：With an open horizon, you can oversee the whole city from the top floor of this building.
由於視野開闊，你可以從這棟建築的頂樓俯瞰整個城市。

5. **interior** *n.* 內部的

例：Let's take a look of the interior design of this room.
讓我們來看看這個房間的內部設計。

6. **audiovisual** *adj.* 影音的

例：If you like the audiovisual effect, you can't miss our latest home game console.
如果喜歡影音效果的話，那你絕不能錯過我們最新的電玩主機。

7. **chef** *n.* 主廚

例：May I show my appreciation in person to the chef?
能讓我親自跟主廚道謝嗎？

8. **fitness** *n.* 健身

例：This fitness center features 1 on 1 lecture
這間健身中心主打一對一課程。

重點句型分析

1. **It is a... for... Just filled with...** 意思為「這是個讓…的地方。感覺到…對吧！」，可用於說明並強調某個地方有如夢想之地。

   例：It is a dream come true for online game addicts. Filled with excitement. Huh?

   這是個讓遊戲癡美夢成真的地方。感覺到興奮對吧！

2. **Situated in..., N is just... away from...** 意思為「坐落於…，N 僅離…之遙。」，可用於說明房地產位置的優缺點。

   例：Situated in the science park, this company is just one mile away from us

   坐落於科學園區內，這間公司僅離我們一英里之遙。

3. **With the view of..., N is suitable for...** 意思為「擁有…景緻，N 適合…」，可用於說明房地產周遭有哪些景觀，以及其適合的族群。

   例：With the view of the seashore, the villa is suitable for the people who love scenery of nature to live in.

   擁有海濱的景致，這棟別墅適合喜愛大自然風景的人居住。

4. **The... in... allow you to...** 意思為「在…裡的…讓你可以…」，可用於說明房地產格局能有哪些效用。

   例：The closet and drawers in the dressing room allow you categorize all the clothes you have.

   在更衣間裡的衣櫥和抽屜讓你可以分類你所有的衣物。

本單元以房仲向客戶介紹別墅的四周環境與內部格局為場景，發展一段完整對話，其內容中一共提到四個行銷的常用概念，以下針對每個概念做進一步說明：

1. 以公共設施（public facility）說明便利性：

- 對應句型：**The environment around this villa also worth being mentioned. Half mile away is the public complex gym, so we can walk there for fitness or ball games.**

  若介紹過地產物件的內部設施後，客戶仍興趣缺缺，此是房仲人員可說明附近有哪些公共設施來提高客戶的購買意願。這些設施可以提高居民的生活便利性，足以成為吸引客戶的誘因。**以本範例為例，Jason 提到這間別墅半英里外就有公共的複合式體育館，可以去運動健身與看球賽，非常方便。**

2. 以景觀（view）創造討論度：

- 對應句型：**With the view of open horizon, the place is suitable for people who want to relax after work.**

  除了客觀的各項設外，建築物周邊的景觀也是客戶考量的重點之一。若是銷售高樓，能夠俯瞰城市會是賣點，若是銷售別墅，能夠看見大自然是重點。**以本範例為例，Jason 特別提出這間別墅的視野是非常開闊的，非常適合下班後希望享受大自然氛圍的人購買。**

3. 從回應中追加誘因（incentive）：

- 對應句型：**If we look out from the yard of the villa, the mountain and forest are just few miles away. You can simply sit on the grass to watch the sun rise or sunset during the daytime as well as stars during the night time.**

在銷售地產時，傾聽客戶需求然後投其所好是非常重要的。當銷售人員發現客戶對某種要素特別重視時，就增加這部分的介紹，以增加客戶的購買慾望。**以本範例為例，由於 Lance 對於所謂的享受自然有些疑問，Jason 就依此問題完整描述此想特點，說明在此別墅你可以白天看日出日落，晚上可以看星星，充分感受自然界的變化。**

4. 以格局（pattern）引起注意：

- 對應句型：**When you step into this villa, a spacious living room is revealing in front of you. It is a dream come true for audiovisual lovers. Full of excitement, Huh? The 100-inch projector screen and surround speakers allow you to watch a film with the greatest satisfaction.**

不論地產四周的條件多吸引人，建物內本身的格局還是相當重要。雖然格局可以事後施工加以變更，但由於會增加花費，初始的格局是否符合客戶的需求，其實深深左右客戶的購買意願。**以本範例為例，一進入別墅 Jason 就馬上介紹寬敞客廳，強調這裡可以享受絕佳的影音效果，希望可以馬上吸引客戶的注意。**

看《歡迎光臨布達佩斯飯店》（*The Grand Budapest Hotel*），學習向顧客推銷餐點

篇章重點搶先看

1. 以《歡迎光臨布達佩斯飯店》（*The Grand Budapest Hotel*）男主角 M. Gustave 經典台詞學習如何向客顧客推銷餐點。
2. 以 M. Gustave 的經典台詞 *"Some things make you grow up overnight, and some people you'll be grateful for your entire life."*

   「總有一些事，讓你一夜長大；總有一個人，讓你一生感謝。」學習本單元核心句型：

   ★Some N make you... and some N you will be...「有些…，讓你…總有…讓你…。」
3. 搭配學習本單元其他三大重點句型：

   a To make sure..., we only...（為確保…我們只…。）

   b Knowing the... of...well, Sb can...（熟知…的…，…可以…。）
4. 將四種句型放入實境對話練習，學習四大行銷概念：

   a 以等級（grade）強調選材。

   b 以專業（expertise）提高價值。

   c 以搭配（collocation）增加消費。

   d 以氣氛（atmosphere）創造享受。

影片背景介紹

本片的時空始於一名女子在墓園內某個作家的墓碑閱讀其作品。接下來故事就切換至書中年輕作家於 1968 年時前往某虛構國度中的布達佩斯飯店入住，並與飯店經理討論 1932 年發生在飯店內的往事。在 1932 年時，當時的飯店經理古斯塔夫對於各個房客的喜好瞭若指掌。時空再次切回 1968 年，年老的 Zero 告訴作家，即使現在飯店業績很差，但由於年輕時的記憶難以割捨，他還是不忍脫手。時空又再轉換到現代，那名女子還在讀這本書。片中，經理對於人事物變化的感慨，若將其句法應用在強調產品或服務的特點，實為一份良好教材。

The film begins with a girl who approaches a monument to a writer in a cemetery. When she starts to read the writer's work, the time goes back to the timeframe of that book. In that book, a young writer lives in the Grand Budapest Hotel in year 1968 and talks about one thing happened in 1932. The manager of the hotel M. Gustave at that time clearly knows the preferences of every guest. Then, the time goes back to 1968 again, old Zero, who used to be the lobby boy of the Grand Budapesf Hotel, tells the young writer he refuses to sell this hotel because of the memory in his youth time. The time swifts to the present again, and the girl reads the book still. If we apply the words that M. Gustave uses to show his regret towards the past to the marketing field, it turns out to be good materials for us to learn how to emphasize the features of a product or a service.

看影片怎麼說、怎麼用

In ABC Steakhouse. Jason, a server of ABC Steakhouse, is going to take an order for Leo and Ivy.

（在 ABC 牛排餐廳。ABC 牛排餐廳的服務生 Jason 正要替 Leo 和 Ivy 點餐。）

Leo: This is our first time to have meals in your restaurant, can you give us some recommendations?

Leo：我們是第一次來用餐，可以替我們推薦餐點嗎？

Jason: Of course.(1) Some **ingredients** make you hard to resist and some **flavors** you will be fascinated for long. (2) To make sure the good quality of our beef, we only use US Prime grade. For guests who prefer the **tenderness** of the steak, I would recommend our 6 oz. fillet. For guests who want to have some **texture**, our 8 oz. sirloin is a good choice. If you want both, 10 oz. T- bone is waiting for you.

Jason：當然可以。有些食材會讓你難以抗拒，有些風味會讓你深深著迷。為確保每塊牛排都能保有良好品質，我們只使用 Prime 等級的美國牛。對於喜愛軟嫩口感的顧客，我會推薦 6 盎司菲力。若想要感受嚼勁，可以選擇 8 盎司的沙朗。如果想兩者兼具，可以點 10 盎司的丁骨。

Leo: I think I would prefer fillet. What steak doneness is the most recommended?

Leo：我想我會點菲力。有推薦的熟度嗎？

Jason: Rare is the best. (3) Knowing the texture and the distribution of the fat of each steak well, our chef can fully keep the juice and flavor in this doneness level. And that is the secret why our steak tastes better.

Jason：三分熟最好吃。我們的主廚熟知每塊牛排的紋理與油花分布，在此熟度下肉汁與風味都能完整保留。這也是我們牛排美味的原因。

Leo: I see. Rare, please.

Leo：我了解了。就三分熟，謝謝。

Jason: How about you, madam?

Jason：女仕您要點什麼呢？

Ivy: The same as what he just ordered.

Ivy：跟先生的一樣就好。

Jason: I got it. Besides the main meals, do you want to have some **appetizers** or salad? They are delicate and delicious.

Jason：我了解了。除了主餐外，有想要點開胃菜或是沙拉嗎？精緻又好吃喔！

Leo: A Caesar salad and two **seared** prawns with garlic, please.

Leo：一份凱薩沙拉和兩份香煎大蝦佐大蒜，謝謝。

Jason: I see. Here let me repeat what you just ordered. You ordered two rare 6oz fillets, one Caesar salad and two seared prawns with garlic, right?

Jason：好的，這邊讓我重複一下您剛所點的餐點。您點了兩份三分熟 6 盎司菲力、一份凱薩沙拉、兩份香煎大蝦佐大蒜，對嗎？

Leo: Right.

Leo：沒錯。

Jason: To provide the best dining atmosphere for you, the light could be darker or lighter in accordance with your need.

Jason：為提供您最佳的用餐氣氛，燈光可依照您的需求調亮或調暗。

Leo: It is good enough now. Thank you, sir.

Leo：目前這樣就很好了。謝謝您。

Jason: You are welcome.

Jason：不客氣。

對話單字說分明

1. **ingredient** *n.* 原料

例：To keep the good quality of our dishes, we only use the ingredients grown by our contract farmer.

為保持餐點的的一定品質，我們只使用契作農夫所種植的食材。

2. **flavor** *n.* 風味

例：To keep the flavor of the steak, we cook it with few seasoning.

為保有牛排的自然風味，烹調時僅簡單調味。

3. **tenderness** *n.* 柔軟度

例：Rare is the most appropriate level to keep the tenderness of this steak.

三分熟是保有這塊牛排軟嫩口感的最佳熟度。

4. **texture** *n.* 質地

例：If you prefer the texture of the steak, I would recommend our sirloin to you.

如果您喜歡有嚼勁的牛排，我會推薦莎朗給您。

5. **appetizer** *n.* 開胃菜

例：Roasted potato is our best-selling appetizers.

烤馬鈴薯是開胃菜的必點菜色。

6. **sear** *v.* 燒烤

例：To enjoy the flavor of the fish, you can sear it with salt.

若要品嚐魚的新鮮風味，你可以加鹽調味後加以燒烤。

7. **prawn** *n.* 蝦子

例：This seafood combo has fish, prawn, and oyster.

這個海鮮套餐有魚、蝦和牡蠣。

重點句型分析

1. **Some N make you... and some N you will be...** 意思為「有些…，讓你…總有…讓你…」，可用於說明事物或人所帶來感受。

   例：Some steaks give you unforgettable memories and some wine you will be surprised in your first sip.

   有些牛排讓您一吃難忘，有些紅酒讓您一嚐驚艷。

2. **To make sure..., we only...** 意思為「為確保…，我們只…。」，可用於說明為維持某一特性所需保有的堅持。

   例：To make sure the ingredients we use is fresh, we only use seasonal vegetable and fruit.

   為確保所用食材的新鮮，我們只使用當季的蔬果。

3. **Knowing the... of...well, Sb can...** 意思為「熟知…的…，…可以」，可用於說明熟悉某種特性與否所產生的差異。

   例：Knowing the feature of each ingredient, our chef can make the best cuisine for you.

   熟知各項食材的特性，我們的主廚能為您製做最美味的餐點。

職場補給站

本單元以餐廳服務人員向顧客推薦餐點為場景，發展一段完整對話，其內容中一共提到四個行銷的常用概念，以下針對每個概念做進一步說明：

1. 以等級（grade）強調選材：

- 對應句型：**To make sure the good quality of our beef, we only use US Prime grade.**

  對於懂吃的消費者來說，食材的好壞等級也會是他們在意的重點。以牛肉為例，有高級的和牛，也有相對便宜的 choice 等級。若顧客前往高級餐廳用餐，也會希望所吃的餐點食材品質具有一定水準。**在本範例中，Jason 強調本餐廳為確保牛排的品質能在水準之上，所以只選用 Prime 等級的牛肉。**

2. 以專業（expertise）提高價值：

- 對應句型：**Rare is the best. Knowing the texture and the distribution of the fat of each steak well, our chef can fully keep the juice and flavor in this level.**

  除食材之外，廚師的烹調技術是餐點美味的關鍵。當顧客對於餐點有任何疑問時，相關人員若能給予專業的回答，顧客會覺得自己花的錢是值得的。**在本範例中，顧客詢問菲力得最佳熟度，Jason 告知三分熟的肉汁與風味最佳，建議點此熟度。這樣的回覆展現對於烹調手法的熟悉，會讓顧客可以感受到餐廳的用心。**

3. 以搭配（collocation）增加消費：

- 對應句型：**Besides the main meals, do you want to have some appetizers or salad? They are delicate and delicious.**

  做為餐廳的服務人員，除了對於每項餐點的特性要熟悉外，各餐點之間的搭配性也是重點。向顧客介紹如何搭配除可讓各食材彼此相得益彰外，對整體的業績也是正向成長。**在本範例中，點完主餐後，Jason 便詢問顧客是否要加點開胃菜或是沙拉做搭配。**

4. 以氣氛（atmosphere）創造享受：

- 對應句型：**To provide the best dining atmosphere for you, the light could be darker or lighter in accordance with your need.**

顧客前往餐廳用餐時，除食物本身外，用餐氣氛也會影響其消費意願。若兩間餐廳在食材與價格上皆相去無幾，但在氣氛尚有差異，多數顧客應該會選擇前往氣氛較好的那間消費。**在本範例中，Jason 表示為了給顧客更好的用餐氣氛，貼心提醒顧客燈光可隨其需求調整，讓顧客除了品嚐美食外，心情也可以更加愉悅。**

看《料理鼠王》（*Ratatouille*），學會用不同的方式向顧客介紹餐點

篇章重點搶先看

1. 以《料理鼠王》（*Ratatouille*）中美食評論家 Ego 經典台詞學習如何從不同的方式向顧客介紹餐點。
2. 以美食評論家 Ego 的台詞 *"Not anyone can become a great artist, but a great artist can come from anywhere."*「不是誰都可以成為藝術家，但任何地方都可能有藝術家。」學習本單元核心句型：

   ★Not any... can..., but a... can... from...「不是每一個…都可以…，但任何…都可能有…。」
3. 搭配學習本單元其他三大重點句型：

   a. N is enough for..., so I...（N 夠…來…，所以我…。）

   b. To..., we will... for you（為了…，我們將會替您…。）

   c. After Ving..., you will...（…之後，您將…。）
4. 將四種句型放入實境對話練習，學習四大行銷概念：

   a. 以經典（classic）產生誘因。

   b. 以份量（quantity）強調實惠。

   c. 以桌邊服務（table service）提升滿意度。

   d. 以優惠券（coupon）吸引回流。

影片背景介紹

老鼠雷米（Rémy）和他的兄弟和父親及其他老鼠一起住在法國一棟老房子裡。受到剛去世的法國食神的啟發，雷米很嚮往美食家的生活。由於他的嗅覺異常靈敏，被族長賦予檢查食物是否有鼠藥的工作。後來屋主發現老鼠們的藏身處，讓老鼠們逃之夭夭。雷米也因此與家人失散，但也找到食神的餐館。雷米陰錯陽差地協助一位來應徵廚師但卻毫無廚藝的年輕人留在餐廳工作。兩人選擇交換條件，年輕人讓雷米留下，雷米幫他做菜。雷米做出的菜色大受歡迎，也讓嚴苛的美食評論家 Ego 決定上門品嚐。片中 Ego 感嘆原來廚師可以來自任何地方，甚至可能是隻老鼠的台詞，若應用在介紹餐點上，恰可做為我們學習改變切入點的良好教材。

Rémy's family and all the other rats live in an old house in France. Inspired by the deceased chef, Rémy wants to live a life as a cook. Rémy is good at smelling, so he's designated to check whether the food is poisoned or not. Found by the house owner, all rats run away. Rémy is separated from his family as well, but finds the restaurant of the chef he admires by accident. He helps a young man to keep his job over there, and has some negotiation with this man. The man lets Rémy stay and Rémy helps him to cook. The cuisine that Rémy makes become popular, making the strict food critics Ego come to taste in person. If we apply the words that Ego says to show his surprise when he knows Rémy is the chef to the introduction of the dishes, they turn out to be good materials for us to learn how describe dishes from different aspects.

看影片怎麼說、怎麼用

In ABC American Restaurant. Jason is at the table of Mark's family, who is first time at ABC American Restaurant.

（在 ABC 美式餐廳。Jason 站在 Mark 一家人的桌旁。這是 Mark 一家人第一次來 ABC 美式餐廳。）

Jason: Sure. For new guest, Buffalo chicken **wings** is a must-eat. (1) Not all dishes can become classic, but a classic dish can be in any place. Though we are not in the US, we can taste the **original** flavor of this appetizer.

Jason：當然可以。對於新顧客，水牛城雞翅是必點餐點。不是每道餐點都能成為經典，但任何地方都可以有經典菜色。雖然我們人不在美國，但我還是能品嚐這道開胃菜的原味。

Mark: Besides the appetizer, what is your best selling main meal?

Mark：除了開胃菜外，主餐的銷售冠軍是？

Jason: For seafood lovers, seafood **platter** is the most popular cuisine. It includes baked **lobsters** with cheese topping, roasted fish fillets, and deep fried oysters. (2) The dish is enough for three people, so I suggest you order two if you like it. For meat lovers, our BBQ ribs rank number one. We **marinated** the ribs with our secret **recipe** for one day, making its taste hard to forget. The ribs are enough for five to six people, so I suggest you order one if you like it.

Jason：針對海鮮愛好者，海鮮拼盤是最受歡迎的。這道菜有焗烤龍蝦、嫩烤魚排與炸牡蠣，份量夠三人食用。如果喜歡這道菜我建議點兩份。對於愛吃肉的顧客，我們的 BBQ 肋排是點餐排行榜的第一名。我們以獨家配方醃製肋排一天後烹調，這道菜讓你一吃難忘。肋排一份夠六人分食，所以如果想吃這道菜，我建議點一份即可。

Mark: We like the ribs more, but my two kids are too young to use knives and forks. Do you have any solution concerning this **consequence**?

Mark：我們比較喜歡肋排，但我的兩個小孩年紀太小不會使用刀叉。針對這樣的情況，你有任何解決的方法嗎？

Jason: (3) To provide the best service to our guests, I will slice the ribs into six portions or remove the bones for the kids if needed when I serve the food for you.

Jason：為了要給顧客最好的服務，上菜時我可以先幫您把肋排分成六份。如有需要，也可以幫小朋友去骨。

Mark: Great. I would like a slab of ribs. Besides, please give me two Buffalo chicken wings and one salad with roasted beef.

Mark：太棒了。那我要點一份肋排。此外，再給我兩份水牛城雞翅和一份烤牛肉沙拉。

Jason: Any **soft** drinks?

Jason：需要任何非酒精飲料嗎？

Mark: Please give me two cokes and four orange juices, thank you.

Mark：兩杯可樂跟四杯柳橙汁，謝謝。

Jason: OK. Let me repeat what you just ordered. You ordered two Buffalo chicken wings, one salad with roasted beef, a BBQ rib, two cokes, and four orange juices. Besides, we have a special event to celebrate our 10th anniversary. (4) After paying the bill today, you will get a 30% discount coupon for the next time.

Jason：好的，讓我重複一遍您的餐點，您點了兩份水牛城雞翅、一份烤牛肉沙拉、一份 BBQ 肋排、兩杯可樂和四杯柳橙汁。此外，為了慶祝開幕十周年，我們有特別活動，今日您付完帳，會得到一張下次用餐享七折的優惠券。

對話單字說分明

1. **wing** *n.* 翅膀

例：Chicken wings are widely used in many cuisines.
許多料理都有使用雞翅作為食材。

2. **original** *adj.* 最初的

例：To keep the original flavor, we cook this fish with salt alone.
為保有魚的新鮮風味，我們烹調時只以鹽調味。

3. **platter** *n.* 拼盤

例：If you want to have our best sellers at once, the chef's platter is your best choice.
如果想要一次品嚐多種熱門餐點，主廚拼盤是您的最佳選擇。

4. **lobster** *n.* 龍蝦

例：Boiled lobster is the cuisine highly recommended in our restaurant.
水煮龍蝦是我們餐廳最推薦的菜色。

5. **marinate** *v.* 醃製

例：The pork is marinated with BBQ sauce before roasting.
這塊豬肉在燒烤前經過 BBQ 醬醃製。

6. **recipe** *n.* 食譜

例：This risotto is made in accordance with our secret recipe.
這道燉飯是按照我們的獨家食譜所做成。

7. **consequence** *n.* 情況

例：To treat every guest as our VIP, we won't limit the dinning time in any consequences.
視每名顧客為貴賓，不管情況如何，我們不會去限制他的用餐時間。

8. **soft** *adj.* 無酒精的

例：You can get a soft drink for me if you order this combo.
點這個套餐可以免費獲得一杯無酒精飲料。

重點句型分析

1. **Not any... can..., but a... can... from...** 意思為「不是每一個…都可以…，但任何…都可能有…」，可用於強調人或物只要特色，不管在何處都能發光發熱。

   例：Not any cook can be a famous chef, but a famous chef can from any place.

   不是每一位廚師都可以成為知名主廚，但任何地方都可能有知名主廚。

2. **N is enough for..., so I...** 意思為「N 夠…來…，所以我…」，可用於食物的份量與建議的點餐數量。

   例：This seafood platter is enough for four people to eat, so I suggest you order two.

   這個海鮮拼盤夠四人食用，所以我建議您點兩份。

3. **To..., we will... for you.** 意思為「為了…，我們將會替您…」，可用於表示為了達成某事，而願意做其他事來達成。

   例：To provide a better service, we will send one waiter to slice and deliver the ribs for you.

   為了提供更好的服務，我們將會派一名服務生為您分肋排。

4. **After Ving..., you will...** 意思為「…之後，您將…」，可用於表示完成某事後會得到的某物。

   例：After paying the bill, you will receive a 20% discount coupon that you can use next time.

   結帳過後，你將獲得一張下次消費享八折的優惠券。

本單元以餐廳人員向顧客推銷餐點為場景，發展一段完整對話，其內容中一共提到四個行銷的常用概念，以下針對每個概念做進一步說明：

1. 以經典（classic）產生誘因：

- 對應句型：**Not all dishes can become classic, but a classic dish can be in any place. Though we are not in the US, we can taste the original flavor of this appetizer.**

 相較於創意菜色，許多顧客對於名菜的接受度較高。其原因在於前者雖然新奇，但在口味的接受度上可能見仁見智，後者則是因為味道已為多數人接受，餐廳人員在推薦時可以以此做為吸引顧客的誘因。**在本範例中，Jason 向 Mark 介紹水牛城雞翅，並強調我們雖然不在美國，但在這可以品嚐這道經典美式餐點。**

2. 以份量（quantity）強調實惠：

- 對應句型：**It includes baked lobsters with cheese topping, roasted fish fillets, and deep fried oysters. The dish is enough for three people, so I suggest you order two if you like it.**

 對於家庭或是食量大的顧客，餐點的份量絕對是他們點餐時的考量之一。針對此客群，餐廳人員應依其人數給予份數上的建議，讓他們能夠吃飽也吃巧。**在本範例中，Jason 介紹海鮮拼盤內容有龍蝦、魚排和牡蠣，且一份夠三人食用，建議有六人的 Mark 家庭點兩份。**

3. 以桌邊服務（table service）提升滿意度：

- 對應句型：**To provide the best service to our guests, I will slice the rib into six portions or remove the bones for the kids if needed when I serve the food for you.**

  除了餐點本身外，餐廳的服務也是顧客在意重點。若服務人員能讓顧客感覺賓至如歸，顧客自然願意回流。當餐廳提供桌邊服務，對於整體印象是有加分作用的。**在本範例中，由於 Mark 表示他的小孩因為年紀太小無法用自己餐具吃肋排，Jason 表示可以把肋排先切成六份或是為小孩直接去骨，這樣的服務肯定能讓 Mark 一家感受到餐廳的用心。**

4. 以優惠券（coupon）吸引顧客回流：

- 對應句型：**Besides, we have a special event to celebrate our 10th anniversary. After paying the bill today, you will get a 30% discount coupon for the next time.**

  從行銷的角度切入，若顧客此次用餐後，下次就不會再來，就表示餐點可能不夠好吃或是價格太貴。為避免這樣的情況發生，發送優惠券是很好的手法。當顧客獲得這樣的票券，回流的機率會獲得提升。**以本範例為例，Jason 表示適逢餐廳開幕十周年，今日結帳後，Mark 一家可獲得下次享七折的優惠券。**

看《女傭變鳳凰》（*Maid in Manhattan*），學會化解顧客的不合理要求

篇章重點搶先看

1. 以《女傭變鳳凰》（*Maid In Manhattan*）女主角瑪麗莎經典台詞學習如何巧妙化解顧客的不合理要求。
2. 以以女傭變鳳凰女主角瑪麗莎經典台詞 *"Although we serve, we are not their servant."*「我們提供服務，但我們絕對不是他們的傭人。」。學習本單元核心句型：

   ★ Although we..., we are not...「我們…但我們不是…。」
3. 搭配學習本單元其他三大重點句型：
   a. Knowing you..., we...（知道您…，我們…。）
   b. Because..., this is the 最高級 we can...（因為…，這是我們所能…的…。）
   c. Being a part of..., ... always comes first（身為…的一份子，…是最優先的。）
4. 將四種句型放入實境對話練習，學習四大行銷概念：
   a. 以職業道德（professional ethics）維持底限。
   b. 以替代方案（alternative）化解刁難。
   c. 以諒解（forgiveness）避免尷尬。
   d. 以體貼（consideration）創造回流。

影片背景介紹

本片主角瑪麗莎是一位在貝瑞斯佛旅館（Beresford Hotel）工作的單親媽媽，與兒子泰同住。由於這是間豪華旅館，瑪麗莎常常幻想自己也能過更好的生活。有一天參議員候選人克里斯多福因為參加活動而入住，瑪麗莎在同事的慫恿下偷穿了賓客的華服，而被他誤認為瑪麗莎就是社交名媛卡洛琳。兩人一見傾心，但兩人懸殊的身分也成為交往的阻礙。片中瑪麗莎對於旅館服務人員身分所下的一番定義，恰可做為學習如何透過闡述職業道德化解客戶的不適當要求。

Marisa is a single mother who works as a maid in Beresford Hotel. She lives with her son Ty. Since this is a luxurious hotel, she often expects one day she could live a better life. One day the senatorial candidate, Christopher lives in this hotel for an up-class event. Under her co-worker's encouragement, Marisa wears one guest's designer dress and happens to be seen by Chris. Regarding she is the socialite Caroline, Chris is attracted by Marisa. Soon, they fall in love. However, the difference in the social status becomes the obstacle of their relationship. The words Marisa uses to define her job turn out to be good materials for us to learn how to use professional ethics as a tool to respond unreasonable requests from guests.

看影片怎麼說、怎麼用

In the front desk of ABC Hotel.

（在 ABC 飯店的前檯。）

Jason: Good afternoon, sir. What can I do for you?

Jason：先生午安。有什麼能為您服務的嗎？

Parker: I need a double room with the seashore view on the high floor. A King size bed.

Parker：我需要一間高樓層的海景雙人房，雙人大床一張。

Jason: Sorry sir, all double rooms are **booked**. Would you mind changing the room type.

Jason：非常抱歉，所有的雙人房都被訂滿，您介意更換房型嗎？

Parker: Not a chance. Giving me a double room today is not that difficult. Just cancel any guest with **reservation**, but haven't finished the procedure of check-in.

Parker：別想叫我換。弄間雙人房沒這麼困難，就隨便取消一個還沒完成入住手續旅客的訂房就好了啊！

Jason: (1) Though we serve, we are not your servants. Every guest is our VIP. They shall enjoy the same right, so I can't cancel the booking without their **permission**. (2) Meanwhile, knowing you have a need of a double room, we will try to find an **alternative** for you.

Jason：我們提供服務，但我不是您的傭人。所有房客都是我們的貴賓，所以他們都應享有相同權利，除非獲得他們的許可，不然我不會取消訂房。於此同時了解到您雙人房的需求，我們會替您尋找替代方案。

Parker: Ok, I will wait and see what you can do for me.

Parker：好啊！我倒要瞧瞧你能怎樣做。

Jason: After checking our system, we found one guest just checked out from the **premium** single **suite** few hours ago. This size of is almost as same as a standard double room. And very lucky, this room is on our 25th floor with an open horizon. It perfectly meets you requirement. (3) Because the room type you firstly requested is not available, this is the best solution we can provide now.

Jason：查詢系統過後，我們發現有名入住頂級單人套房的房客幾小時前剛退房。這種房型的大小跟標準雙人房差不多。而且非常幸運的是，這間套房位在本飯店25 樓，視野開闊，可說是完全符合您的要求。因為你最初要求的房型客滿，這是我們所能提供給您的最佳解決方案。

Parker: I should say this option is even better. I think I have to apologize for my rudeness.

Parker：我必須說這個選項更好。我想我需要為我剛才的魯莽道歉。

Jason: Don't mention it. There must be some reasons behind your behavior, so I don't feel **offended**. Being a part of the service industry, guests' needs always come first.

Jason：別這樣說，行為背後都有原因，所以我並沒有覺得被冒犯。身為服務業的一份子，顧客的要求優先。

Parker. Your quick reaction and good emotional management really **impress** me. I will recommend your hotel to my friends.

Parker：你快速的反應與良好的情緒管理真的讓我印象深刻，我會向朋友們推薦你們的飯店。

Jason: Thank you, sir. Now let me help you to check in. May I have your passport for few seconds?

Jason：謝謝。現在就讓我幫你完成入住。可以借用你的護照進行登記嗎？

Parker: OK.

Parker：好的。

Lesson 19
Lesson 20
Lesson 21
Lesson 22
Lesson 23
Lesson 24

對話單字說分明

1. **book** *v.* 預定

例：You can book the ticket online twenty days before the concert.

演唱會前 20 天可以上網訂票。

2. **reservation** *n.* 預約

例：We will keep your reservation for ten minute.

我們會保留您的預約十分鐘。

3. **permission** *n.* 允許

例： Without manger's permission, I can't give you reference.

除非有經理的允許，否則我無法把這份參考資料給你。

4. **alternative** *n.* 替代方案

例：Please find an alternative for this project.

請找出此專案的替代方案。

5. **premium** *adj.* 高級的

例：This is premium suit we just release two days.

這是我們兩天前新推出的西裝。

6. **suite** *n.* 套房

例：I need a single suite with a king size bed.

我需要一間有大床的單人套房。

7. **offend** *v.* 冒犯

例：If my words offend you, please accept my deepest apology.

如果我的話語有冒犯到您，請接受我最誠摯的道歉。

8. **impress** *v.* 使…印象深刻

例：Your vivid description really impresses me.

你生動的敘述讓我印象深刻。

重點句型分析

1. **Although we..., we are not...** 意思為「我們⋯，但我們不是⋯」，可用於說明各職業所堅守的某些底限。

   例：Although we sale, we are not their agents.
   我們銷售商品，但我們不是他們的代理商。

2. **Knowing you..., we...** 意思為「知道您⋯，我們⋯」，可用於說明我方將如何處理客戶所提出的需求。

   例：Knowing you have the need of vegetarian food, we have asked our chef to prepare it for you.
   知道您有茹素的需求，我們已經要求主廚為您準備素食餐點。

3. **Because..., this is the 最高級 we can...** 意思為「因為⋯，這是我們所能⋯的⋯」，可用於說明在某一情況下所能做出的最佳處置。

   例：Because all conference rooms are booked, this is the biggest place we can provide now.
   由於所有的會議室都已被預訂，這是目前所能提供的最大場地。

4. **Being a part of..., the... of... always comes first.** 意思為「身為⋯的一份子，⋯是最優先的⋯」，可用於說明各職業所應優先處理的事項。

   例：Being a part of the technology industry, the need of the production line always comes first.
   身為科技業的一份子，生產線的需求是最優先的。

本單元以飯店櫃台人員處理客戶無理要求為場景，發展一段完整對話，其內容中一共提到四個行銷的常用概念，以下針對每個概念做進一步說明：

1. 以職業道德（professional ethics）維持底限：

- 對應句型：**Though we serve, we are not you servants. Every guest is our VIP.**

  在服務客戶或是銷售商品時，客戶的要求並非一定要照單全收，如果這些要求會影響到其他客戶的權益，本著職業道德，應當與以拒絕，改用其他方式處理其需求。**在本範例中，客戶 Parker 要求 Jason 取消別人的訂房好讓他有雙人房可住，本著平等對待每為客戶的職業道德，Jason 選擇拒絕這樣的不合理要求。**

2. 以替代方案（alternative）化解要求：

- 對應句型：**After checking our system, we found one guest just checked out from the premium single suite few hours ago. This size of is almost as same as a standard double room.**

  雖然客戶的要求不合理，但因為他也是客戶，銷售或是服務人員應以其他方式滿足其需求，也就是尋找替代方案。**在本範例中，為了要在雙人房全滿的情況下滿足 Parker 的要求，Jason 透過查詢系統發現目前尚有一間頂級單人套房是空的，該房間的大小與標準雙人房差不多，應當可以滿足其需求。**

3. 以諒解（forgiveness）避免尷尬：

- 對應句型：**Don't mention it. There must be some reason behind your behavior, so I don't feel offended. Being a part of the service industry, guests' needs always come first.**

當客戶感覺到自己的要求或是行為有不合理之處，欲向服務或是銷售人員道歉時，此時我方應盡量選擇接受，讓其有台階下，以免造成雙方的尷尬。**在本範例中，Parker 覺得自己一開始要求 Jason 退別人訂房的行為很魯莽，Jason 以諒解的方式接受致歉，不讓 Parker 難堪。**

4. 以體貼（consideration）創造顧客回流率：

- 對應句型：**Your quick reaction and good emotional management really impress me. I will recommend your hotel to my friends.**

當銷售人員能進行換位思考，設身處地為客戶著想，客戶通常都會表示未來願意在此來此消費，或是將其推薦給其親朋好友，進而創造出相當的回流率。**在本範例中，雖然 Parker 的要求不合理，但 Jason 還是和顏悅色地為他找出替代方案，讓 Parker 十分滿意並表示會向他人推薦 ABC 飯店。**

看《巴黎拜金女》（*Priceless*），學習展現商品與服務價值

篇章重點搶先看

1. 以《巴黎拜金女》（*Priceless*）女主角經典台詞學習如何展現商品或服務價值。
2. 以巴黎拜金女女主角 Irene 的經典台詞 “But charm is more valuable than beauty. You can resist beauty, but you can't resist charm.”
   「迷人本身比美貌更有價值，美貌可以抵抗，但魅力是抵抗不了的。」學習本單元核心句型：
   ★A is 比較級 than B. We can... A but we can't... B.「A 比 B 更…，A 可以…，但 B 是不可以…。」
3. 搭配學習本單元其他三大重點句型：
   a A is for the... of... while B is for the... of...（A 是針對…的…，而 B 針對…的…。）
   b Though sth is..., what you can... is...（雖然…是，但你能…的也…。）
   c Sth include... but the... is 比較級，making it a/the...（…包含…，但…的…卻才…，是一個…。）
4. 將四種句型放入實境對話練習，學習四大行銷概念：
   a 以套裝（package）加乘效益。
   b 使廉價（cheapness）不是唯一。
   c 以同理心（empathy）進行推薦。
   d 用計算（calculation）說明細節。

影片背景介紹

本片女主角 Irene 是個超級拜金女，總是有辦法以性與陪伴讓富豪願意花大筆鈔票讓她過奢華日子。有天她與略為年長的男友前往男主角 Jean 工作的豪華飯店慶生，席間男友不勝酒力醉倒，所以 Irene 跑到飯店酒吧續攤，與服務生男主角首次相遇。幾杯雞尾酒下肚後，兩人跑到飯店皇家套房共度春宵，但隔天醒來 Jean 卻以不見 Irene 蹤影。直到片尾時，兩人發現其實彼此是相愛的，物質並沒有想像中的那樣重要。片中 Irene 用來比較美貌與魅力的台詞，若應用在服務或商品的價值展現上，實為值得我們學習的好教材。

The protagonist of *Priceless,* Irene is a super material girl. She always uses sex and companionship to exchange a lavish life. One day when she celebrates her birthday with her elderly boyfriend in one luxury hotel where Jean works in. During the party, her boyfriend is too drunk to accompany her, so she goes to the bar in the hotel and firstly meets Jean. They spend the night together, but Jean finds Irene is gone the next morning. When the movie is about to end, Irene and Jean find that they love each other and material is not that important. If we apply the words that Irene uses to compare beauty and charm to marketing, they can turn out to be good materials for us to learn to emphasize the value of a product or service.

看影片怎麼說、怎麼用

At the counter of ABC Hotel. Nancy tells Jason that she needs a family room for two double beds or four single beds.

（在 ABC 飯店的櫃檯。Nancy 跟 Jason 說她需要一間家庭房，兩張雙人床或是四張單人床都行。）

Jason: Our system shows that there are several rooms are available, so here let me briefly introduce our latest package to you for more options. (1) **Astonishment** is more attractive than specialty. You can control your curiosity to specialty, but you can't control you curiosity to astonishment. To make every journey unforgettable, now we combine the must-go and must-eat in our hotel all together.

Jason：系統顯示目前尚有多間空房，所以讓我簡單為您介紹目前最新的套餐活動，讓您可以有更多選擇。驚奇比特別更加吸引人，你可能對特別的事物不感好奇，但驚奇的事物絕對讓你好奇。為了讓每趟旅程令人難忘，我們現在將本飯店與必去景點與必吃食物做結合。

Nancy: It sounds great, but I think the package will definitely go beyond my budget.

Nancy：聽起來很棒，但我想這樣的套裝行程一定超過我的預算。

Jason: You are right, partially. (2) Though accommodation alone is cheaper, what you can enjoy is less. What we put in this special project will never disappoint you and makes every **penny** you pay worthy.(3) The must-go is for the witness of amazing world cultural **heritage**, while the must-eat is the

Jason：你只說對了一部分。雖然單購住宿比較便宜，但你所享受的項目也較少。這個特別行程的內容絕對不會讓您失望，也讓您所花的每一分錢都值得。必去景點是為了您親眼目睹驚人

taste of fresh local food. The **spirit** of this package is to create the most wonderful memory for the tourists as if they can only visit here for one time in their life.

的世界文化遺產，必吃食物是為了讓您品嚐新鮮的當地食材。這個活動的精神就是當成每位遊客這一生只會來這一次，而這趟行程能替他們創造最好的回憶。

Nancy: After your explanation, I am more interested in the package. What's the total charge if I upgrade to this project?

Nancy：經過你的解釋後，我對這個套裝行程更有興趣了，請問升級到此套裝的總價是多少呢？

Jason: It will be 400 USD. For the standard accommodation alone, we charge 300 USD. For the tour alone, the fee is 300 USD. For the **cuisine** alone, you have to pay 200 USD. (4) The package includes the three parts mentioned above but only charges you 400 USD, making it a good **bargain**.

Jason：是 400 美金。單算標準住宿，我們收您 300 美金。單就旅遊部分的費用是 300 美金，若只用餐，您需支付 200 美金。這個套組包含上述三項，但卻只收您 400 美金，一個非常划算的價格。

Nancy: The price is affordable. Only 100 USD more, my family and I can have more fun. I will like to have an upgrade. Here is my credit card and the passport, please help me to check-in.

Nancy：這個負擔的起的價格。只要再多花 100 美金，我和我的家人就能享受更多樂趣。我要升級成套裝行程。這邊是我的信用卡與護照，請幫我辦理入住手續。

Jason: OK.

Jason：好的。

對話單字說分明

1. **astonishment** *n.* **令人驚訝的事物**

例：To my astonishment, this smart phone could be used in the water.

讓我驚訝的是這支智慧型手機可在水中使用。

2. **specialty** *n.* **特殊性**

例：The specialty of this tour is you can see the whales in a short distance.

本旅遊的特殊之處在於能夠近距離觀賞鯨魚。

3. **penny** *n.* **一分錢**

例：To make every penny you spend worthy, we check the quality strictly before shipment.

為確保您花的每一分錢都是值得的，出貨前我們嚴格確認品質。

4. **heritage** *n.* **遺留物**

例：Cultural heritage is an important resource for the local tourism.

文化遺產是當地重要的觀光資源。

5. **spirit** *n.* **精神**

例：Holding the spirit of going natural, our products are chemical additive free.

秉持追求自然的精神，我們的產品不含化學添加劑。

6. **cuisine** *n.* **餐點**

例：If needed, we can customize the cuisine for you.

如有需要，我們可以替您特製餐點。

7. **bargain** *n.* **交易**

例：The deduction in the freight makes this order a good bargain.

運費的減免讓此交易更顯划算。

8. **voucher** *n.* **票券**

例：Please keep this voucher in the coming two days.

未來兩天內請您妥善保管此票券。

重點句型分析

1. **A is 比較級 than B. We can... A but we can't... B...** 意思為「A 比 B 更…，A 可以…，但 B 是不可以…」，可用於強調商品或是某種不可取代或是難以超越的特質。

   例：Safety is more important than aesthetics in a car. You can neglect aesthetics when you drive, but you can't neglect safety when you drive.

   一輛車的安全性比美感更重要。開車時你可以忽略美感，但安全是不可忽略的。

2. **A is for the... of... while B is for the... of...** 意思為「A 是針對…的…，而 B 針對…的…。」，可用於說明套餐式銷售各部分的主要訴求。

   例：Home-made food is for the experiencing of a local culture, while the massage is for the relaxation of the body.

   家常餐點是針對當地文化的體驗，而按摩是針對身體的的放鬆。

3. **Though A is..., what you can... is...** 意思為「雖然…是，但你能…的也…」，可用於說明產品或服務。

   例：Though the package tour is more expensive, what you can enjoy is more.

   雖然這個套裝行程比較貴，但你能享受的項目也較多。

4. **Sth include... but the... is 比較級, making it a/the...** 意思為「…包含…，但…的…卻才…，是一個…」，可用於說明組合式銷售的內容共有哪些，以及優點為何。

   例：This package includes runner apparels, runner shoes, and smart watches, but the price is only 500 USD, making it the best choice for advance runners.

   這個套組包含跑服、跑鞋與智慧腕表，但價格卻才只有 500 美金，是進階跑者的最佳選擇。

職場補給站

本單元以飯店櫃檯人員向遊客推薦住房升級為場景，發展一段完整對話，其內容共提到四個行銷的常用概念，以下針對每個概念做進一步說明：

1. 以套裝（package）加乘效益：

- 對應句型：**Astonishment is more attractive than specialty. You can control your curiosity to specialty but you can't control you curiosity to astonishment. To make every journey unforgettable, now we combine the must-go and must-eat in our hotel all together.**

在銷售產品時，倘若單一商品無法引起消費者的購買意願時，套裝組合就是可以使用的輔助手法之一。此種組合的優勢在於內容多元且價格上具競爭性，可提高成交的機率。**在本範例中，Jason 強調這個組合包含景點與美食，會讓您覺得特別而且驚訝，希望藉此引起 Nancy 想進一步了解的動機。**

2. 使廉價（cheapness）不是唯一：

- 對應句型：**Though accommodation alone is cheaper, what you can enjoy is less. What we put in this special project will never disappoint you and makes every penny you pay worthy.**

若從價格面切入，消費者當然希望產品或是服務越便宜越好，但便宜有時並不能滿足需求，而這也是為何強調價值能夠打動消費者的原因。**在本範例中，Jason 強調單純住宿確實比較便宜，但能享受的項目就變少了，然後自信地向 Nancy 保證這個套裝行程不會讓她失望。**

Lesson 19
Lesson 20
Lesson 21
Lesson 22
Lesson 23
Lesson 24

3. 以同理心（empathy）進行推薦：

- 對應句型：**The spirit of this package is to create the most wonderful memory for the tourists as if they can only visit here for one time.**

  在消費市場中，消費者往往都會認為銷售方只關注商品是否售出，並非真的為消費者著想。若要破除這樣迷思，銷售人員在推薦商品時應去思考不同的消費者會有怎樣的需求，然後給予最佳的建議。**在本範例中，Jason 提到這格套裝行程就是當成消費者只能來此旅遊一次，要替他們創造難忘的回憶。**

4. 用計算（calculation）說明細節：

- 對應句型：**For the standard accommodation alone, we charge 300 USD. For the tour alone, the fee is 300 USD. For the cuisine alone, you have to pay 200 USD. The package include the three parts mentioned above but only charge you 400 USD, making it a good bargain.**

  由於商品組的內容眾多，若要突顯其划算程度，以簡單的加減乘除一項項計算給客戶看是非常實用的銷售技巧。這樣的說明方式讓消費者感覺自己省了很多，消費意願自然會提高。**在本範例中，Jason 告訴 Nancy 單購住宿要 300 美金、單買旅遊要 300 美金，單吃飯要 200 美金，三者相加原本要 800 美金，但現在只需 400 美金，非常划算。**

看《當幸福來敲門》（*The Pursuit of Happyness*），學習向客戶闡述產品與服務的核心價值

篇章重點搶先看

1. 以《當幸福來敲門》（*The Pursuit of Happyness*）男主角克里斯賈納經典台詞學習如何向客戶闡述產品或服務的核心價值。
2. 以當幸福來敲門男主角克里斯賈納 *"The source of our greatest courage is always those who we want to protect the most."*

   「我們總是能在想要守護的人身上，找到自己最大的勇氣。」學習本單元核心句型：

   ★The...of... is always...「我們總是能在…上找到…。」
3. 搭配學習本單元其他三大重點句型：

   a To find..., we collect...（為了找出…，我們蒐集…。）

   b Aided with..., the new...can（輔以…，新的…能夠…。）

   c Showing our... to..., I would like（為表示我們…，我要…。）
4. 將四種句型放入實境對話練習，學習四大行銷概念：

   a 以閒聊（chat）做為開頭。

   b 以動機（motive）說明核心價值。

   c 以統計數據（statistic figure）佐證效果。

   d 以專業性（specialty）說服消費者。

影片背景介紹

本片是改編自美國賈納理財公司執行長克里斯賈納創業的故事。賈納以銷售醫療器材為業，雖然他熱愛這份工作，但因為收入無法維持家計，妻子選擇與之離婚，為了自己與兒子的未來，他爭取到擔任證券經紀無薪實習生的機會。為了終結困頓的生活，賈納更加努力，最後完成實習也成功進入該公司任職，並於 1987 年時自己成立賈納理奇證券經紀公司。片中賈納用來自我鼓勵的台詞，若將其語法應用在行銷上，恰可做為我們學習透過闡述產品或服務的核心價值的良好教材。

The Pursuit of Happyness is adapted from the true story of Chris Gardner. Gardner is a sales of medical equipment. He loves this job, even though the income is low and brings the end to his marriage. To have a better future for himself and his son, he tries his best to work as an internship with no salary in a stock brokerage firm. Finally, Gardner finishes the internship and works in this company. Gardner also establishes his own company in 1987. If we apply the words that Gardner uses to encourage himself to marketing, they turn out to be good materials for us to learn how to illustrate the core values of our products or services to the consumers.

看影片怎麼說、怎麼用

In the retailer store of ABC Sports Goods Company.

（在 ABC 體育用品公司的門市。）

Jason: Long time no see, Sam. How are you? I heard you won the **champion** in this badminton open. You are really a good player.

Jason：好久不見，Sam。最近好嗎？聽說你榮膺本次羽球公開賽冠軍，您真是位優秀選手。

Sam: Don't mention that. I won the game with some luck. During the game, I also found some flaws of my **sneakers**.

Sam：別這麼說，我這次贏的有點幸運。比賽過程中我也發現這雙羽球鞋的一些缺點。

Jason: Can you explain more specifically?

Jason：可以更詳細的說明是怎樣的缺點嗎？

Sam: Sure. When I shift the center of **gravity** of my body to hit the ball, sometime I feel that I tend to move forward.

Sam：當然可以。當我移動身體重心去擊球時，有時會感覺人向前傾。

Jason: Many consumers have reflected this situation to our company, and to be honest that is the reason I invite you to our store today. (1) The motive of the improvement is always the strictest critics from our supporters. Sport injury could end the career of the professional **athletes**, making the modification of this shoes our priority.

Jason：許多顧客都已向我們反映此問題。坦白說，這也是邀您來公司的原因。我們總是能從支持者所給予的嚴厲批評上找到進步的動機。運動傷害可能會終結一位專業運動員的職業生涯，這讓我們視改良此鞋款為優先事項。

Sam：True. Healthy body is the most valuable **property** of an athlete. What is the main cause of this problem?

Sam：沒錯，健康的身體是運動員最重要的資產。那產生缺陷的原因是什麼呢？

Jason: (2) To find the reason, we invite 100 players to have an experiment in our lab, and we collect the data detected from the sensor that we installed on the ankles and inside the soles of shoes. The figures indicate that the soles can't fully **absorb** the pressure created by movements. To solve this problem in a scientific way, we upgrade the shoes' materials. (3) Aided with **composite** materials, the new edition can give you the better support.

Jason：為了找出原因，我們邀集 100 位球員至公司的實驗室做實驗，並收裝置在受測員腳踝上與鞋底內的數據。這些數字指出此鞋款的鞋底無法完全吸收因為移動所產生的壓力。為了解決這個問題，我們升級鞋材。輔以複合型材料，新鞋款給您更好的支撐性。

Sam: It sounds great. Can I try this now?

Sam：聽起來很棒。我可以體驗看看嗎？

Jason: Of course. What is your size?

Jason：當然可以。您穿幾號鞋？

Sam: US 9.5. Thank you.

Sam：美規 9 號半，謝謝。

Jason: How do you feel? Please either jump or move forward or backward with certain speed. I think you can tell the difference.

Jason：感覺如何呢？請跳躍看看，或是有速度的前後移動。我相信您能感受出差別的。

Sam: It is more stable indeed and somehow lighter. I would like to buy two. What is the price?

Sam：真的更穩定而且似乎更輕量化了。我要兩雙，請問多少錢呢？

Lesson 19
Lesson 20
Lesson 21
Lesson 22
Lesson 23
Lesson 24

對話單字說分明

1. **champion** *n.* 冠軍

例：Our brand representative just gets the champion in Taipei Badminton Open. 我們的品牌代言人甫獲台北羽球公開賽冠軍。

2. **sneaker** *n.* 運動鞋

例：To produce the best sneakers, we conduct many experiments to test the materials we use.
為了做出最棒的運動鞋，我們對於使用素材進行多項實驗。

3. **gravity** *n.* 重力

例：To keep the center of the gravity in the same place, we redesign the base of the machine.
為保持重心的位置，我們重新設計機器的底座。

4. **athlete** *n.* 運動員

例：Professional athletes are our target customers.
職業運動員是我們的目標客群。

5. **property** *n.* 資產

例：The expertise in recycled materials is our most important property.
再生素材上的專業技術是我們最重要的資產。

6. **sole** *n.* 鞋底

例：The new material makes the soles of our boots more durable.
新素材讓我們的靴子的鞋底更加耐磨。

7. **absorb** *v.* 吸收

例：The function of the soft pad is to absorb the vibration.
軟墊是要用來吸收震動用的。

8. **composite** *adj.* 複合的

例：To keep durability and lightness at once, we develop composite materials. 為達到質輕且耐用，我們研發出複合材質。

重點句型分析

1. **The...of... is always...** 意思為「我們總是能在…上找到…」，可用於說明事物產生變化的原因。

   例：The spark of the breakthrough is always from the inconvenience we encounter.

   我們總是能在所遭遇的不便上找到突破的切入點。

2. **To find..., we collect...** 意思為「為了找出…，我們蒐集…。」，可用於說明為取得某項資訊所對應的做法。

   例：To find the reason of the abnormality, we collect all the signals received in the past one week for the further analysis.

   為了找出異常的原因，我們收集過去一週所接收知訊號以利進一步分析。

3. **Aided with..., the new...can...** 意思為「輔以…，新的…能夠…」，可用於說明加上有種新的事物後所產生的差異為何。

   例：Aided with our latest technology, the new smart phone can overturn your fixed image to our brand.

   輔以最新科技，我們的新款智慧型手機會顛覆您對我們品牌的既有印象。

4. **Showing our.... to..., I would like...** 意思為「為表示我們…，我要…」，可用於說名支持某種想法或事活動的具體作為。

   例：Showing our support to the domestic industry, I would like to use the parts made in Taiwan.

   為表示我們對國內產業的支持，我要使用台製零件。

本單元以運動鞋銷售員向專業運動員推薦新款運動鞋為主題，發展一段完整對話，其內容中一共提到四個行銷的常用概念，以下針對每個概念做進一步說明：

1. 以閒聊（chat）做為開頭：

- 對應句型：**Long time no see Sam. How are you? I heard you won the championship in this badminton open. You are really a good player.**

  若從顧客的角度來看，當銷售人員一見面就馬上滔滔不絕的推薦自家產品，很容易對之反感。相反地，若以閒話家常方式開頭，顧客會比較願意去聆聽後段的介紹。**在本範例中，Jason 一看到 Sam 並不是馬上向他介紹新鞋，而是向他問好，恭賀他拿下羽球公開賽的冠軍。**

2. 以動機（motive）說明核心價值：

- 對應句型：**The motive of improvement is always the strictest critics from our supporters. Sport injury could end the career of the professional athletes, making the modification of this shoe our priority.**

  任何產品或是服務都有其核心價值，這樣的價值往往也是左又顧客購買與否的關鍵。以產品改版為例，通常其原因都是因為發現舊版有缺點需要修正。**在本範例中，Jason 表示進步來自於批評。由於運動傷害可能讓運動員的運動生命劃下終點，因此修正舊款的缺失是當務之急。**

3. 以統計數據（statistic figure）佐證效果：

- 對應句型：To find the reason, we invite 100 player to have an experiment in our lab, we collect the data detected from the sensor that we installed on the ankles and inside the soles of shoes. The figures indicate that the soles can't fully absorb the pressure create by movements.

　　越是精明的消費者，對於銷售人員的話術的信任程度往往越低，因為他們會認為這些話語存在太多誇大不實之處。為說服這類消費者，使用統計數據是可行的方法。正所謂數字會說話，統計學能夠呈現許多客觀事實。**在本範例中，Jason 提到為修正舊款缺失，公司邀請 100 位羽球選手進行實驗，以監測的方式找出原來是因為鞋底無法完全吸震，因而造成不穩。**

4. 以專業性（specialty）說服消費者：

- 對應句型：To solve this problem in a scientific way, we upgrade the materials. Aided with composite materials, the new edition can give you the better support.

　　為了提高消費者對於產品的信心，銷售人員在推薦時一定要具備專業性，對於各項細節有一定的掌握，這樣當消費者詢問時，才能給予適當的回答。**以本範例為例，Jason 表示公司使用科學方式來解決鞋款缺點，藉由使用複合材質，新款球鞋可給予使用者更穩定的支撐。**

看《第五元素》（*The Fifth Element*），學習推銷產品

篇章重點搶先看

1. 以《第五元素》（*The Fifth Element*）經典台詞學習如何推銷產品。
2. 以本片中的經典台詞 *"Even if we're just a matchstick, we can still spark and ignite at the most critical moment."*「即使我們只是一根火柴，也要在關鍵的時刻有一次閃耀。」學習本單元核心句型：

   ★Even if..., ... can still...「即使…，…也能…。」
3. 搭配學習本單元其他三大重點句型：

   a Through..., the... is controlled in...（透過…，…被控制在…。）

   b If the...is below..., you can...（如果…低於…，你可以…。）

   c Finding..., we...at the speed of...（找出…，我們以…的速度…。）
4. 將四種句型放入實境對話練習，學習四大行銷概念：

   a 以功用性（functionality）擴大價值。

   b 以精確度（precision）強調技術。

   c 以良率（yield rate）確保品質。

   d 以效率（efficiency）吸引下單。

Lesson 19
Lesson 20
Lesson 21
Lesson 22
Lesson 23
Lesson 24

影片背景介紹

1914 年時，外星人自埃及古神廟取走四塊石頭與一具石棺。相傳惡魔每 5000 年就會試圖摧毀宇宙中的所有生物一次。兩百多年後，惡魔攻擊地球。人類戰艦隊發動攻擊卻反遭消滅。外星人在地球的聯絡人告訴地球總統，這四塊被帶走石頭分別代表四種元素，加上神秘的第五元素就能形成擊敗惡魔的武器。片中男主角自我鼓勵的台詞，若將其句構運用在強調產品的功能性上，實為一個良好的學習教材。

In 1914, aliens take four stones and one stone coffin from an Egyptian temple. According to legend, the devil tends to destroy all creators every 5000 years. Two hundred years later, the devil attacks the Earth. Human's warship fights it back but is destroyed. If we apply the words that Dallas uses to encourage himself to the marketing, they turns out to be good materials for us to learn how to emphasize the functions of a product or a service.

看影片怎麼說、怎麼用

At the conference room of ABC Screw Company. Jason, the sales of the International Sales Department, is going to have a short presentation.

（在 ABC 螺絲公司的會議室。擔任國貿部業務人員的 Jason 將做個小報告。）

Jason: OK. As we know, screws are not eye-catching products.(1) Even if the size of screw is small, it can still have a great impact on a product. A good screw can tightly combine two parts, while the improper machining screws could cause the crash of an airplane. To provide the best screws to our customers, we upgrade the hardware and software this year. (2) Through the usage of new machine program, the errors are controlled in a range between plus or minus 0.01 mm. This inaccuracy is tolerable to most products. Not willing to be just good but the best, we give you more promises. (3) If the yield rate is below 99%, you can return the lot you order and we will cover the freight.

Jason：好的。我們都知道在個螺絲在一個產品上看起來並不起眼。但即使它的尺寸很小，也能有很大的影響力。好的螺絲可以讓緊密零件緊密結合，但加工不良的螺絲可能會導致墜機。為了提供給客戶最好的螺絲，今年我們軟硬體都同步升級。透過使用新的加工軟體，誤差的範圍控制在 0.01 公厘內。這是多數產品所容許的一個範圍。好還要更好，今年我們給您更多保證。如果良率未達百分之九十九，您可以整批退貨，我們替您出運費。

Thomas: It seems that you are confident of your screws. What I want to ask here is the guarantee for all screws or for standard ones only?

Thomas：看來您對自家的螺絲很有信心。這邊想請問得是上述的保證是針對所有類型的螺絲，還是僅限標準型的？

Jason: Generally speaking, for all. But in some cases, we have some negotiations with our customers because sometimes the structure they request is too complicated. We set a compromised rate for this customization.

Jason：一般來說，是全部的螺絲。但在某些特殊情況下，我們會因為客戶所要求的結構過於複雜，而與之協商。雙方為此客製化零件重新訂定一個彼此同意的誤差範圍。

Thomas: I got it. What if I need the screw in urgency, how fast can you deliver 10,000 pieces to me?

Thomas：我了解了。如果需要一萬顆螺絲，最快何時可以出貨給我呢？

Jason: (4) Finding the best arrangement of the machining process, we can produce the screws at the speed of 3000 to 3500 pieces a day. In other words, you can receive the screws four or five days, if you place the order now.

Jason：由於我們已找出最佳的加工程序，目前每天以三千至三千五百顆的速度生產螺絲。換言之，如果您現在下單，四到五天後就能收到螺絲。

Thomas: You are a company with high efficiency. Here is the specification of the screws I need. Please send me your quotation to my secretary. I will sign it when I go back to the office today.

Thomas：貴公司真得很有效率。這邊是我需要的規格。請把報價單寄給我的秘書。我今日返回辦公室後就會簽署。

Jason: I see. Thank you for showing confidence in our product. If you have any problem, please contact me.

Jason：了解。感謝您對敝公司的螺絲有信心。如有任何問題，請與我連絡。

對話單字說分明

1. **screw** *n.* **螺絲**

例：Though the size of a screw is small, its function is great.
螺絲雖然尺寸小，但功用確非常大。

2. **eye-catching** *adj.* **吸引目光的**

例：To gain the publicity, the new banner is eye-catching.
為增加曝光度，新的橫幅廣告訴求吸引目光。

3. **crash** *v.* **損毀**

例：The document is crashed due to the abnormal accessing.
檔案因為不當存取而所損毀。

4. **tolerable** *adj.* **可容忍的**

例：Plus or minus 0.01 centimeter is a tolerable range in the case of the machine.
就此機殼而言，正負 0.01 公分的誤差是個可接受的範圍。

5. **yield** *n.* **產量**

例：The average yield per day is 4,000 to 5,000 pieces.
日均產量為 4,000 到 5,000 件。

6. **compromised** *adj.* **妥協的。**

例：To finalize the deal soon, we are willing to provide a compromised price to you.
為了能夠盡快成交，我們願意在價格上讓步。

7. **arrangement** *n.* **安排**

例：To find the best arrangement of production line, we adjust the position of the machine for many times.
為找出生產線的最佳安排，我們多次調整機器的位置。

8. **confidence** *n.* **信心**

例：Thank you for showing confidence in our latest products.
感謝您對我們的新產品有信心。

重點句型分析

1. **Evenif..., ... can still...** 意思為「即使…，…也能…」，可用於說明產品或服務的功能性。

   例：Even if the size of the chip is small, it can still keep the efficiency.
   即使晶片的尺寸的很小，也能保有效能。

2. **Through..., the...is controlled in...** 意思為「透過…，…被控制在…」，可用於說明如何控至某向變因或是誤差在一定範圍內。

   例：Through the precise calculation, the error is controlled in plus or minus 1 mm.
   透過精準的計算，誤差被控制在正附一厘米之內。

3. **If the... is below..., you can...** 意思為「如果…低於…，你可以…」，可用於向客戶保證產品或服務可達一定水準。

   例：If the yield rate is below 98%, you can return this lot.
   如果良率低於百分之九十八，你可以整批退貨。

4. **Finding..., we... a tthe speed of...** 意思為「找出…，我們以…的速度…。」，可用於說明提生產效能的關鍵為何。

   例：Finding the best production arrangement, we produce the machine at the speed of 5 sets per hour.
   找出最佳的生產線安排，我們以每小時 5 台的速度生產機器。

本單元以螺絲公司業務向客戶推銷自家螺絲為場景，發展一段完整對話，其內容中一共提到四個行銷的常用概念，以下針對每個概念做進一步說明：

1. 以功用性（functionality）擴大價值：

- 對應句型：Even if the size of screw is small, it can still have a great impact on a product. A good screw can tightly combine two parts, while the improper machining screws could cause the crash of an airplane.

  在銷售零組件時，由於客戶購買的目的是將其再組裝為完整產品售出，強調零件的功用性可提高成交機率。當一個零件可以廣泛的使用於許多領域，其價值性自然提高。**在本範例中，Jason 強調螺絲雖然很小，但功用確很大。好的螺絲能使各組件緊密接合，設計不良的螺絲可能會讓飛機故障，因而墜機。**

2. 以精確度（precision）強調技術：

- 對應句型：Through the usage of new machining program, the errors are controlled in a range between plus or minus 0.01 mm. This inaccuracy is tolerable to most products.

  針對高精密度的產品，各組件的精密度是客戶要求的重點。每一組件間的誤差必須控制在一定範圍內，才不會使成品出現問題。**在本範例中，Jason 強調自家的螺絲因為使用新的加工軟體來製造，誤差值控制在 0.01 公厘，是多數產品所能接受的數值範圍。**

3. 以良率（yield rate）確保品質：

- 對應句型：**Not willing to be just good but the best, we give you more promises. If the yield rate is below 99%, you can return the lot you order and we will cover the freight.**

  針對大量生產的貨品，買賣雙方會訂立品質上的基本要求。若成品的品質低於此要求，買方可已要求退貨，甚至可根據契約要求賠償。**以本範例為例，Jason 表示自家公司對於產品很有信心，所以只要良率低於百分之九十九，就接受退貨，並支付相關運費。**

4. 以效率（efficiency）吸引下單：

- 對應句型：**Finding the best arrangement of the machining process, we can produce the screws at the speed of 3000 to 3500 pieces a day. In other word, you can receive the screws four or five days if you place the order now.**

  當客戶有緊急需求時，肯定會希望賣方能夠為其趕工。此時若賣方的效率足以為其完成需求，雙方後續合作與交易的機會就會大增。**在本範例中，Jason 提到公司因為找到怎樣生產最具效率，因此日產量來到 3,000 到 3,500 顆，10,000 顆的訂單約三個工作天便可完成，加上運送時間，四到五天便可送達。**

看《班傑明的奇幻旅程》（*The Curious Case of Benjamin Button*），學習業務人員產品推銷技巧

篇章重點搶先看

1. 以《班傑明的奇幻旅程》（*The Curious Case of Benjamin Button*）經典台詞學習如何推銷產品。
2. 以本部的台詞之一 “Age doesn't make you mature; experience does.”「讓你成熟的是經歷，而不是歲月」。學習本單元核心句型：

   ★N1 doesn't make...; N2 does.「能讓 N1…的是…，而不是…。」
3. 搭配學習本單元其他三大重點句型：

   a ...is the...that determine the...of...（…是影響…的…。）

   b All...is/are Ved...before, but we still...（所有的…在…之前都…，但我們仍…。）

   c Since..., the chance is... to V...（因為…，…的機會很…。）
4. 將四種句型放入實境對話練習，學習四大行銷概念：

   a 以產品生命週期（product life cycle）說明未來性。

   b 以線性迴歸（linear regression）解釋影響因子。

   c 以保固（guarantee）增加保障。

   d 以抽獎（lottery）提高購買慾望。

影片背景介紹

本片以倒敘開頭，由臨終前的女主角黛西與其女兒讀出主角班傑明所留下的日記開啟故事的序幕。班傑明的身體奇特，出生時就像是八十歲的老人。自此班傑明以此方式逆向生長。班傑明 11 歲時首次與黛西相遇。17 時班傑明離開黛西開始周遊四海，兩人再次相遇是九年後，當時黛西的舞者生涯正達顛峰，與一位男舞者相戀。班傑明選擇再次離去。若我們將片中班傑明用來闡述成長真義的台詞應用在銷售上，其句構洽可用於說明產品或服務的獨特處為何。

The Curious Case of Benjamin Button begins with the time that dying Daisy reads the diary of Benjamin with her daughter. Benjamin's body is special because he looks like an eighty-year-old man ever since he is born. He is growing in a reversed way. He meets Daisy for the first time when he is 11 and starts his journey on the sea when he is at the age of 17. When they meet each other 9 years later, Daisy reaches her career peak as a top dancer and falls in love with one male dancer from the same dance group. Benjamin chooses to leave again. If we apply the words that Benjamin use to define growth into the marketing, they turns out to be good materials for us to learn how to emphasize the feature of a product or a service.

看影片怎麼說、怎麼用

At the conference room of ABC Computer Company. Jason is going to start a presentation.

（在 ABC 電腦公司的會議室。Jason 正要開始報告了。）

Jason: Ok. Let me begin with the current status of the notebook market. (1) High specification alone doesn't make high end notebook popular; high specification plus with **multifunction** does. Digital devices have revolutionized the way of our daily life and work. (2) How a notebook functions and **serves** is the key factor that determines the intension of purchase. The more, the better. In consumers' mind, the definition of a best notebook now is light, multifunctional, and efficient. The one with these three characteristics can have the longest product life cycle. And our latest notebook Ommi-75 is the product that perfectly meets this requirement.

Jason：好的，讓我先從當前筆電的市場狀況說起。只有高規格並不能受消費者青睞，要再加上多功能才可以。數位裝置已經徹底改變我們的生活與工作方式。一台筆電所擁有的功能數是左右消費意願的關鍵因素，功能是越多越好。同時具備質輕、多功能與高效的產品可享有最長的產品生命週期。而我們的 Ommi-75 完全符合這樣的要求。

Andy: It sounds reasonable. Because you just said that Ommi-75 is multifunctional, can you demonstrate the functions for me?

Andy：聽起來很合理。因為您提到 Ommi-75 有很多功能，可以跟我展示一下每項功能嗎？

Jason: Yes, I can. This notebook **consists** of three parts: a keyboard, monitor, and the **box**. The monitor plus with the thin box can

Jason：當然。我們的新筆電可分為三大部分：鍵盤、螢幕、主機。螢幕加上薄型

be transformed into a pad. The keyboard alone can **pair** with other digital device through blue tooth. The monitor alone can be connected with other computers.

主機可以變成平板。鍵盤可透過藍芽與其他裝置配對。螢幕也可以再於其他電腦連接。

Andy: It would be a tool for our sales representatives. However, I really concern the after-sale service because we use notebooks all the time. How long is the **warranty**?

Andy：這會是我們業務所能使用的一項好工具。但因為我們成天使用筆電，所以很在乎售後服務這塊。你們的筆電保固多久呢。

Jason: Since we are confident in our product, we can give you the following promises. (3) All notebooks are strictly checked before shipment, but we still provide a two-year warranty. If you find any flaws under the proper usage within the period, we will repair or replace it for free.

Jason：我們對於自家很有信心，所以給您以下保證。所有筆電出貨前都經過嚴格品檢，但我們還是給您兩年保固，在這段期間內，所有正常使用下所產生的瑕疵，我們都免費更換或維修。

Andy: I see. By the way, do you have any promotion campaigns recently?

Andy：我了解了。順帶一提，最近有什麼促銷活動嗎？

Jason: We do have one this month. A **lottery** activity is launched to those who buy our computers. (4) Since we prepare more than 300 gifts, the chance is high to win a **grand** prize.

Jason：這個月真的有。本月購買電腦的消費者可以參加抽獎。因為我們準備了三百份獎品。抽中大獎的機會很高。

Andy: Got it. I will contact you when I confirm the amount we need this time.

Andy：了解。確定需要多少台後會與您聯絡。

對話單字說分明

1. **multifunction** *n.* 多功能

例：Multifunction has become a trend in smart devices.
多功能已在智慧裝置上形成一股風潮。

2. **serve** *v.* 提供

例：This new ultrabook serves the function of pad.
此款新型輕薄筆電同時具備平板功能。

3. **consist** *v.* 組成

例：This audio equipment consists of five speakers and one remote control. 這套音效設備由五個喇叭與一個遙控器所組成。

4. **box** *n.* 主機

例：Since the motherboard is on sale, it is the best for you to upgrade your box. 因為主機板降價了，現在是升級電腦的好時機。

5. **pair** *v.* 配對

例：You can pair these two smart watches through the blue tooth.
你可以使用藍芽配對這兩隻智慧腕錶。

6. **warranty** *n.* 保固

例：To give you the most comprehensive after-sale service, we provide a three year warranty.
為了給您最全面的售後服務，我們提供三年保固。

7. **lottery** *n.* 抽獎

例：To show our appreciation to the customers, we launch a lottery activity this month.
為了表達對於消費者的感激，我們本月舉辦抽獎活動。

8. **grand** *adj.* 豪華的

例：If you purchase the notebook today, you have the chance to win the grand price of the monthly lottery activity.
若今日購買筆電，有機會讓你贏的本月抽獎的大獎。

重點句型分析

1. **N1 doesn't make...; N2 does...** 意思為「能讓 N1…的是…，而不是…」，可用於釐清造成某現象的原因為何。

   例：Fad doesn't make your product mature; trend does.
   能讓產品成熟的是趨勢，而不是風潮。

2. **...is the... that determine the... of...** 意思為「…是影響…的…。」，可用於說明事件發生與否的關鍵因素為何。

   例：The freight is the key factor that determines the intention of purchase in this project.
   運費是影響這次專案採購意願的關鍵因素。

3. **All... is/are... before, but we still...** 意思為「所有的…在…之前都…，但我們仍…」，可用於說明銷售方所願意做出的保證。

   例：All machines are strictly checked before shipment, but we still accept the return if you find any flaws.
   所有機器在出貨之前都經過嚴格檢查，但如您發現任何缺陷，我們仍願意接受退貨。

4. **Since..., the chance is... to V...** 意思為「因為…，…的機會很…」，可用於說明事情發生的機率高低。

   例：Since we provide more than 200 gifts for consumers to draw the lottery, the chance is high to win the items you like.
   因為我們準備超過兩百分的禮物讓消費者抽獎，抽到您喜歡品項的機率很高。

職場補給站

本單元以電腦公司業務項客戶推銷高階電腦為場景，發展一段完整對話，其內容中一共提到四個行銷的常用概念，以下針對每個概念做進一步說明：

1. 以產品生命週期（product life cycle）說明未來性：

- 對應句型：In consumers' mind, the definition of a best notebook now is light, multifunctional, and efficient. The one with the three characteristics can have the longest product life cycle. And our latest notebook Ommi-75 is the product that can perfectly meet this requirement.

產品週期指的是產品進入市場到被市場所淘汰的時間長度。時間越長，代表消費者的接受度高，或產品不易被取代。反之，代表消費者不接受，或是產品易被模仿。**在本範例中，Jason 提到消費者對於筆電的要求是質輕、多功能與高效，而公司的產品正好符合所有要求，產品生命週期相對較長。**

2. 以線性迴歸（linear regression）解釋影響因子：

- 對應句型：How a notebook functions and serves is the key factor that determine the intension of purchase. The more the better.

線性迴歸簡單來說指的就是某項變因會造成某種影響。舉例來說，假設天氣冷熱會影響冰品的銷售，天氣熱時冰品銷售量加就是一種線性迴歸。**在本範例中，Jason 表示當前市場趨勢是強調多功能。若將功能視為影響銷售的變因，越多功能就夠賣得越好。**

3. 以保固（guarantee）增加保障：

- 對應句型：**All notebooks are strictly checked before shipment, but we still offer you a two-year warranty. If you find any flaws under proper usage within the period, we will repair or replace it for free.**

  為了確保產品出廠時品質達到一定水準，廠商對於消費者都會給予一定的承諾。若產品不符這樣的承諾，可以予以維修或更換，藉此提高消費者對於產品的信心。**在本範例中，Jason 表示自家筆電品管良好，但還是願意提三年保固。只要這段期間內正常使用出現問題都可以免費維修甚至更換。**

4. 以抽獎（lottery）提高購買慾望：

- 對應句型：**A lottery activity is launched to those who buy our computers. Since we prepare more than 300 gifts, the chance to win a grand prize is high.**

  除了產品本身外，促銷活動也是影響購買意願的因素，而抽獎就是其中一種手法。雖然消費者知道並非人人有獎，但因為當中包含大獎，而產生期待。這樣的期待可能使原本猶豫的消費者考慮購買，進而提高整體銷售。**在本範例中，Jason 提到本月有舉辦抽獎。獎項有兩百個，所以只要參加抽獎，抽到大獎的機會很高。**

看《真愛每一天》（*About Time*），學習在業務上點出關鍵要素

篇章重點搶先看

1. 以《真愛每一天》（*About Time*）經典台詞學習如何業務上的銷售技巧。
2. 以本片經典台詞 *"What you need for a second chance in life to happen isn't by changing anything from the past, but by cherishing everything in the present."*「想要有第二次機會，你需要的不是改變過去的任何事，而是學會珍惜現在的每一刻。」學習本單元核心句型：
   ★What you need for...isn't by...but by...「想要…，你需要的不是…，而是…。」
3. 搭配學習本單元其他三大重點句型：
   a Equipped with..., the... of... can reach...（配備…，…的…可達…）
   b The usage of... make the... of N1 is 比較級 than N2（…的使用，讓 N1 的…比 N2…還…。）
   c For... with.., N is...（對於…的…，N 是…。）
4. 將四種句型放入實境對話練習，學習四大行銷概念：
   a 以誤解（misunderstanding）做為反證。
   b 以最優化（optimization）強調性能。
   c 以材質（material）突顯差異。
   d 以規格（specification）區分客群。

影片背景介紹

男主角提姆的父親在他 21 歲生日時，告訴提姆這個家族的男性都穿越時空的天賦。但這項超能力也有其限制，雖然可以攜伴，但只能回到彼此都曾出現過的時間與地點。提姆決定運用這項能力來追求愛情。若將片中提姆對生活真義的一番體會應用在銷售上，其句構實為我們學習如何點出關鍵要素的良好教材。

On Tim's 21 year-old birthday, his father tells him that the men in this family all have the ability to travel in time. But this ability has one limitation. Though the man can bring partners to travel in time, they can only go back to the time that they had been to. Tim uses this ability to pursue love. If we apply the words that Tim uses to express his true feeling to life, the structures turn out to be the good material for us to learn how to clarify the factors in a market trend.

看影片怎麼說、怎麼用

At the exhibition hall of ABC Heavy Motor.

（在 ABC 重機館。）

Jason: Afternoon, sir. Welcome to ABC Heavy Motor. How can I help you?

Jason：先生，午安。歡迎來到 ABC 重機館。有什麼需要幫忙的嗎？

Sean: I would like to buy my first heavy motor in my life, so can you give some recommendations?

Sean：我想要買我人生中的第一不重機，所以可以請你為我推薦嗎？

Jason: Of course. To give you the best suggestion, let me ask you one question here. What kind of **route** do you use the most if you buy a bike today?

Jason：當然可以。為了給您最佳建議，這邊讓我先問你一個問題。如果今天買車了，你會最常騎的路線是哪種？

Sean: I think I will ride to the mountain area to enjoy the atmosphere of the nature.

Sean：我想我會騎到山區去享受大自然的氛圍。

Jason: I see. (1) What you need for a smooth ride in this kind of **topography** isn't by the speed, but the climbing ability Trail Bike is suitable for you. Currently, we have three models available, GT550, GT650, and GT750.

Jason：我了解了。想要在這類地形下享受舒適的騎乘，你需的不是速度，而是爬坡力。越野車符合你的需求。目前我們共有三種車款：GT550、GT650、GT750。

Sean: I got it. Can you tell me a little more about the features of your bikes?

Sean：嗯。可以為我簡單介紹一下車款的特色嗎？

Jason: Sure.(2) Equipped with our latest engine, the **horsepower** of three models mentioned above reaches 150 or faster. This is the best motors of the same performance we can offer. Besides, (3) the usage of the carbon **fiber** make the weight of the bike lighter than that of the similar models.

Jason：當然可以。配有我們的最新式引擎，這三種車款的馬力都超過 150 匹，是同級車中最佳。此外，碳纖維材質的使用，也讓車重比相似車款還輕。

Sean: OK. Few more questions. Are the three models named after the engine **volume**? And which model will be my top choice with a budget of 15000 USD?

Sean：嗯。這邊還有幾個問題想問。請問車款是按照排氣量還命名嗎？以及在我 15000 美金的預算下，哪一款是最適合我的車款？

Jason: Yes, they are. (4) With the budget of 15000 USD, GT650 is your **must-buy**. The efficiency of GT650 is much higher than that of GT-550, making it my recommendation for the beginner with a high budget.

Jason：沒錯。針對預算有 15000 美金的客戶，GT-650 您的最佳選擇。GT-650 的性能比 GT-550 好很多，所以推薦給預算較高的入門車主。

Sean: Can I have a ride nearby with my helmet on?

Sean：我可以帶上安全帽在附近試騎嗎？

Jason: Sure. Please filled this form and keep your ID as the **collateral** here. I will give you the key when you finish this process.

Jason：可以。請填寫這張表格，並以身分證做抵押。完成手續後我就會把鑰匙給你。

Sean: I see. Please give me the form.

Sean：好的。請把表格給我吧。

Lesson 19
Lesson 20
Lesson 21
Lesson 22
Lesson 23
Lesson 24

對話單字說分明

1. **route** *n.* 路線

例：This route is designed for the beginner to practice.
這條路線是設計給新手練習用的。

2. **topography** *n.* 地形

例：To have a smooth ride in this topography, you need to adjust the flexibility of cushion.
為了要在此種地形下舒適騎乘，你需要調整避震器的軟硬。

3. **horsepower** *n.* 馬力

例：The more powerful the horsepower is, the higher the torque could be. 馬力越大，扭力也跟著增強。

4. **fiber** *n.* 纖維

例：The usage of carbon fiber can reduce the weight of the case.
使用碳纖維可以降低外殼的重量。

5. **bike** *n.* 自行車

例：For most female riders, the bikes with lighter weight is crucial.
對多數的女性騎士而言，車重的輕量化是必要的。

6. **volume** *n.* 容量

例：The volume of the engine determines how much it will be taxed.
排氣量決定這台機車的繳稅額。

7. **must-buy** *n.* 最值得購買商品

例：Considering the cost-performance ratio, this ultrabook is the must-buy. 若考量其性價比，這台輕薄型比電是最值得購買商品

8. **collateral** *n.* 抵押品

例：If your credit record is not very good, banks will request collateral when you need loans.
如果信用狀況不佳，你貸款時銀行會要求抵押品。

重點句型分析

1. **What you need for... isn't by... but by...** 意思為「想要…，你需要的不是…，而是…」，可用於釐清造成某一現象的關鍵因素為何。

   例：What you need for a longer usage life isn't by machine structure, but by the correct operatio.

   想要有較常的使用年限，不是靠機器本身的結構，而是靠正確的操作方式。

2. **Equipped with..., the...of... can reach...** 意思為「配備…，…的…可達…。」，可用於說明某項配備所能達到的效果為何。

   例：Equipped with our latest sensor, this security system can detect the slightest movement around the building.

   配備本公司最新的偵測器，這套保全系統可以偵測到建築物四周最細微的變動。

3. **The usage of... make the... of N1 比較級 than N2...** 意思為「…的使用，讓 N1 的…比 N2…還…」，可用於使用某種素材所能產生的差異性為何。

   例：The usage of composite materials makes the hardness of the armor stronger than that of the previous editions.

   複合材料的使用讓護甲的硬度比上一代的產品更高。

4. **For... with..., N is...** 意思為「對於…的…，N 是…」，可用於說明各客層所適合的產品類型。

   例：For the consumer with a higher budget, the flagship edition is your top choice.

   對於預算較高的消費者，旗艦版是您的最佳選擇。

本單元以重機館銷售人員向首次購車的新客戶推薦車款為場景，發展一段完整對話，其內容中一共提到四個行銷的常用概念，以下針對每個概念做進一步說明：

1. 以誤解（misunderstanding）做為反證：

- 對應句型：**What you need for a smooth ride in this kind of topography isn't by the speed but the climbing ability. Trail Bike is suitable for you.**

  許多消費者會因為對產品不了解，或是因為聽信市場的一些傳言，而對產品有錯誤的認知。當銷售人員以此做為範例來導引出正確的概念時，消費者的印象會更加深刻。**在本範例中，Jason 提到有許多人認為騎山路只要馬力強就可以，但是事實上爬坡力才是關鍵。藉此讓 Sean 對於越野車有基本認識。**

2. 以最優化（optimization）強調性能：

- 對應句型：**Equipped with our latest engine, the horsepower of three models mentioned above reaches 150 or faster. This is the best the motors of same performance can offer.**

  在銷售車輛時，性能是許多消費者關注的項目之一。由於高規格再高都有可能被新車款超越，因此行銷的重點可放在與同等級的款式的比較上。若該車款具有某項突出的性能，就容易受消費者青睞。**在本範例中，Jason 提到公司的三款越野車的馬力都有 150 匹以上，為同級車之最佳，以此做為吸引 Sean 購買的誘因。**

3. 以材質（material）突顯差異：

- 對應句型：**Besides, the usage of the carbon fiber makes the weight of the bike is lighter than that of the similar models.**

結構相似的尺寸相仿的產品若在材質的使用上有所不同，其特性可能會天差地遠。舉例來說，若兩台尺寸相同的機器安裝外殼的保護，一個裝上金屬殼，一個裝上塑膠殼，金屬殼的耐碰撞度明顯較高。**在本範例中，Jason 提到自家的重機使用碳纖維，因此在車重上比同級車還輕，並以特殊素材做為吸引新客戶的誘因。**

4. 以規格（specification）區分客群：

- 對應句型：**With the budget of 15000 USD, GT650 is your must-buy. The efficiency of GT650 is much higher than that of GT-550, making it my recommendation for the beginner with high budget.**

各客層所需要的商品可能因為預算高低或是需求差異而有所不同，若要提高成交機率，銷售人員應對其進行差異推薦。以車輛來說，入門規格適合推薦給預算有限的消費者，而頂級規格則是給高需求或高預算的車主。**在本範例中，Jason 因為 Sean 告知購車預算為 15000 美金，因而選擇中階的 GT-650 做為推薦車款。**

Part 3

國際貿易篇

看《金牌特務》（*Kingsman: The Secret Service*），了解事前準備的重要性

篇章重點搶先看

1. 以《金牌特務》（*Kingsman: The Secret Service*）主角之一哈特經典台詞學習如何透過事前的準備來降低競爭所帶來的影響。
2. 以哈特的經典台詞 “If you're prepared to adapt, you can transform.”「如果你能適應，你將會脫胎換骨」。學習本單元核心句型：

   ★ If you are...to..., you can...「如果你能…，你將會…。」
3. 搭配學習本單元其他三大重點句型：
   - a The raise/drop in... indicates that..., making N a/the... in...（…的提高／下降意謂…，使…成為…的…。）
   - b Through the... of..., the N can be transformed into...（透過…的…，the N 可以轉變為…。）
   - c To utilize the..., the duty of... is specialized in...（為了善用…，…的職責被設定為…。）
4. 將四種句型放入實境對話練習，學習四大商業概念：
   - a 以方向（direction）決定後續策略。
   - b 按市場訊息（message）解讀趨勢。
   - c 將員工能力化做資產（asset）。
   - d 以工作站（job shop）形成專業分工。

影片背景介紹

金士曼表面上是一間裁縫店，但事實上是一個歷史悠久的民間諜報組織。在某次任務中，特務哈特因為一時不察，導致同伴英勇犧牲。耿耿於懷的哈特將一個徽章交給已故探員的家屬，告知只要撥打特定號碼並報出暗號就可以完成任何事。若將片中哈特用來鼓舞伊格西（為已故探員的兒子）的台詞應用於解釋商場的競爭上，其句構實為我們良好的學習教材。

Kingman is a tailor's shop from its appearance, but it is also a secret intelligent organization. In one mission Hart causes his partner's death due to his carelessness. Feeling guilty, Hart gives his partner's family a badge and tells them that if they dial the number behind the badge and speak out the password, they can do anything. If we apply the words that Hart uses to encourage Eggsy (the son of the killed agent at the beginning) to the explanation to the competition in the market, they turn out to be good learning materials.

看影片怎麼說、怎麼用

At the conference room of ABC Company.

（在 ABC 公司的會議室。）

Manager Chen: Good morning, my **colleagues**. Since the performance of our department in the last quarter is worse than that of the previous year, I hope we can find the solution through the meeting today. Please feel free to express what you have found concerning this **phenomena**.

陳經理：各位同事早安，由於本部門上一季的績效就去年同期表現較差，我希望透過今日的會議找出解決方法。請各位針對此一現象盡量發表意見。

Jason: As the leader of my team, I think the direction of the strategy is the key to solve the problem we are facing. According to my **observation**, the raise in cost is the reason of the bad performance. (1) If you are prepared to lower the cost, you can have a better performance in the next quarter.

Jason：做為團隊的主管，我認為策略的方向是解決當前問題的關鍵。根據我的觀察，成本的上升是績效變糟的主因。如果能夠降低成本，下一季的績效就會變好。

Lin: Good. Please tell us the actions you will take.

Lin：很好。請告訴我們你的行動計畫。

Jason: (2) The raise in labor cost indicates that our profit will shrink, making it the reason which **dilutes** our margin profit for the whole year. To save our money, using machines to replace **manpower** is a good option. However, considering the experiences are one kind of invisible assets to our company, I have an alternative. (3)

Jason：人力成本的上升會造成利潤的萎縮，使其成為稀釋年度獲利的因素。為了要省錢，以機器替代人力是一個很好的方法，但考量到經驗也屬於公司無形資產的一部分，我想到一個替代方案。透過過經驗的分享，相

Through the sharing of experience, the knowledge and expertise can be transformed into our visible assets like manuals or video clips.

關的知識與專業可以轉化為有形資產，例如教學手冊或是影片。

Harper: What you just said is about how to keep the resources, can you tell me more about it?

Harper：您剛所說的部分是關於如何保留現有資源，可以多說一點嗎？

Jason: (4) To utilize the resources we have now, the duty of the senior technicians can be specialized in the development of new technology and the sharing of previous experiences. Forming a new working pattern to improve the **productivity** to lower cost of each product is the way to solve the trouble we have now.

Jason：為了善用現有資源，資深技術人員的職責可被設定為新技術的研發與舊技術的傳承。組織新的工作戰可以增加產量來降低平均成本，解決我們當前所遭遇的麻煩。

Lin: Your action plan sounds practical. Do have any **pocket** list for the new working pattern you just mentioned? I will submit your report to our General Manager, and the chance to get his **approval** is high.

Lin：你的行動計畫似乎可行。你有新工作站人員的口袋名單嗎？我會把你的報告上呈總經理，我覺得核准的機會相當高。

Jason: About the candidates, I will recommend Mark, Copper, and Addison. All of them have worked here for more than ten years, so their experiences can generate more profit, if they are promoted to this position. About the proposal, I will start to write right after this meeting. I will finish it by this Friday.

Jason：在適當人選的部分，我會推薦 Mark、Copper 和 Addison。他們三位都已到任超過十年，如果讓他們升官擔任此職位，能替公司創造更多利潤。而在報告書的部分，會後我就會開始撰寫，並於本週五前完成。

對話單字說分明

1. **colleague** *n.* 同事

例：Having a good performance or not this year lies in the cooperation among colleagues. 今年績效是否良好有賴各位同事間的合作。

2. **phenomena** *n.* 現象

例：It will take us four to five days to analyze the reason behind this weird phenomena, so please be patient.
需要四至五天我們才能分析出造成此奇怪現象的主因，所以請您耐心等候。

3. **observation** *n.* 觀察

例：Though a six month observation, the sale of our original edition ranks No.1 among the similar products in the market. 透過為期六個月的觀察，我們一般版的產品的銷售在市面上相似產品中榮膺第一。

4. **dilute** *v.* 稀釋

例：The raise in the freight will dilute the profit of each shipment.
運費上漲會稀釋每次出貨的獲利。

5. **manpower** *n.* 人力

例：The cost in manpower shall be considered in our new project.
新專案應把人力成本也算入。

6. **productivity** *n.* 生產力

例：To enhance the productivity, the arrangement of the assembly lines needs to be changed. 若要提高生產力，裝配線的安排要進行調整。

7. **pocket** *n.* 口袋

例：Here is the pocket list of the experts we will hunter next year.
這邊就是我們明年度打算挖角的專家的口袋名單。

8. **approval** *n.* 核准

例：To get the approval from the General Manager, you have to write a proposal with an estimated budget.
若要獲得總經理的許可，你必須撰寫一分附上預算表的企劃書。

重點句型分析

1. **If you are... to..., you can...** 意思為「如果你能…，你將會…」，可用於說明做好準備能夠降低影響的程度為何。

   例：If you are ready to face the completion, you can survive to the end.
   如果你能準備好面對競爭，你將會有辦法熬到最後。

2. **The raise/drop in... indicates that..., making N a/the... in...** 意思為「…的提高／下降意謂…，使…成為…的…。」，可用於說明某種物料價格上漲所代表的意涵，以及對公司所帶來的影響為何。

   例：The raise in the price of raw materials indicates the margin will shrink in the coming month, making it a great impact on our performance in 2015.
   原物料價格的上升意味我們的利潤會將低，使其成為影響 2015 年整體績效的因素。

3. **Through the... of..., the N can be transformed into...** 意思為「透過…的…，the N 可以轉變為…」，可用於說明透過何種方法可將無形的技術或知識轉化為有形的資產。

   例：Through the manual writing of the core concepts, the experiences of the senior technicians can be transformed into the asset of our company.
   透過核心概念的手冊撰寫，資深技術人員的經驗可以轉化為公司有型的資產。

4. **To utilize the..., the duty of... is specialized in...** 意思為「為了善用…，…的職責被設定為…」，可用於說明如何透過分工，讓整體效益發揮至最大。

   例：To utilize the expertise in machining, the duty of the lab is specialized in the testing of flaws in new pieces.
   為了善用加工技術上的專業，本實驗室的職責被設定為測試新工具的缺點為何。

職場補給站

本單元以管理階層討論如何不靠導入機器，但維持既有生產力為場景，發展一段完整對話，其內容中一共提到四個商業的常用概念，以下針對每個概念做進一步說明：

1. 以方向（direction）決定後續策略：

- 對應句型：**According to my observation, the raise in cost is the reason of bad performance. If you are prepared to lower the cost, you can have better performance in the next quarter.**

在進行決策時，其大方向會左右後續成效。若判斷正確，問題可以很快獲得改善，反之，則可能毫無效果，甚至導致狀況惡化。為避免此種情況產生，管理階層務必要在通盤了解後，再做出決定。**在本範例中，Jason 根據自身觀察發現成本上升是影響業績的主因，故應當以此大方向來制定後續的應變策略。**

2. 按市場訊息（message）解讀趨勢：

- 對應句型：**The raise in labor cost indicates that our profit will shrink, making it the reason which dilutes our margin profit for the whole year. To save our money, use machines to replace manpower is a good option.**

面對市場競爭，首先要懂得如何解度市場訊息。市場訊息能傳達出市場中的各項變化，若我們能夠發現個訊息間的關聯性，要做出應變也較為容易。**在本範例中，Jason 提到人力成本上升會稀釋獲利，因此建議導入機器生產，透過縮減人力的方式降低人事成本。**

3. 將能力化做資產（asset）：

- 對應句型：**Through the sharing of experience, the knowledge and expertise can be transformed into our visible assets like manuals or video clips.**

除相機設備這樣的有形資產外，技術人員所具備的專業也是資產的一種。而這樣能力可透過經驗傳承、手冊撰寫等方式加以具體化，變成能夠管理的有形資產。**在本範例中，Jason 提到可以運用寫手冊或拍教學影片的方式，將資深的技術人員的知識與經驗加以具象化，供其他人員交流使用。**

4. 以工作站（job shop）形成專業分工：

- 對應句型：**Forming a new working pattern to improve the productivity to lower cost of each product is the way to solve the trouble we have now.**

當營運效能出現問題，其原因有可能是既有的任務分組無法發揮最佳效果。若要解決這樣的問題，重新專業分工形成新的工作站是很有效的方法。由於這樣編組是依照現況加以安排，在效能上絕對可以獲得改善。**在本範例中，Jason 提到新的工作模式可以提高生產力，降低單位成本，如此一來當前人力成本升高的影響就被稀釋了。**

看《功夫熊貓》（*Kung Fu Panda*），學習按照可行性做出對應措施

篇章重點搶先看

1. 以《功夫熊貓》（*Kung Fu Panda*）經典台詞學習如何按照可行性做出對應措施。
2. 以功夫熊貓中的經典台詞 "Respect cannot be given, you have to earn it."「尊敬不是別人給的，是自己爭取來的。」。學習本單元核心句型：
   ★N cannot be Vpp, you have to...「…不是…，而是要…的。」
3. 搭配學習本單元其他三大重點句型：
   a With the habit of..., many... prefer...（因為有…的習慣，很多…偏好…。）
   b Regarded as the..., N is... in all...（被視為…，N 在所有…中都可以…。）
   c Owing the... in, we can put the focus on（擁有…，我們可以將重心放在…。）
4. 將四種句型放入實境對話練習，學習四大商業概念：
   a 從可行性（feasibility）決定執行方向。
   b 以消費者偏好（preference）進行初步分析。
   c 以常態分布（normal distribution）找出競爭區段。
   d 以競爭對手找到市場定位（market positioning）。

影片背景介紹

《功夫熊貓》（*Kung Fu Panda*）是一個關於笨拙熊貓立志成為武功高手的故事。在和平谷裡，有隻充滿熱情的胖熊貓名叫阿波，他非常崇拜由武功大師以及他所訓練出來的功夫五俠。但現實中的阿波只能幫他的爸爸賣麵，無法去追求自己的學武之夢。不久之後，被囚禁的武功高手殘狼從監獄逃脫，為了找出能夠與之對抗的對手，和平谷舉辦了一場武術錦標賽，阿波陰錯陽差地被烏龜宗師認為是傳說中的神龍大俠。若將片中有關如何得到尊重的台詞的句法應用在闡述如何順應市場趨勢做出應變上，實為一個良好的學習教材。

Kung Fu Panda is a story about a clumsy panda who wants to be a Kung fu master. In the Valley of Peace, there is a fat panda with great passion named Po. Po views the kung-fu master and the Furious Five as his idols. Days by days, Po helps his father sell noodles in their restaurant, so learning kung fu is always his dream for long. Later, a gangster with great kung fu named Tai Lung escapes from the prison. To find a person who has the ability to fight against Tai Lung, a kung fu tournament is held in the Valley of Peace. Po wins the competition accidentally and is regarded as the Dragon Warrior by the grand master Oogway. If we apply the lines about how to win the respect in this movie to the illustration of the actions based the market trend, they turns out to a good reference for us.

看影片怎麼說、怎麼用

At the conference room of ABC Company.

（在 ABC 公司的會議室。）

Manger Marcos: Good morning all. We have good sales figures in the USA last year, so I think it is good time for us to evaluate the possibility of entering the market in Canada. Later, Jason will have a briefing about the survey he have **conducted** for weeks. Now Jason will have the table. Please pay attention to his talk.

Marcos 經理：各位早安，我們去年在美國的銷售數字相當漂亮，所以我覺得現在是我們評估是否進軍加拿大市場的好時機。接下來，Jason 會針對他已進行數週的調查進行簡報。現在我把發言權轉交 Jason。請各位仔細聆聽。

Jason: Manager Marcos and all my other colleagues, good morning. Now I will illustrate what I have found in this survey. (1) Popularity can't be given, you have to create it. As a new LED TV brand in Canada, we are undoubtedly **hardly** known by the consumers. To have a stable foothold in this market, knowing the consumers' preference is crucial. (2) With the habit of watching DVDs at home, many consumers in this region prefer big size TVs. This preference is not a secret, so the competition here is **definitely** fierce. To get more specific information about the best-selling sizes, I collect the statistics published on the

Jason：Marcos 經理、各位同事早安，現在我要開始說明我在此次研究中所得到的發現。知名度不是別人給的，是要靠自己創造的。作為加拿大市場的新 LED 電視品牌，我們無疑不太為當地消費者所知。為了要獲得穩定的市佔率，了解消費者的偏好是必要的。因為有在家看 DVD 的習慣，此地區許多消費者偏好大電視。為了要獲得關於銷售最佳尺寸的進一步資料，我蒐集當地有關當局公布在網站上的統

website of local **authority** and find 42 inch ranks number one among all sizes. To dig out why this size is chosen, I check the reference about furnishing and find out whether it has something to do with TV **stand**. (3) Regarded as the standard size for most TV stands, 42 inch is available in all brands in this region. I will stop here temporarily to ask you one question: should we join the completion or find another war **field**?

計數字，從中發現 42 吋榮膺第一。為了瞭解為何是這個尺寸，我查詢了關於裝潢的資料，然後發現原來是與電視櫃有關。被視為多數電視櫃的標準尺寸，此地區所有的電視品牌都有 42 吋電視。講道這邊我要先暫停一下問大家，覺得我們該加入競爭，還是應該另闢戰場呢？

Ken: From you analysis, I think the competition in popular size is too fierce to enter at the very beginning. However, I am not sure which size can own the greatest strength in Canada.

Ken：從你的分析，我覺得熱門尺寸的競爭太過激烈，不適合在初進新市場就踏入。但我不確定在加拿大主打哪種尺寸對我們最有優勢。

Jason: You have the same thought as I do. We should find another field to begin. Thinking of the success we have in the 55 inch in USA, I check the sales status of the same size in Canada. Surprisingly, the marketing is booming but only one brand produces this size. Owning the **cutting-edge** technology in field, we can put the focus on TVs of 55 inch or above.

Jason：你跟我有一樣的想法。我們應該另尋開端。想起我們在美國市場 55 吋電視銷售上所得到的成功，我去查詢同樣尺寸在加拿大的銷售狀況。令人驚訝的是，這個市場正在發展，但目前只有一個品牌有生產。擁有生產大型電視的頂尖技術，我們可以把主力放在 55 吋或是更大的電視上。

Marcos: I agree with this idea. Copying a **mode** is easy, but modifying it in accordance with the actual situation is difficult. You do find the **niche** market we have in Canada. Good job Jason. Now, we need to think where to set retailer stores and the pricing of the TVs. Emily, please collect the data about the distribution map of the home appliance shops in Canada after this meeting. If nothing to add, let us wrap it up here.

Marcos：我同意這個想法。複製模式很容易，但根據實際狀況再去調整就很變得困難。Jason 真的發現了我們公司在加拿大的利基市場，做得很好。現在我們該去思考零售店的位置以及如何定價。Emily，會後請開始收集關於加拿大家電商店地點分布的資料。另外如果各位沒有要補充的，今天會就先開到這邊。

1. **conduct** *v.* **進行**

   例：This experiment is conducted to find out the key reason of the drop in sales figure.

   進行此實驗是為了要找出造成銷售數字下滑的原因。

2. **hardly** *adv.* **幾乎不**

   例：Neglecting the consumer preference, the machine is hardly purchased.

   忽略掉消費者偏好這項因素，該商品幾乎無人購買。

3. **authority** *n.* **權威**

   例：We are waiting for the approval from related authorities.

   我們正在等待有關當局的許可。

Lesson 25
Lesson 26
Lesson 27
Lesson 28
Lesson 29
Lesson 30

MEMO

4. **stand** *n.* 座

例：This stand is set for keeping the balance of the machine.

這個基座是設計來保持機器平衡用的。

5. **field** *n.* 領域

例：To gain a share in the athletic apparel, we develop the new fiber this year.

為了要在運動服飾市場佔有一席之地，我們今年研發出新的纖維材質。

6. **cutting-edge** *adj.* 頂尖的

例：With the cutting-edge machining technology, we can produce the parts with a complicated structure.

擁有頂尖加工技術，我們可以生產結構複雜的零件。

7. **mode** *n.* 模式

例：The performance could be better, if we apply this mode.

若採用此模式，我們績效可以更好。

8. **niche** *n.* 利基

例：High-end speaker is the niche market we have in this region.

高階喇叭是我們在此區域的利基市場。

重點句型分析

1. **N cannot be Vpp, you have to...** 意思為「…不是…，而是要…的」，可用於說明某些現象的不可變動性。

   例：Popularity cannot be granted, and you have to create it.
   流行不是靠給予，而是要自己創造的。

2. **With the habit of..., many... prefer...** 意思為「因為有…的習慣，多數…偏好…」，可用於解釋習慣所造成的選擇差異。

   例：With the habit of using Wi-fi, many smart phone users prefer to eating in the restaurant with this service.
   因為有使用 Wi-Fi 的習慣，許多智慧型手使用者偏好在有提供此項服務的餐廳用餐。

3. **Regarded as the..., N is... in all...** 意思為「被視為…，N 在所有…中都可以…」，可用於說明大眾普遍的想法。

   例：Regarded as the most comfortable size, 4.7 inch phones are available in all brands in the market.
   被視為最舒適尺寸，市面上所有手機品牌都有推出 4.7 吋手機。

4. **Owing the... in, we can put the focus on...** 意思為「擁有…，我們可以將重心放在…」，可用於解釋並說明某事的原由，以及後續的可能行為。

   例：Owning the leading expertise in composite materials, we can put the focus on the development of armors for riders.
   擁有製造複合材料的頂尖技術，我們可以將重心放在騎士護甲的研發上。

本單元以員工向總經理與執行長報告行銷策略為場景，發展一段完整對話，其內容中一共提到四個行銷的常用概念，以下針對每個概念做進一步說明：

1. 從可行性（feasibility）決定執行方向：

- 對應句型：**Popularity can't be given, you have to create it. As a new LED TV brand in Canada, we are undoubtedly hardly known by the consumers. To have a stable foothold in this market, knowing the consumers' preference is crucial.**

在進入新市場或推出新產品前，公司一定會對其可行性進行評估。而這樣的評估通常會依照一些準則進行。此處的準則通常是商業定律，透過規則上的輔助，我們可以判斷該市場是否值得進入或該如何進入。**在本範例中，Jason 認為自家品牌在當地的知名度可能不如既有品牌，因此有必要先去了解當地消費者的喜好，才能做出正確的評估。**

2. 以消費者偏好（preference）進行初步分析：

- 對應句型：**With the habit of watching DVDs at home, many consumers in this region prefer big size TVs.**

在銷售商品時，符合消費這偏好是非常重要的一環。因為如果產品與市場需求有落差，即便產品再好也可能不受歡迎，讓這些商品淪為庫存或是滯銷品。**在本範例中，Jason 發現加拿大的消費者常會在家看 DVD，因此大型電視的購買率很高。**

3. 以常態分布（normal distribution）找出競爭區段：

- 對應句型：**Regarded as the standard size for most TV stands, 42 inch is available in all brands in this region.**

　　在統計學上，大部分的數值都會落在一個平均值附近，極端高數值的比率相對較少。若將這樣的分布應用在銷售上，消費者的偏好也會有集中的現象。雖然這個客群的人數最多，但也意味競爭可能最激烈，所以此區段不見得適合作為新品牌的市場切入點。**在本範例中，Jason 提到由於多數電視櫃將 42 吋電視當成標準尺寸，基於置放的方便，多數消費者也會購買同尺寸的電視。**

4. 以競爭對手找到市場定位（market positioning）：

- 對應句型：**Surprisingly, the marketing is booming but only one brand produces this size. Owning the cutting-edge technology in field, we can put the focus on TV of 55 inch or above.**

　　當公司要推出新產品或是打算進軍新市場時，去研究競爭對手都可以讓我們更加清楚應採取何種定位進行銷售。當競爭十分激烈，我方又打算挑戰既有品牌，就須檢視自身條件，審視是否具備足夠競爭力。**在本範例中，Jason 透過資料得知當前市場大電視的需求增加，但競爭對手少。加上自家公司本身就對此有高度競爭力，故當以此種尺寸進軍。**

看《華爾街之狼》（*The Wolf of Wall Street*），學習闡述概念或想法

篇章重點搶先看

1. 以《華爾街之狼》（*The Wolf of Wall Street*）Jordan Belfort 經典台詞學習如何闡述我方所奉行的某些概念或想法。
2. 以 Jordan Belfort 的經典台詞 “I'm a student of history, Roland, and I'm a firm believer that he who doesn't study the mistakes of the past is doomed to repeat them.”「我是歷史的學生，Roland，而且我深信那些不去研究過去錯誤的人，注定會再次犯錯」。學習本單元核心句型：
   ★I am a student of..., and I am a... believer that he who... is doomed to...「我是…的學生，我深信那些…人注定會在…。」
3. 搭配學習本單元其他三大重點句型：
   a Realizing the... of..., we would like to...（了解…的…，我們會…。）
   b To have a... cooperation/connection with...., the... is added to...（為了能與…有更…的合作／連結，…的…加入…。）
   c The... of... shall be examined every..., assuring the... is/are...（每…會針對…的…進行檢驗，以確保…有…。）
4. 將四種句型放入實境對話練習，學習四大商業概念：
   a 以案例分析（case study）理解影響因子。
   b 針對變因（variable ）加以控制。
   c 以在地化（localization）創造市場差異。
   d 以問卷（questionnaire）推估預期成效。

影片背景介紹

《華爾街之狼》（*The Wolf of Wall Street*）改編自華爾街傳奇人物喬丹貝爾福特的自傳。1987 年時，貝爾福特剛失去華爾街上某間公司股票經紀人的工作，失業的他轉擔任鍋爐室（boiler room）的電話推銷員，向客戶推銷有問題的水餃股（penny stock）。貝爾福特的舌粲蓮花讓他很快又東山再起，快速地累積財富，年僅 26 歲就身價千萬。憑藉著自己優異的口才與清晰的思維，貝爾福特用盡各種骯髒手段遊走法律灰色地帶賺錢，也用這些賺來的錢享盡各種奢華生活，獲得華爾街之狼的封號。若將片中貝爾福特用來表達自己所奉行的概念的句構，應用在闡述商業競爭上，實為我們良好的學習教材。

The Wolf of Wall Street is adapted from the autobiography of Jordan Belfort. In 1987, Belfort just loses the job working as a stockbroker in a firm in Wall Street. But very soon, he gets a job in a boiler room brokerage company that specializes in selling questionable penny stocks. Belfort uses his eloquence to return to live the life by making thousands of money a day. Not long, Belfort earns more than ten millions. With great eloquence and clear thinking, Belfort uses many dirty tricks to make money illegally. He uses the money to lead a lavish life and gambling, earning himself the title: the wolf of Wall Street. If we apply the words that Belfort uses to illustrate the faith he believes in to the explanation of business competition, they turn out to be a good reference for us.

看影片怎麼說、怎麼用

At the conference room of ABC Clothing Company.

（在 ABC 服飾公司的會議室。）

Manager William: Last year, two more budget fashion brands Qup and U&M entered this market. To keep the market share we own now, the headquarters want us to develop a strategy to be prepared to the white-hot completion. Now let's begin the discussion. Please feel free to express your ideas.

William 經理：去年又有兩個平價時尚品牌 QAP 和 U&M 進軍此市場。為了保持現有的市佔率，總公司希望我們擬出對策以面對白熱化競爭。

Jason: Let me say something first. (1) I am a student of history, and I am a firm believer that he who doesn't find the reason of the mistake is doomed to repeat the same mistake again. Repeating the mistake of D&P, YCK tastes **failure**, which as well indicates the fact that putting the local **elements** into consideration is needed.

Jason：讓我先發表一些意見。我是歷史的學生，而且我深信那些不去找出錯誤原因的人，注定會再犯相同的錯誤。犯了與 D&P 相同的錯誤，YCK 的失敗點出加入在地元素有其必要性。

Leo: True. As a foreign **corporate** here, eliminating the **gaps** between our design concepts and the expectations of local consumers is an important task to us. (2) But realizing the importance of **localization**, we would like to add some local **totems** in the new series next season.

Leo：的確是。做為一間外國公司，我們的設計理念可能跟在地消費者有些落差。但了解到在地化的重要性，我想要在下一季的新系列產品加入在地圖騰。

William: Good idea. Can you tell us what kind of totems you are planning to use?

William：好主意。可以告訴我們你預計使用哪類型的圖騰嗎？

Leo: Aboriginal totems are my first choice. With a long history and comprehensive interaction with other cultures, their art is an important cultural heritage in this region. (3) To have a closer connection with this art, the **abstract** totems are added to the design draft of our T-shirts, pants, jackets, and so on.

Leo：原住民圖騰是我的首選。歷史悠久加上歷經多元文化交流，原住民藝術是此地區的重要的文化遺產。為了要與此文化有更緊密的連結，我們將其抽象圖騰加入我們 T 恤、褲款、外套等的設計初稿中。

William: The thought itself is good, but we have to make sure this innovation matches consumers' preference. Thus, doing some survey is inevitable. Do you have any idea about this?

William：想法本身很好。但我們要確定這樣的創新符合消費者的喜好。因此做些研究是無可避免的。各位有任何想法嗎？

Jason: To evaluate the acceptability of this design, questionnaires can be used. The result of the survey shall be examined every week for one month, assuring the acceptability is above certain level.

Jason：若要評估此設計的接受度，可以使用問卷。調查的結果要持續一個月每週檢驗一次，以確保接受度有達到一定水平。

William: Here let me integrate what you all just said. You think using aboriginal totems to our clothing is a good option to face the competition. To make sure this option is workable, using questionnaires to collect and analyze the responses from consumer is needed.

William：這邊讓我統整一下各位的說法。各位覺得將原住民圖騰加入服飾設計是面對競爭的好方法。為了確保此方法可行，需要使用問卷收集與分析消費者反應。

對話單字說分明

1. **white-hot** *adj.* **白熱化**

例：Since the cost of the core parts has dropped, the competition will become white-hot this year.

因為核心零件的成本下降，今年度的競爭會變得白熱化。

2. **failure** *n.* **失敗**

例：The failure of this campaign indicates that we should shift the focus to the customer in the top of the pyramid.

此活動的失敗意味我們應將重心轉移至金字塔頂端的客戶。

3. **element** *n.* **元素**

例：If you want to have a clear market segmentation, adding local elements to your design is a good option.

如果你想要有清楚的市場區隔，加入在地元素是個好方法。

4. **localization** *n.* **在地化**

例：Though we live in a global village, localization is still needed in many marketing strategies.

雖然我們都生活在地球村，但許多行銷策略中仍需考量在地化。

5. **corporate** *n.* **公司**

例：As a new International corporate in this region, we have lower publicity compared with that of local brands.

做為此地區的新國際公司，我們的知名度比當地品牌低。

6. **gap** *n.* **落差**

例：To eliminate the gap between our products and the expectations of consumers, we conduct several surveys to find solutions.

為了弭平產品與消費者期待之間的落差，我們進行許多研究來找出解決方法。

7. **totem** *n.* **圖騰**

   例：The usage of some totems can make our logo more eye-catching.
   使用圖騰讓我們的商標更加引人注目。

8. **abstract** *adj.* **抽象的**

   例：The idea you use in the project is abstract, so can you give us some examples? 你專案中所使用的概念很抽象，所以可以舉例說明嗎？

MEMO

重點句型分析

1. **I am a student of..., and I am a... believer that he who... is doomed to...** 意思為「我是…的學生，我深信那些…人注定會在…」，可用於說明我方所堅信的原則或是理念。

   例：I am a student of experience, and I am a firm believer that he who refuses to review the mistakes is doomed to make the same mistakes again.

   我是經驗的學生，我深信那些不願檢視錯誤的人注定會再犯相同的錯誤。

2. **Realizing the... of..., we would like to...** 意思為「了解…的…，我們會…」，可用於說明在理解某事物的影響程度後，所做出的對應措施為何。

   例：Realizing the importance of discount, we would like to sell our latest products with a favorable price.

   了解到折扣的重要性，我們會以優惠價販售最新商品。

3. **To have a... cooperation/connection with..., the... is added to...** 意思為「為了能與…有更…的合作／連結，的…加入…」，可用於說明達成合作所要做的行動。

   例：To have a closer cooperation with the local designer, the totem of aboriginal is added to our new series.

   為了能與當地設計師有更多的合作，我們新的系列產品加入原住民的圖騰。

4. **The... of... shall be examined every..., assuring the... is/are...** 意思為「每…會針對…的…進行檢驗，以確保…有…」，可用於。

   例：The performance of the new project shall be examined every quarter, assuring the related activities are carried out as scheduled.

   每一季會針對新專案的績效進行檢驗，以確保相關活動有如期舉行。

職場補給站

本單元以平價服飾業人員討論如何面對品牌競爭為場景，發展一段完整對話，其內容中一共提到四個行銷的常用概念，以下針對每個概念做進一步說明：

1. 以案例分析（case study）理解影響因子：

- 對應句型：**Repeating the mistake of D&P, YCK tastes failure, which as well indicates the fact that putting the local elements into consideration is needed.**

  在制訂銷售策略時，過去成功或失敗案例都是很好的參考資料。成功代表當中值得學習之處，失敗代表當中有需要避免之事。善用這些資源，我們就可以發展出適合我們的方式。**在本範例中，Jason 所提出的就是失敗案例，其原因是忽略在地化元素，而這也是公司新策略所應避免重蹈覆轍之處。**

2. 針對變因（variable）加以控制：

- 對應句型：**As a foreign corporate here, eliminating the gaps between our design concepts and the expectations of local consumers is an important task to us.**

  了解失敗或成功案例的關鍵因素後，接下來就是根據這些因子來制訂相關策略。若能控制得當，產品或時服務的銷售就會順利，反之則可能滯銷。**在本範例中，Leo 提到因為我們是國際公司，設計理念不見得完全符合在地需求，因此透過方法來弭平這樣的落差。**

3. 以在地化（localization）創造市場差異：

- 對應句型：**But realizing the importance of localization, we would like to add the some local totems in the new series next season.**

  在地化指的就是加入適合當地的元素，使產品或服務更加符合消費者需求。舉例來說，當某些圖案在該地區被視為禁忌時，就會在當地推出產品時與以避免。相反地，若某元素再當地深受歡迎，可將其與自家設計結合，吸引更多消費者購買。**在本範例中，Leo 提到可在設計中加入原住民圖騰，其理由便是其文化具備歷史性且與多種文化融合，深具文化價值。**

4. 以問卷（questionnaire）推估預期成效：

- 對應句型：**To evaluate the acceptability of this design, questionnaires can be used. The result of survey shall be examined every week for one month, assuring the acceptability is above certain level.**

執行策略之前，若要評估其可行性，可以對消費者做問卷調查。透過回覆資料蒐集與分析，從中得出相關數據。若數據顯示反映良好，則可考慮執行。反之，則代表有需要修正之處。**在本範例中，為了了解結合原住民圖騰是否恰當，Jason 建議執行為期一個月的問卷調查，每週小計一次結果，看看此策略是否符合消費者期待。**

MEMO

看《救救菜英文》（*English Vinglish*），學習視自家產品或服務的缺點

篇章重點搶先看

1. 以《救救菜英文》（*English Vinglish*）主角 Godbole 的經典台詞學習如何檢視自家產品或服務的缺點為何。
2. 以救救菜英文主角 Godbole 的台詞 “The best way to gain confidence is by doing what you're afraid to do.”「增加自信最好的方法，就是去做令你害怕的事情。」學習本單元核心句型：

   ★The 最高級 way to... is by Ving what you are.... to do...「…的最…方法，就是去做令你…的事情。」
3. 搭配學習本單元其他三大重點句型：

   a To enhance/improve the... of..., the... of... shall be adjusted from... to...（為了增加…的…，…的…以從…調整至…。）

   b The 比較級 the N..., the 比較級 the N...（當…越…，…的…就越…。）

   c Considering the... of..., a... is established/set to V...（考量到…，我們建立／設計一個…來…。）
4. 將四種句型放入實境對話練習，學習四大行銷概念：

   a 以行動計畫（action plan）確立方向。

   b 以組織再造（reconstruction）解決困境。

   c 以媒體佔有率（share of voice）說明廣告效果。

   d 以即時／線上（real time/online）平台加速需求處理。

影片背景介紹

《救救菜英文》(*English Vinglish*)是一部典型的寶萊塢電影，劇情環繞家庭主婦 Shashi Godbole 加以開展。有天 Godbole 接到在美國生活姐姐的來電，希望他們一家人到紐約參加她女兒的喜宴。Godbole 的丈夫希望她先提早一個月過去幫忙。Godbole 因為自己英文不好而推拖，但最後來是隻身前往。到了美國後，語言的障礙更加困擾 Godbole。所幸後來姪女的鼓勵下，她去參加一個秘密的英語訓練課程。這個課程讓 Godbole 逐漸找回自信，也許其他學員相互交流。若將片中 Godbole 自我鼓勵的台詞應用在解釋商業競爭上，其句構實為我們學習的良好教材。

English Vinglish is a typical Bollywood movie. The storyline is around the housewife Shashi Godbole. One day Godbole gets a call from her sister in the US, and she invites Godbole and her family to attend her daughter's wedding ceremony in New York. Godbole's husband wants her to get there one month earlier to help her sister, but Godbole refuses to go due to her poor English at the very beginning. When she stays in the USA, the language obstacle bothers her even more. But under her niece's encouragement, she takes a secret English training class. This class helps Godbole confident in her English and she has more interactions with her classmates. If we apply the lines that Godbole uses for self-encouragement to the explanation of business competition, they turns out to be a good reference for us.

看影片怎麼說、怎麼用

At the conference room of KODAA Company.

（在 KODAA 公司的會議室。）

General Manager: After reading the balance sheet of Q3, I found our market share has dropped for 5 percent due to the white-hot competition since Q1. To get what we lost back, I hope today we can come up with some ideas to turn the table. If there have been some solutions in your mind, please don't **hesitate** to tell us.

總經理：看完第三季的損益平衡表後，我發現我的市佔率因為從第一季就開始的白熱化競爭而下跌了百分之五。為了拿回我們所失去的，我希望今年能夠想出一些概念來逆轉情勢。如果各位腦中已經有想法，請別猶豫，儘管告訴我們。

Jason: (1) The best way to change is by doing what we haven't done so far. Though we own the **top-notch** manufacturing technology in digital camera, we pay less attention to the public relation and advertisement. Living in an information era, I think high publicity sometimes equals to high sales figures. In my opinion, maybe now is a good timing for us to think out of the box.

Jason：改變的最好方法就是增加過去你沒去做的。我們雖然擁有頂尖的數位相機製造技術，但我們不注重公關與廣告。生在資訊世代，我認為有高知名度等同高銷售。就我看來，也許現在是我們跳脫舊思維的好時機。

GM: Good analysis. Holding the faith about expertise always comes first, we did neglect the importance of **propaganda** in the past. To make up this gap, do you all have any suggestions?

總經理：分析的很好。秉持專業永遠至上的精神，我們過去的確忽略了文宣的重要性。為了彌補這樣的落差，各位有什麼建議嗎？

Peterson: According to the company regulation, our PR department has one director and two specialists. If we want to utilize the power of media, the **existing** manpower **deployment** is definitely not enough. (2) To enhance the efficiency of this department, the number of the employees shall be adjusted from three to six or more.

Peterson：根據公司規章，公關部編制一名主任與兩名專員。如果我們要善用媒體的力量，現行的人力部署絕對不足。為了增進該部門之效能，員工數應從三人調整至六人或更多。

GM: It sounds reasonable. What will you do next when the reconstruction is done?

總經理：聽起來相當合理。那組織再造過後，你的下一步是？

Peterson: (3) The more frequent our camera could be seen, the higher the chance the consumers buy them. Using **celebrity endorsement** can create high publicity in a short time.

Peterson：當我們相機的曝光度越高，消費者購買的機會就越高。請名人代言可以在短時間內創造高知名度。

GM: Since our competitors do the same thing, I think we should catch up.

總經理：因為競爭對手也會找人代言，所以我們理當跟上腳步。

Jason: I would like to say something more here. To optimize the media resource we have, I think we should also upgrade our website. (4) Considering the convenience of the after-sale service, I think an in-time interaction platform has to be established to meet consumer's need if necessary.

Jason：這邊我要補充一下，為了要善用現有媒體資源。我覺得應該升級公司網站。考量到進行售後服務的方便，我認為如有需要，建立一個即時互動平台有其必要，以符合顧客的需求。

GM: You are right.

總經理：沒錯。

對話單字說分明

1. **hesitate** *v.* 猶豫

例：If you have come up with any solutions, please don't hesitate to tell us. 如果您有想到解決方法，請別猶豫，儘管告訴我們。

2. **box** *n.* 框架

例：Once you see the project in a bigger picture, you can think out of the box. 一旦能以更宏觀的角度看待此專案，你就能跳脫框架。

3. **top-notch** *adj.* 頂尖的

例：The goal we set this year is being the top-notch smart watch producer in this region.
本年度目標是成為此地區頂尖的智慧腕表製造商。

4. **propaganda** *n.* 文宣

例：Knowing the importance of propaganda, we make two ads this year.
深知文宣的重要性，我們今年推出兩支廣告。

5. **existing** *adj.* 現有的

例：The workload will be too heavy, if we carry out the project with the existing manpower. 如以現有人力執行此專案，工作負擔會太重。

6. **deployment** *n.* 佈署

例：Finding the workload is uneven. The manpower deployment is adjusted.
發現到工作分配並不平均，人力佈署以進行調整。

7. **celebrity** *n.* 名人

例：Celebrity endorsement is one common propaganda.
名人代言是常見的宣傳手法。

8. **endorsement** *n.* 背書

例：With the endorsement of the related authorities, you can trust our quality. 有了主管機關的背書，您可以信任我們的品質。

重點句型分析

1. **The 最高級 way to... is by Ving what you are... to do...** 意思為「…的最…方法，就是去做令你…的事情」，可用於說明如何透過面對自身弱點獲得實質上的強化。

   例：The best way to find the weakness is by challenging what you are feared to do.

   找出弱點的最佳方法就是去挑戰你所害怕的事情。

2. **To enhance/improve the... of..., the... of... shall be adjusted from... to...** 意思為「為了增加…的…，…的…以從…調整至…」，可用於說明為提高某種能力或指標所做出的調整為何。

   例：To improve the performance of international sales, the employee number of this team shall be adjusted from three to five.

   為提升國貿的銷售績效，該團隊的員工數以從三名調整至五名。

3. **The 比較級 the N..., the 比較級 the N...** 意思為「當…越…，…的…就越…」，可用於說明提升或改變某種要素所帶來的影響。

   例：The more frequent you check the machine, the lower the chance for the unexpected shutdown you will have.

   當你越常檢查機器，無預警當機的機會就越小。

4. **Considering the... of..., a... is established/set to V** 意思為「考量到…，我們建立／設計一個…來」，可用於。

   例：Considering the growth in online shopping, an e-shop is established to meet the needs of our customers.

   考量到線上購物的成長，我們設計一個線上商店來滿足顧客的需求。

本單元以數位相機製造商主管與員工討論如何改善市佔率下滑為場景，發展一段完整對話，其內容中一共提到四個行銷的常用概念，以下針對每個概念做進一步說明：

1. 以行動計畫（action plan）確立方向：

- 對應句型：**Living in an information era, I think high publicity sometimes equals to high sales figures. In my opinion, maybe now is a good timing for us to think out of the box.**

  在執行策略前，首先需要釐清方向，才能事半功倍。為達到此目標，擬定行動計畫方真是很有效的方法。**在本範例中，Jason 表示我們生在資訊世代，高知名度有時真的能夠帶來高收益，因此有必要去思考是否應當跳脫舊思維，在媒體行銷上多加著墨。**

2. 以組織再造（reconstruction）解決困境：

- 對應句型：**If we want to utilize the power of media, the existing manpower deployment is definitely not enough. To enhance the efficiency of this department, the number of the employee shall be adjusted from three to six or more.**

  當既有編制無法應付相關業務時，調整人員數量、增減單位數量都是常見的組織再造方式。希望經由這樣的變革，始運作效能得到提升。**在本範例中，Peterson 提到公關部現有人力並不足以應付新的業務分配，因此建議增加編制，將人員倍增。**

Lesson 25
Lesson 26
Lesson 27
Lesson 28
Lesson 29
Lesson 30

3. 以媒體佔有率（share of voice）說明廣告效果：

- 對應句型：**The more frequently our camera could be seen, the higher the chance the consumers buy them. Using celebrity endorsement can create high publicity in a short time.**

  若從媒體曝光度來看，當一個產品越常被消費者看見，留下印象的機會就越高，相對的也越有被購買的可能性。根據這樣的原則，若商品廣告的媒體佔有率達一定水平，必能產生一定的效益。**在本範例中，Peterson 就是根據此原則，向總經理提出使用名人代言的建議，期望在短期內創造知名度。**

4. 以即時／線上（real time/online）平台加速需求處理：

- 對應句型：**Considering the convenience of after-sale service, I think an in-time interaction platform has to be established to meet consumer's need if necessary.**

  售後服務一直是銷售中重要的一環。當顧客對於產品有疑問，或是產品出現問題，都會尋求幫助。為了提升服務品質與處理速度，建立線上平台是許多公司的做法。**在本範例中，Jason 便是以即時平台能夠更快處理客戶需求，而向總經理建議執行此方案。**

看《亞果出任務》（*Argo*），學習分析狀況、解決問題並提升品質

篇章重點搶先看

1. 以《亞果出任務》（*Argo*）主角東尼經典台詞學習如何分析狀況，解決問題或提升品質。
2. 以亞果出任務主角東尼的台詞 "It's often in the deepest despair that we find the strength to surpass ourselves."

   「往往只有在最深的絕望裡，才能找到超越自我的動力。」學習本單元核心句型：

   ★It is often in... that we....「往往在…，我們…。」
3. 搭配學習本單元其他三大重點句型：

   a The...will focus on..., so that the... be truly Vpp（…的…會放在…，使…真的被…。）

   b Not to miss..., we collect all... we...（為了不要遺漏…，我們記錄所有…的…。）

   c With... unrevealed, the... of... can be Vpp as...（不揭露…，…的…可被…為…。）
4. 將四種句型放入實境對話練習，學習四大行銷概念：

   a 以批評（criticism）發現須修正區塊。

   b 從癥結點（sticking point）對症下藥。

   c 以思想構圖（mind mapping）延伸既有思維。

   d 以單盲（single blind test）檢驗修正成效。

影片背景介紹

本片改編自 1979 伊朗人質事件，當時伊朗的美國大使館遭到當地群眾與革命聯隊示威抗議，要求引渡前伊朗領導人。使館人員接獲銷毀敏感資料指令，開始大量銷毀檔案。不久後使館被佔領，使館人員與平民成為人質。但有六名外交人員脫逃成功，躲至加拿大使官邸。美方要求其按兵不動，想辦法解決人質問題。但由於僵持持續，國務院要求中情局先行營救這六人。在無計可施的情況下，國務院同意主角東尼提出的偽裝拍片取景的救援方案。若將片中東尼面對困境時自我鼓勵的台詞的句構，可應用在闡述如何透過解析困境，找出突破或改進的方法。

Argo is adapted from the Iran hostage crisis in1979. USA Embassy in Iran is enclosed by the local civilians and the army with the request of the extradition of former Supreme Leader. Diplomats receive the order of destroying all sensitive documents. Soon the embassy is occupied, making the diplomats and some US civilians become the hostages. Finding no solution, State Council accepts the plan of the fake film making proposed by Tony. If we apply the structure of the words that Tony uses for self-encouragement to the aspect of marketing, they turn out to a good reference for us to learn how to find the solutions by analyzing the difficulties.

看影片怎麼說、怎麼用

At the conference room of ABC Software Company.

（在 ABC 軟體公司的會議室。）

Manger Lance: Before we leave the office to enjoy the holiday, I hope we can have some discussions concerning our CAD software. After checking messages in our service platform, I found our software has some **loopholes** needed to be fixed. The reference in front of you is the criticism I regard important, you can spend few seconds reading them and share your opinion.

Lance 經理：在我們下班享受假日之前，我希望可以就自家的電腦輔助設計系統進行一些討論。在看完客服平台的訊息後，我發現這個軟體真的有些漏洞需要補強。各位看到的參考資料是我覺得重要的一些批評，請大家花點時間閱讀，並分享你的看法。

Jason: (1) It is often in the strictest **criticism** that we find the incentive to improve. Though Customer Livingston uses some **emotional** words to criticize our software, he points out the delay in big data receiving has become a serious **defect** in our system. To precisely fix this problem in the shortest time, a workload maximum testing is needed. (2) The test will focus on the data receiving, so that the delay can be truly improved.

Jason：往往在在最嚴厲的批評中，我們找到進步的誘因。雖然我們的客戶 Livingston 用了一些情緒字眼批評本軟體，但他也點出巨量資料接收延遲已經成為本軟體的一個嚴重瑕疵。為了能夠在最短的時間內精確解決問題，有必要進行最大工作負荷量測試。測試的重心會放在資料接收上，讓延遲問題獲得真正的改善。

Lance: True. I will ask Dante to start the testing next Monday. About the correction

Lance：的確是。我會請 Dante 下週一起開始進行

error problem, do you all have any solutions?

測試。關於出現修正的部分，各位有想到任何解決方式嗎？

Anson: Wrong **default** value and the abnormality in program codes are the possible reasons. To prove which **assumption** I make is right, we will need to conduct time-consuming code examinations. (3) Not to miss any possible section, we will collect all results we get from the test for a further analysis.

Anson：預設值錯誤和程式碼異常是可能的原因，為了要驗證我的哪個假設是正確的，我們需要進行耗時的程式碼檢驗。避免錯過任何可能區段，我們會收集所有測試資料作進一步分析。

Lance: Just as you said, either one could be the cause. How do you evaluate the effect of the modification?

Lance：就像你所說的，兩種原因都有可能，那你要如何檢測修正後的效果？

Anson: Except for the **interior** test, we will find a third **party** to have the single blind test. (4) With the brand names and related designs unrevealed, the responses of the examinees can be collected as a reference.

Anson：除了內部測試外，我們會找第三方進行單盲測試。在不揭露品牌名稱與相關設計的情況下，受測者的反應可做為我們的參考資料。

Lance: This method is practical but somehow money-consuming. Please check how much money we have to pay for a verification you just mention.

Lance：這個方法可行，但有點花錢。請去確認進行你剛所說驗證要花多少錢。

Anson: I see. I will contact Mia after this meeting.

Anson：了解。會後我就會去聯絡 Mia。

對話單字說分明

1. **loophole** *n.* **漏洞**

例：To fix the loophole of this software in time, our engineers have conducted few tests.

為了及時修復漏洞，我們的工程師已進行多項測試。

2. **criticism** *n.* **批評**

例：The criticism from the consumer is the incentive for us to make a progress. 消費者的批評是我們進步的動力。

3. **emotional** *adj.* **情緒化的**

例：As a part of service industry, emotional words shall be avoided when you work.

身為服務業的一份子，上班時應避免使用情緒性字眼。

4. **defect** *n.* **瑕疵**

例：If you find the shoes with any defects, you can return them.

如您發現這雙鞋有任何瑕疵，您可以退貨。

5. **default** *adj.* **預設的**

例：Keep the setting in default value, or your machine may be damaged.

請將設定保持在預設值，否則機器可能會壞掉。

6. **assumption** *n.* **假設**

例：The experiment result proves my assumption wrong.

實驗結果證明我假設錯誤。

7. **interior** *adj.* **內部的**

例：All products should pass the interior quality examination before shipment. 所有產品出貨前應通過內部品質檢驗。

8. **party** *n.* **當事人**

例：To prove our product is toxic substance free, we find an examining organization as the third party for verification.

為證明產品不含有毒物質，我們找了一個檢驗機構做第三方驗證。

重點句型分析

1. **It is often in... that we...** 意思為「往往在…，我們…」，可用於說明如何透過分析狀況，從中得到省思或啟發。

   例：It is often in the smallest changes that we find the most important message.

   往往在最微小的改變中，我們發現最重要的訊息。

2. **The... will focus on..., so that the... be truly Vpp** 意思為「…的…會放在…，使…真的獲得…。」，可用於說明調整或修改的重點為何。

   例：The modification will focus on the alignment of figures, so that problems can be truly solved.

   修正的的重點會放在數據的校正，使問題真正獲得解決。

3. **Not to miss..., we collect all... we...** 意思為「為了不要遺漏…，我們蒐集所有…的…」，可用於說明如何確保接受訊息或事物時不會錯過任何部分。

   例：Not to miss any feedback, we will collect all messages we receive from the consumers.

   為了不要遺漏任何回饋，我們蒐集所有顧客傳給我們的訊息。

4. **With... unrevealed, the... of... can be Vpp as...** 意思為「不揭露…，…的…可被…為…」，可用於說明進行盲測時所設定的相關條件。

   例：With the logos being unrevealed, the responses of examinees can be collected as the data for a further analysis.

   不透漏商標，受測者的反應可作為進一步分析的資料。

本單元以員工向軟體公司內部會議為場景，以處理軟體缺陷為主題發展一段完整對話，其內容中一共提到四個行銷的常用概念，以下針對每個概念做進一步說明：

1. 以批評（criticism）發現須修正區塊：

- 對應句型：**Though Customer Livingston uses some emotional words to criticize our software, he points out the delay in data receiving has become a serious defect in our system.**

  沒有產品是完美的，因此消費者對於產品有所批評實屬正常。若以更正面的態度看待批評，其實這些評論是在替公司進行品質修正，使產品更加優質。**在本範例中，Jason 認為顧客 Livingston 雖然留言內容帶情緒字眼，但卻也點出軟體的大問題，對於後續修正大有幫助。**

2. 從癥結點（sticking point）對症下藥：

- 對應句型：**To precisely fix this problem in the shortest time, a workload maximum testing is needed. The test will focus on the data receiving, making the delay be truly improved.**

  若要有效且快速地解決產品問題，就一定要先找處問題的癥結點。透過這樣的邏輯思考，我們可以精確找出造成問題的主因，然後將之改善。**在本範例中，由於本軟體常會接受巨量資料，會延遲極可能是因為負荷量出問題，Jason 據此提出作最大負荷測試的建議。**

3. 以思想構圖（mind mapping）延伸既有思維：

- 對應句型：**Wrong default value and the abnormality in program code are the possible reasons. To prove my assumption, we will need to conduct time-consuming examinations.**

找出問題癥結點後，由於我們無法一下子思考到多個面向，因此可以透過思想構圖的方法去找尋每個想法之間的關聯性，然後將其組合。**在本範例中，Anson 先提出預設值錯誤或是程式編碼異常是兩個可能主因，然後提出程式碼測試的建議。整個處理過程其實就是思想構圖的實踐。**

4. 以單盲（single blind test）檢驗修正成效：

- 對應句型：**Except for the interior test, we will find a third party to have single blind test. With the brand names and related designs unrevealed, the responses of the examinees can be collected as reference.**

進行盲測是為了要排除受測者的一些主觀影響因子，使測試結果更具公正性。舉例來說，在看到商標的情況下，受測者可能因為品牌形象等因素，影響產品本身客觀因素的判斷。而單盲指的是受測者不知道產品資訊，但施測者知道，其主要目的多是用來檢測改良的成效。**在本範例中，Anson 認為造成修正誤差的原因有二，工程師檢測過後會提供兩種修正版給第三方檢測效果，以確保問題有真正改善。**

看《星際異攻隊》（*Guardians of the Galaxy*），學習掌握商機

篇章重點搶先看

1. 以《星際異攻隊》（*Guardians of the Galaxy*）主角彼得奎爾經典台詞學習如何掌握先機，贏得高市佔率。
2. 以星際異攻隊主角彼得奎爾的台詞 "Losers watch it happen; winners make it happen."「輸家看著它發生；贏家讓它發生」。學習本單元核心句型：
   ★N1 watch it..., N2+ make it...「N1 等其⋯，N2 讓其⋯。」
3. 搭配學習本單元其他三大重點句型：
   a By adding... to..., our... is 比較級 than that of...（將⋯加入⋯，我們的⋯比其他的⋯還⋯。）
   b Though... is..., the... will... when you...（雖然⋯很⋯，但當你⋯時，其⋯會⋯。）
   c Once... become the symbol of..., the value of... is...（當⋯成為⋯的象徵，⋯的價值會⋯。）
4. 將四種句型放入實境對話練習，學習四大行銷概念：
   a 以主動創造市場性（marketability）。
   b 以形象塑造（image making）提升價值。
   c 以邊際效用（marginal utility）找出最適規格。
   d 以高度涉入（high evolvement）為長期目標。

影片背景介紹

《星際異攻隊》（*Guardians of the Galaxy*）改編自漫威同名漫畫。故事始於 1988 年主角彼得奎爾被一群名為破壞者的盜賊軍團帶離地球。18 年後，長大成人的彼得在盜賊首領的訓練下，也成為一名大盜。彼得成功從威脅宇宙安危的大反派羅南手上盜取一顆宇宙靈球，但也因此成為賞金獵人追殺的目標。被捕入獄後，彼得認識了一群特異人士，分別是浣熊火箭（Rocket）、樹人格魯特（Groot）、葛摩菈（Gamora），以及毀滅者德克斯（Drax the Destroyer）。在一干人等彼此合作，成功逃獄。若將片中彼得鼓勵夥伴的台詞，應用在產品銷售上，其內容實為學習闡明主動（正面）與被動（負面）所產生差異的良好教材。

Guardians of the Galaxy is adapted from the Marvel comics of the same name. The story begins with year 1988 when the protagonist, Peter Quill is taken away by the space pirates, Ravagers. Eighteen years later, the grown-up Peter becomes a pirate under the training of leader of this group. Later Peter successfully steals an orb from the bad guy Ronan and becomes the target of a treasure hunter. After being captured, Peter knows few guys with special talents in the jail. They are Rocket, Groot, Gamora, and Drax the Destroyer. In order to escape from the jail, they cooperate. If we apply the words that Peter says to encourage his partners to the sale of products, they turn out to a good reference for us to learn how to illustrate the difference between being positive and being negative.

看影片怎麼說、怎麼用

At the conference room of ABC Company. Jason is asking if Ryder needs a cup of coffee as the **refreshment** before the discussion.

（在 ABC 公司的會議室。Jason 詢問 Ryder 在討論前，是否需要來杯咖啡提神。）

Ryder: Good idea. A latte, please.

Ryder：好阿。請給我一杯拿鐵。

Jason: As we discussed in the phone call, our company wants to launch a special campaign to create a trend in the coffee market this year. The followers watch it happen; the **pioneers** make it happen. We want to be the pioneer who make the bottle coffee different. And you are the key element to realize the goal.

Jason：如同我們電話中所討論的，本公司希望舉辦一個特別活動來開創瓶裝咖啡的新風潮。跟隨者等其發生，開創者讓其發生。我們想做讓瓶裝咖啡不同的第一人。而您是實現此目標的關鍵元素。

Ryder: Because our two companies are from different fields, in what way can we help you?

Ryder：因為我們兩間公司來自不同領域，我們可以怎樣協助您呢？

Jason: Being the most outstanding **hand-made** clothing and bag manufacturer, you are the pronoun of **elegance**. We all know the first impression sometimes determines whether the consumers buy this product or not. (2) By adding your elegant element to the bottle, our coffee is definitely more eye-catching than that of the competitors.

Jason：做為業界最頂尖的手工服飾與包款的製造商，你是優雅的代名詞。我們都知道有時對方品的第一印象會決定消費者最終的購買與否。將您的優雅元素加入瓶身，我們的咖啡一定會比他牌更加吸睛。

Ryder: Thank you for your compliment. However, the clothing or bag is much bigger, so I have to **ponder** how to convey the **soul** of design in such a limited space. What's the volume and the size of the bottle you plan to use in this activity?

Ryder：感謝您的稱讚。但我們包款或是服飾尺寸大多了，所以我需要思考如何在這樣有限的空間內傳達出設計的靈魂。這次活動所預計使用的尺寸與容量是？

Jason: The round bottle with the volume of 400c.c. and the **radius** is 3 cm. Here let me explain why this specification. Though the flavor of our coffee is good, the delicious feeling will decease when you drink more than this amount. To leave the best impression in consumers' mind, we prefer the smaller specification.

Jason：半徑 3 公分的 400 CC 圓形罐。這邊讓我解釋一下為何是這個規格。雖然我們的咖啡風味很好，但超過這個份量美味度還是會下降。為了要在顧客心中留下好印象，我們偏好小罐裝。

Ryder: I see. If this program hits the market, what is your **followup**?

Ryder：我了解了。如果這個活動成功掀起潮流，你接下來的盤算是？

Jason: (4) Once this crossover becomes the symbol of elegance, the value of our coffee is higher. Consumers may view this coffee not as a beverage but an art piece. We can extend the design to mugs, coasters, and so on so that the cooperation can go further.

Jason：一旦這樣的跨界合作變成優雅的象徵，我們咖啡的價值會提高。消費者可能會是這個產品為藝術品而不只是飲料。我們還可以延伸此設計到馬克杯、杯墊等商品上，讓這樣的合作更開枝散葉。

Ryder: I got it. Let's call it a day here. I will send you some drafts later.

Ryder：知道了。我們就先討論到這吧，我晚點會寄一些草圖給你。

對話單字說分明

1. **refreshments** *n.* 提神物

 例：Since the meeting has lasted more than 3 hours, let's take a break to have some refreshments.

 因為我們已經開會開三小時了，先休息吃點或喝點東西提神一下吧。

2. **pioneer** *n.* 先驅

 例：As the pioneer in this field, we learn from failure and mistakes.

 做為此領域的先驅，我們在失敗與錯誤中學習。

3. **hand-made** *adj.* 手工的

 例：If you have a higher budget, I recommend you buy our hand-made bags. 如果您的預算較高，我推薦您購買手工包款。

4. **elegance** *n.* 優雅

 例：This dress perfectly matches your elegance.

 這件洋裝完全襯托出您的優雅。

5. **ponder** *v.* 深思

 例：Since the competition is fiercer than I think, I need some time to ponder my next step.

 因為競爭比我想得還激烈，我需要點時間去深思下一步該怎麼做。

6. **soul** *n.* 靈魂

 例：The design with no soul can't touch people's heart.

 沒有靈魂的設計無法感動人心。

7. **radius** *n.* 半徑

 例：Please keep the area in operation radius clean after 2PM.

 下午兩點後請保持操作半徑內的區域淨空。

8. **followup** *n.* 後續動作

 例：Since this product hit the market, we need to outline the follow up soon. 因為這個產品風潮，我們需要快點構思出後續動作。

重點句型分析

1. **N1 watch it..., N2+make it...** 意思為「N1 等其…，N2 讓其…」，可用於說明態度或想法所帶來的差異。

   例：The shallow watches it work; the insightful makes it work.
   膚淺的人等其生效，有洞見的人讓其生效。

2. **By adding... to..., our... is 比較級 than that of...** 意思為「將…加入…，我們的…比其他的…還…」，可用於說明增加某要素後，可產生的差異為何。

   例：By adding the old-school feeling to our design, the appearance of our phone is more eye-catching than that of other competitors.
   在設計中加入復古感，我們手機的外觀比它牌更加吸睛。

3. **Though... is..., the... will... when you...** 意思為「雖然…很…，但當你…時，其…會…」，可用於說明產生滿足感的界線是在哪邊。

   例：Though the taste of the beverage is special, the freshness will decrease when you drink the second glass.
   雖然這飲料口味很特別，但喝到第二杯新鮮感就沒那麼重了。

4. **Once... become the symbol of..., the value of... is...** 意思為「當…成為…的象徵，…的價值會…」，可用於說明產品的價值。

   例：Once wearing our clothing becomes the symbol of fashion, the value of the clothing itself will be upgraded.
   當穿著本品牌服飾成為時尚象徵，服飾本身的價值會得到提升。

職場補給站

本單元以咖啡公司跟手工設計公司洽談跨界合作一事為場景，發展一段完整對話，其內容中一共提到四個行銷的常用概念，以下針對每個概念做進一步說明：

1. 以主動創造市場性（marketability）：

- 對應句型：**The followers watch it happen; the pioneers make it happen. We want to be the pioneer who makes the bottle coffee different.**

  在商場上，機會往往是自己創造的。如果我們的觀察力購敏銳，當嗅到改變或是發展的氣息時，若提早準備，等時機成熟，我們早已大幅領先其他競爭者。**在本範例中，Jason 提到先驅者創造潮流，跟隨者追逐潮流。本公司希望能夠使瓶裝咖啡不同於以往。**

2. 以形象塑造（image making）提升價值：

- 對應句型：**By adding your elegant element to bottle, our coffee is definitely more eye-catching than that of the competitors.**

  消費者選購商品時，其品牌形象也是考量因素之一，顧客會選擇自己熟悉或認同的品牌去消費，這也是許多大廠願意投入大筆經費塑造品牌形象的因素。**在本範例中，Jason 提到若加入 Ryder 公司的優雅形象，自家公司咖啡的形象能夠提升，更能受到消費者的注意。**

3. 以邊際效用（marginal utility）找出最適規格：

- 對應句型：**Though the flavor of our coffee is good, the delicious feeling will decease when you drink more than this amount. To leave the best impression in consumers' mind, we prefer smaller specification.**

  邊際效用是每增加一單位產品數量所能帶給消費者的滿足感。舉例來說，在你很口渴時，所喝下的第一罐的運動飲料會讓你感到滿足，但如果喝到第二罐，滿足感會下降。**在本範例中，Jason 提到雖然自家咖啡很好喝，但喝太多美味感還是會下降，所以推出小罐裝，份量與美味兼具。**

4. 以高度涉入（high evolvement）為長期目標：

- 對應句型：**Once this crossover becomes the symbol of elegance, the value of our coffee is higher. Consumers may view this coffee not as a beverage but an art piece.**

  所謂的高度涉入指的是需要該產品的好處，而這樣的產品通常會是高單價且不易相互比較，例如汽車、高級音響等。但有時高度涉入也可能透過銷售手段或是形象塑造而來。原本替換度高的低度涉入商品，因為成功地創造附加價值，成為市場上的搶手貨。**在本範例中，Jason 表示若這樣的跨界成功使公司的咖啡變成優雅的象徵，消費者購買時，就可能不單只是為了飲用，還有收藏的目的在。**

看《決勝 21 點》（*21*），解釋市場趨勢

篇章重點搶先看

1. 以《決勝 21 點》（*21*）主角班經典台詞學習如何解釋市場趨勢。
2. 以決勝 21 點主角班的台詞 "*In the game of life, it's not how good the cards are in your hands, it's how well you play them.*"「人生的牌局，關鍵不在拿了一手好牌，而在打得一手好牌。」學習本單元核心句型：

   ★In the... of..., it is not how adj N is/are...., it is how adv you...「在…的…中，關鍵不在你的…有多…，而是在於你…得多…。」
3. 搭配學習本單元其他三大重點句型：

   a When choosing..., you do it to sacrifice the.... of...（當選擇…時，就是以…為代價。）

   b From the... N provide, we can tell...（從…所提供的…，我們可知道…。）

   c Assuming each... need..., the total... of... is（假設每一…需要…，…的總…是…。）
4. 將四種句型放入實境對話練習，學習四大行銷概念：

   a 以行銷組合（marketing mix）突顯整合之效用。

   b 以機會成本（opportunity）說明選擇之代價。

   c 以試吃（taste test）蒐集市場反應。

   d 以沉入成本（sunk cost）估算行銷費用。

影片背景介紹

《決勝 21 點》（*21*）主角班是天性害羞麻省理工學院學生，因為希望以當醫生為業，畢業前考取了哈佛醫學院，但卻因為付不起高額的學費而傷透腦筋。某天得知有個獎學金可申請，便與同學一起做實驗，好替自己創造優勢。但班知道自己經歷平庸難以獲選，因此改選擇靠打工賺錢。某天上課時因解出教授所出的數學問題，而被邀請加入黑傑社。若將片中班在歷經眾多牌局後，所得到的人生體悟的那句台詞應用在做生意上，其句構實為我們學習如何向顧客說明市場趨勢的良好教材。

Ben is a shy student studying in Massachusetts Institute of Technology, and he passes the entrance test of Harvard Medical School before his graduation. However, the high tuition makes him headache. Upon knowing there is a scholarship open to apply, he cooperates with his classmates to do some experiments to create some competitiveness in this application. Knowing his portfolio is not outstanding, Ben finds a part time job as the alternative to saving money. One day when Ben solves a math question in class, he is invited to attend the blackjack club. If we apply the words that Ben says to the business field, they turns out to be materials for us to learn how to illustrate the market trend to the consumers.

看影片怎麼說、怎麼用

At the conference room of ABC Company.

（在 ABC 公司的會議室。）

Manager Lai: Good morning my colleagues. The topic we will cover today is the distribution channel for our new **desserts**. The reference in front of your seat is the **locations** of supermarkets and convenience stores in this city. Please spend one minute to read it and tell us what you find as detailed as possible.

賴經理：各位同事早安。今天的會議主題是新推出點心的銷售通路。各位座位前方的參考資料是此城市超市與便利商店的分布圖，請各位花個一分鐘閱讀，並盡可能詳地地告訴大家你的發現。

Jason: (1) In the game of business, it is not how comprehensive your channels are, it is how well you use them in accordance with your needs. Since we view this product as **delicate** food, we should consider its positioning in the point of sales. In my opinion, it shall be sold in the high class supermarkets to attract the consumers with a high purchase power.

Jason：在商業競賽中，關鍵不在你的通路有多全面，而是在於您有多能運用它們。我們視此產品為精緻食品，因此需要去思考它在銷售點的定位為何。就我個人看來，我認為應該選擇在高檔超市銷售，吸引高消費力的客層。

Mandy: It might be a good direction. (2) But when choosing the channel for the top, you do it to sacrifice the guests of the middle and bottom. You have to check which one can **generate** better sales figures for us.

Mandy：這也許是個好的方向，但當你選擇賣給頂級客，就是以中間客與底層客為代價。必須去思考何者能提供我們的較好銷售數字。

Jason: What you just said is right. To test which one is better, taste test is needed. The desserts will be **sliced** into the one **bite** size as the sample for consumers to try. (3) From the feedback they provide, we can tell which flavor is accepted and whether the pricing is appropriate or not. Though the activity needs certain cost, it can help us revise the direction.

Jason：您說的對。點心會切成一口可食的大小讓消費者試吃。從它們的回饋我們可以得知口味與訂價的接受度為何。雖然這樣的活動需要一定的成本，但可以幫助我們修正銷售方向。

Lai: What is the estimated product **assumption**?

Lai：那預計會消耗多少產品呢？

Jason: I would like to hold ten events in different places which include supermarkets, convenient stores. Assuming each place needs ten boxes, the total boxes for this activity is about 100. In other words, the budget of product alone is 10,000 USD. Plus the other expense, the total cost will reach 12,000 to 13,000 USD.

Jason：我想要辦在包含超市與便利商店的十個不同地點辦試吃會。假設每個地點需要用掉十盒，這次活動的總消耗量就是 100 盒。換言之，單產品消耗的金額是一萬美金。加上其他支出後，總花費會在一萬二到一萬三美金之間。

Lai: This is an acceptable range. To convince the General Manager, we need to write a proposal that integrates what we have discussed today. Who wants to be the volunteer to finish the task?

Lai：這是一個可接受的範圍。但為了要說服總經理，我們需要寫一份整合今天討論內容的提案。誰自願做這份工作呢？

Jason: I will do it.

Jason：交給我吧。

對話單字說分明

1. **dessert** *n.* **點心**

   例：The demand of the desserts grows year after year.

   點心的需求年年成長。

2. **location** *n.* **地點**

   例：The location of the shops can greatly affect the sales figure.

   店址會大大影響銷售數字。

3. **delicate** *adj.* **精緻的**

   例：With the delicate decoration, this phone case is really eye-catching.

   這個手機殼上的裝飾精緻，真得很吸睛。

4. **generate** *v.* **產生**

   例：To generate more profit, we have to expand our business to the neighboring cites

   為了能有更多獲利，我們應該把事業擴展至鄰近都市。

5. **slice** *v.* **切割**

   例：The chef is slicing the roasted beef for the guest.

   主廚正在替顧客切烤牛肉。

6. **bite** *adj.* **一口大小的**

   例：To make it easy to take, the cookie is made in a bite size.

   為了方便攜帶，這個做成一口可食的大小。

7. **assumption** *n.* **消耗**

   例：The assumption of consumables shall be considered in the budget.

   預算中需將消耗品的耗損列入考量。

8. **convince** *v.* **說服**

   例：Once the consumers are convinced by your words, there is a high chance that they will buy the product.

   一旦你的話術說服了客戶，他們很可能就會購買商品。

重點句型分析

1. **In the... of..., it is not how adj N is/are..., it is how adv you...** 意思為「在…的…中，關鍵不在你的…有多…，而是在於你…得多…」，可用於說明某種趨勢或形況的核心要素為何。

   例：In the game of business, it is not how wide your coverage is, it is how well you run the business in each region.
   在商業的競賽上，關鍵不是在於你的涵蓋範圍有多廣，而是在於你經營每個區域的方式有多好。

2. **When choosing..., you do it to sacrifice the... of...** 意思為「當你選擇…時，就是以…為代價。」，可用於說明選擇時所需承擔的代價或支付的成本。

   例：When choosing to take the high speed rail way, you do it to sacrifice the cheaper transportation like bus.
   當您選擇搭高鐵時，就是以較便宜的交通方式為代價。

3. **From the... N provide, we can tell...** 意思為「從…所提供的…，我們可知道」，可用於說明中所獲得的資訊中包含何種訊息。

   例：From the comment consumers provide, we can tell this flavor is accepted by most people.
   從消費者所提供的評論來看，這個口味為多數人所接受。

4. **Assuming each... need..., the total... of... is** 意思為「假設每一…需要…，…的總…是…」，可用於活動成本的估算。

   例：Assuming each branch will need ten gifts, the total assumption of our souvenirs in this event is 300 pieces.
   假設每一分店需要十份禮品，這次活動的總紀念品消耗量是 300 個。

職場補給站

本單元以食品公司內部分析銷售通路為場景，發展一段完整對話，其內容中一共提到四個行銷的常用概念，以下針對每個概念做進一步說明：

1. 以行銷組合（marketing mix）突顯整合之效用：

- 對應句型：**In the game of business, it is not how comprehensive your channels are, it is how well you use them in accordance with your needs.**

  在商場上，並非資源多就一定能佔優勢，懂得運用現有資源，將其效能發揮至最大，才是重點。透過行銷組合，資源可依功能分類，將其安排在適合的用途上。**在本範例中，Jason 提到銷售通路不在多，而在於有功效。懂得以需求安排通路，才適正確做法。**

2. 以機會成本（opportunity）說明選擇之代價：

- 對應句型：**But when choosing the channel for the top, you do it to sacrifice the guests of the middle and bottom. You have to check which one can generate better sales figures for us.**

  機會成本指的是做選擇所需承擔的代價。舉例來說，今天有火車與客運兩種交通方式供你選擇，因為你不可能同時搭乘兩者，當你選擇其一時，另一個選像就是你的機會成本。**在本範例中，Mandy 提醒 Jason 當選擇頂端市場時，勢必得放棄中間與底層市場，因此需要評估是否值得。**

3. 以試吃（taste test）蒐集市場反應：

- 對應句型：The desserts will be sliced into the one bite size as the sample for consumers to try. From the feedback they provide, we can tell which flavor is accepted and whether the pricing is appropriate or not.

當食品公司推出新產品時，為了要測試消費者的反應，舉辦詩吃是很常見的做法。透過試吃，公司可以了解尚有哪些部分需要調整。**在本範例中，Jason 就建議將點心成可一口吃下的尺寸，讓消費者試吃，以便蒐集市場資訊。**

4. 以沉入成本（sunk cost）估算行銷費用：

- 對應句型：I would like to hold ten events in different places which include supermarkets, convenient stores. Assuming each place needs ten boxes, the total boxes for this activity is 100.

沉入成本指的是無論銷售成功與否皆無法回收的成本。舉例來說，許多公司都會花錢購買廣告時段，但即便最後產品銷售狀況不佳，這些支付給電視台的花費也是無法討回的，因此這就是一種沉入成本。**在本範例中，Jason 提到要辦十場試吃會，如果粗估一場需要消耗十盒產品，因為東西被吃掉後是無法再回復的，所以這次活動的沉入成本就是 100 盒。**

看《怒海劫》（*Captain Phillips*），學習塑造產品的獨特性

篇章重點搶先看

1. 以《怒海劫》（*Captain Phillips*）主角菲利浦的經典台詞學習如何塑造產品的獨特性。
2. 以怒海劫主角菲利浦的台詞 “Leadership is not a position, but an action.”「領導不是一個地位，而是一種行動。」學習本單元核心句型：
   ★N is not a... but a...「N 是一種…，而不是一種…。」
3. 搭配學習本單元其他三大重點句型：
   a N+V for..., making... their...（N 為…而…，使…成為他們的…。）
   b Consider N is not only a... but a..., ...has... to choose（考量到…不僅是…還是…，…有…可供選擇）
   c Continuing the... of..., ...is used in...（延續…的…，…使用…）
4. 將四種句型放入實境對話練習，學習四大行銷概念：
   a 以聯想法（associative method）創造話題性。
   b 從行為區隔（behavior segmentation）找商品定位。
   c 以搭配性（collocability）提升購買意願。
   d 以設計理念（rationale of design）鮮明產品特質。

影片背景介紹

《怒海劫》（*Captain Phillips*）改編自理查菲利浦的真實故事。菲利浦是一艘貨船的船長，2009 年時他帶領船員自阿曼運送物資到肯亞。但在航經索馬利亞公海時，有兩艘載有武裝海盜的小船靠近。菲利浦用計擺脫其中一艘，但海盜首領所搭乘的小船依舊緊追不捨，最後強行登船。之後菲利浦遭海盜俘虜，雙方交涉後，船員同意支付三萬美元贖金換回船長。若將片中菲利浦表現其處變不驚的台詞，應用在商業行為上，其句構恰可做為我們學習如何塑造商品特殊性的良好教材。

Captain Phillips is adapted from the real story of Richard Phillips. Phillips is the captain of a container ship. In 2009, Phillips leads his seamen to ship goods from Oman to Kenya. When sailing by the high sea of Somalia, the vessel is chased by two small boats controlled by armed pirates. Phillips uses tricks to escape one, but the other is getting closer. Later this ship is seized by the pirates. Soon Phillips becomes the hostage, and his seamen agrees to pay 30000 USD ransom for the freedom of Phillips after long negotiation. If we apply the words the Phillips says that shows his calmness and leadership to the field of business, the structure turns out to be a good material for us to learn how to shape the uniqueness of a product or service.

看影片怎麼說、怎麼用

At the International conference room of ABC Company. CEO is going to have the presentation for the product release event.

（在 ABC 公司的國際會議廳。執行長即將在產品發表會上發表演說。）

CEO: All distinguished guests and the press, thank you for sparing your precious time to join our event today. Here, I represent ABC company to show our most sincere appreciation to you. Before I introduce our latest product today, I would like to share some thoughts with you. As running population grows year after year, people often say running is merely a sport. (1) But I would say running isn't just a sport but an **attitude**. People run for different purposes, and that is the **root** of design we put in this runner shoes. (2) Beginners run for exercise, making runner shoes their equipment. Advanced runners run for training, making runner shoes their tool to **pursue** the progress. Professional runners run for **glory**, making runner shoes their weapons to face the challenge. To meet the different needs of runners, this year we release three series runner shoes, RTB-880, RTB-770, and RTB-660 respectively. (3) Considering runner shoes are not only a

執行長：各位貴賓與媒體朋友，感謝您撥空參加我們今日的活動。於此僅代表 ABC 公司表達誠摯的謝意。在我向各為介紹產品之前，想先跟大家分享幾個想法。人們為了不同目的而跑。初學者會了運動而跑，跑鞋時他們的裝備；進階者為了為了訓練而跑，跑鞋是他們追求進步的工具;職業選手為了榮譽而跑，跑鞋是他們面對挑戰的武器。為了滿足不同跑者的需求，今年我們推出了三種跑鞋系列，分別是 RTB-880、RTB-770、RTB-660。另考量到很多跑者視跑鞋不僅為運動用品，還是時尚配件，所以每個系列都有五種配色可供選擇。我現在手上拿的是彩虹配色款，此款在旗艦店限定發售。為延續設計上的精

sports good but a fashion accessory for many runners, each model has five colors to choose. The one in my hand is rainbow RTB-660. The limited edition that is only available in our flagship store. (4) Continuing the soul of our design, composite martial is used in RTB 660 to provide the best support while running. In the upper part, we use fiber with high **breathing** to provide the most comfortable feeling for runners while running. And lastly, let me announce a good news. The listed price of our new shoes is ranged from 100 USD to 200 USD, but we will have a special discount of 20 percent off from today. It is time-limited, so don't miss it.

隨，RTB-660 使用了複合材質來提供跑步時的最佳支撐。鞋身使用透氣纖維，提供跑者跑步最舒適的穿著感。最後再跟各位說個好消息。我們鞋款的訂價在 100 美金到 200 美金之間，但我們從今天起推出八折優惠，這是期間限定的折扣，所以千萬別錯過了。

The press: Few questions here. You just said time- limited, but you don't tell us how long it will be. Does it mean the period has some **flexibility**? Secondly, do you have enough **inventory**, if some sizes are sold out during this period of time?

媒體提問：這邊有幾個問題想問。第一個是你剛提到期間限定，但你沒說時間是多常，是否代表說時間長短是有彈性的？第二個是如果在這段期間有些尺寸售完了，有足夠庫存可以補貨嗎？

CEO: Good questions. Your guess is right. We haven't decided the time **span** of this event, so we shorten or extend the time according to the reaction from the market. Secondly, we provide more than 5000 pairs this time. I think this amount is enough. What if the sales is better than we think. We place extra new orders to the factory. Here I promise all consumers can be freed from worrying this problem.

CEO：問的很好。你的猜測是對的。我們也尚未決定活動的時間長短，所以會根據市場反應縮短或是延長時間。關於第二個問題，我們準備了五千雙的備貨。這個數量我想是很充足的。如果市場反應超出預期的好，我們會向工場追加訂單。於此我向各位保證不用擔心缺貨。

1. **attitude** *n.* 態度

例：The attitude of the supervisor determines the direction of this projects.

主管的態度決定此專案的方向。

2. **root** *n.* 根本

例：The root of our business is to create a shoe for all.

我們事業的根本是做出適合所有人的鞋款。

3. **pursue** *v.* 追求

例：To pursue great profits, we have to review the location of the branches. 為了追求更高的獲利，我們必須檢討分店的選址。

MEMO

4. **glory** *n.* **榮耀**

例：Winning the golden medal in service is the highest glory of our company.

獲得服務金獎是本公司最大的榮耀。

5. **breathing** *n.* **透氣度**

例：The breathe determines the comfort of the shoe while running.

透氣度決定鞋子跑步時的舒適度。

6. **flexibility** *n.* **彈性**

例：We leave some flexibility in pricing.

我們對於定價保留了部分彈性。

7. **inventory** *n.* **存貨**

例：Since the sales is worse than we think, we need a warehouse to place the inventory.

由於銷售狀況不如預期，我們需要倉庫置放存貨。

8. **span** *n.* **範圍**

例：The scheduled time span of this promotion is one week.

表定的促銷時程是一週。

重點句型分析

1. **N is not a... but a...** 意思為「N 是一種…，而不是一種…」，可用於塑造或強化事物的某種特性。

   例：Change is not a slogan, but an action.
   改變是一種行動，而不是一種口號。

2. **N+V for..., making... their...** 意思為「N 為…而…，使…成為他們的…。」，可用於說明不同消費族群間的行為差異。

   例：Beginners play for fun, making rackets their entertainment equipment.
   初學者為好玩而打球，使球拍成為她們的娛樂設備。

3. **Consider N is not only a... but a..., ...has...to choose...** 意思為「考量到…不僅是…還是…，…有…可供選擇」，可用於說明產品的搭配性。

   例：Considering a notebook is not only a tool but an expression of taste, our ultrabook has four colors to choose from.
   考量到筆電不僅是工具也是品味的展現，我們的輕量化筆電有四種顏色可供選擇。

4. **Continuing the... of..., ...is used in...** 意思為「延續…的…，…使用…」，可用於說明設計上的延續性。

   例：Continuing the tradition of our design, rubber material is used in the bottom unit.
   延續設計上的傳統，底部的部分使用橡膠素材。

職場補給站

本單元以鞋業公司執行長擔任產品發表會主講人為場景，發展一段完整對話，其內容中一共提到四個行銷的常用概念，以下針對每個概念做進一步說明：

1. 以聯想法（associative method）創造話題性：

- 對應句型：**But I would say running isn't just a sport but an attitude. People run for different purposes, and that is the root of design we put in this runner shoes.**

  銷售商品時，產品的話題性高低足以左右銷售量。越有話題性的商品，越可能引起消費者的注意。運用聯想法，我們可以讓消費者去思考該想法與產品的關聯性。**在本範例中，執行長表示他認為跑步不是運動，而是一種態度，新產品也是依此概念做設計，成功開啟一個思考空間。**

2. 從行為區隔（behavior segmentation）找商品定位：

- 對應句型：**Beginners run for exercise, making runner shoes their equipment. Advanced runners run for training, making runner shoes their tool to pursue the progress. Professional runners run for glory, making runner shoes their weapons to face the challenge.**

  不同消費族群會有不同的行為表現，針對其行為打造商品方可投其所好。裝備類的產品，常根據使用者的操作專業程度分類。初學者版本功能基本，專業人士版本功能更齊全。**在本範例中，執行長提到公司對於新跑鞋的分類。初學者視跑鞋為裝備，進階者視跑鞋為工具，職業級視跑鞋為爭取榮耀的利器。**

3. 以搭配性（collocability）提升購買意願：

- 對應句型：**Considering runner shoes is not only a sports good but a fashion accessory for many runners, each model has five colors to choose.**

  當市場競爭激烈時，消費者選購商品時除考量功能外，搭配性也是重點。若此產品可以與其它產品相互搭配，其購買意願就會提高。**在本範例中，執行長提到公司的新跑鞋考量到許多跑者視跑鞋為時尚配件，所以每個系列都推出五種配色供消費者選擇。**

4. 以設計理念（rationale of design）鮮明產品特質：

- 對應句型：**Continuing the soul of our design, composite martial is used in RTB 660 to provide the best support while running. In the upper part, we use fiber with high breathe to provide the most comfortable feeling for runners while running.**

  在銷售商品時，特別是新品發表，強調設計理念可提高消費者對於產品的認識，進而有機會提高購買意願。**在本範例中，執行長提到本次鞋款延續過去的設計精神，鞋底使用複合材質加強支撐性，鞋身使用透氣纖維，提供最佳舒適感。**

看《控制》（*Gone Girl*），學習如何與其它公司建立夥伴關係

篇章重點搶先看

1. 以《控制》（*Gone Girl*）男主角尼克經典台詞學習如何與其它公司建立夥伴關係。
2. 以《控制》（*Gone Girl*）男主角尼克 "You don't calculate life, you live it; you don't test a relationship, you protect it."
   「生活是用來經營的，不是用來計較的；感情是用來維繫的，不是用來考驗的。」。學習本單元核心句型：
   ★ You don't..., you... it; you don't..., you... it「你不會⋯，你⋯；你不會⋯，你⋯。」
3. 搭配學習本單元其他三大重點句型：
   a Once we cooperate in..., the... can be reduced to...（當我們在⋯方面進行合作，⋯可以降低至⋯。）
   b Considering the..., people tend to... at the...（考慮到⋯，人們傾向在⋯。）
   c Sharing the goal of..., we shall...（同樣抱持⋯的目標，我們應當⋯。）
4. 將四種句型放入實境對話練習，學習四大行銷概念：
   a 以極大化（maximization）說明合作優點。
   b 以成本分攤（cost sharing）增加誘因。
   c 以地域區隔（geological segmentation）發展最適策略。
   d 以目標一致（goal congruence）確立進程。

影片背景介紹

《控制》(*Gone Girl*)改編自同名小說。主角尼克是寫作客的講師，女主角艾咪是知名童書的作者，兩人是對人人稱羨的夫妻，但在結婚五周年那天，尼克下班返家後發現愛咪無故失蹤了。為了找出原因，尼克請警方協助，卻發現各種證據都指向他就是兇手。這個事件引起媒體關注，尼克的醜聞被一一挖出，但這一切其實艾咪精心策劃的陰謀。若將片中尼克關於經營感情的台詞，應用在商業領域上，其句構洽為我們學習如何與其他公司建立夥伴關係的良好教材。

Gone Girl is adapted from the novel of the same name. Nick is a composition lecturer and Amy is the author of famous children's books. They are couples people envy. On their fifth marriage anniversary, Nick goes home after work but finds Amy is gone. To find what happened to Amy, Nick asks the police for help but finds all evidence indicates he's the murderer. This incident attracts the attention of the media. The scandals of Nick are revealed one after one. However, all schemes are Amy's conspiracy. If we apply the words that Nick says to express his true feeling toward love, the structure turns out to be a good material for us to learn how to establish the partnership with other companies.

看影片怎麼說、怎麼用

At the lobby of MGN Company.

（在 MGN 公司的大廳。）

Ashley: Good afternoon Jason, I am Ashley, Manager Owen's secretary. Mr. Owen is in the conference room. Please follow me.

Ashley：午安，Jason。我是 Owen 經理的秘書 Ashley。經理人已經在辦公室了，請跟我來。

Jason: OK.

Jason：好的。

Owen: Good afternoon, Jason. Actually, I am so surprised that ABC Company wants to cooperate with us. Now let's begin the issue we will cover today.

Owen：午安，Jason。事實上我很驚訝 ABC 公司會想與我們合作。現在就讓我們切入正題吧。

Jason: Though we have certain **fame** in our country, we are area **newbies** in this region. To have a stable foothold, we want to find a partner here. We often say "(1) You don't waste resources you have, you use it; you don't break partnership you establish, you trust it." The integration of our resource can bring greater benefit to us.

Jason：雖然我們在自己國內享有一些知名度，但在此區域是新手。為了要有穩固的立足點，我們想要尋找合作夥伴。人們常說：「你不會浪費手邊的資源，你使用它：你不會破或自己建立的夥伴關係，你信任它。」資源整合能讓我們享有更多利益。

Owen: Our business concentrates on the manufacturing of delicate machines for the **domestic** market, so I am wondering in what way we can become partners.

Owen：我們的事業主要集中在國內市場機密機械銷售，所以我非常好奇我們能怎樣地合作。

Jason: You just point out one key point: the domestic market. The **goodwill** you **accumulate** can be transformed into the **panacea** of cost reduction. (2) Once we cooperate in the machining field, the cost of each machine can be reduced to 8,000 USD due to our expertise in programming. Besides, the distance between we and consumers is important. (3) Considering the transportation, people tend to buy the product with the similar quality at the place with shorter delivery time. The location of your company can make us utilize this strength.

Jason：您剛提到重點了：國內市場。您所累積的商譽可已轉變降低成本的萬靈丹。一旦我們合作，每台機器的成本會因為我們在軟體上的專業降至 8000 美金。此外，我們與消費者的距離很重要；考量到交通時間，當兩個產品的品質相仿時，人們會選擇購買運送時間較短的那個。您的公司地點可讓此特性發揮到淋漓盡致。

Owen: A very **insightful** analysis. Now I am really interested in our possible cooperation. However, there are few questions I want to ask. Firstly, what is the **duration** of our cooperation? What is the specific coverage of our cooperation?

Owen：非常有洞察力的分析。現在我也很有興趣要與您合作。但這邊有幾個問題想請教。第一個，合作期程多長？第二個，確切的合作範圍是？

Jason: One year for the first cooperation. We can extend the duration to save the burden of signing contract every year if we establish a good partnership. About the coverage, CNC machine is one we are most interested in. (4) Sharing the goal of generating more profits, we shall finalize the signing of the contract soon.

Jason：首次合作是一年。但如果合作愉快的話，可以延長時程以免去年年重簽的麻煩。關於合作涵蓋部分，我們最有興趣的是 CNC 機台。同樣抱持著獲取更多利潤的目標，我們應該盡快完成簽約事宜。

對話單字說分明

1. **fame** *n.* 名氣

例：With low fame in this region, we need to launch a promotion campaign periodically.
在此地區默默無名，因此我們需要定期舉行促銷活動。

2. **newbie** *n.* 新手

例：As a newbie in this region, we need to get familiar with the market trend soon.
做為此區域的新手，我們需要趕快熟悉市場趨勢。

3. **domestic** *adj.* 國內的

例：Though we sell this product in the domestic market alone, its margin is still high. 雖然這個產品只內銷，但其利潤豐厚。

4. **goodwill** *n.* 商譽

例：Though the goodwill is invisible, its value is higher than you think.
商譽雖然無形，但其價值高到超乎你想像。

5. **accumulate** *v.* 累積

例：The publicity is accumulated by comments from the consumers.
知名度是從消費者的評論中所累積而來的。

6. **panacea** *n.* 萬靈丹

例：The discount is not the panacea of good sales figures, so you have to find the clear positioning of you product.
不是折扣就能有好銷售，你必須找到商品的清楚定位。

7. **insightful** *adj.* 有洞察力的

例：After hearing your insightful analysis, I think the project seems really feasible. 聽完你深具洞察力的分析，我覺得此專案似乎真的可行。

8. **duration** *n.* 期間

例：The duration of this contract is two year.
這份合約的有效期時間為兩年。

重點句型分析

1. **You don't..., you... it; you don't..., you... it...** 意思為「你不會…，你…；你不會…，你……」，可用於面對事物的態度。

   例：You don't question your faith, you trust it; you don't abandon your dream, you realize it.

   你不會質疑自己的信仰，你相信它；你不會遺棄自己的夢想，你實現它。

2. **Once we cooperate in..., the... can be reduced to...** 意思為「當我們在……方面進行合作，…可以降低至…。」，可用於合作後所能節省的時間量或是金錢總額。

   例：Once we cooperate in the manufacturing of CNC machine, the cost can be reduced to 10,000 USD per set.

   當我們能在在 CNC 機具的生產上合作，每組的成本可以較低至一萬美金。

3. **Considering the..., people tend to... at the...** 意思為「考慮到…，人們傾向在…」，可用於說明考量某因素後所做出的選擇為何。

   例：Considering the convenience of parking, people tend to eat at the restaurant with parking lot.

   若考量到停車的方便性，人們傾向去有停車場的餐廳吃飯。

4. **Sharing the goal of..., we shall...** 意思為「同樣抱持…的目標，我們應當…」，可用於基於何種目標，雙方所需擔負的責任與享受的義務。

   例：Sharing the goal of getting more market share, we shall cooperate rather than compete.

   同樣抱持獲得更高市佔率的目標，我們應該合作不是競爭。

本單元以外國公司尋求與本地公司合作為場景，發展一段完整對話，其內容中一共提到四個行銷的常用概念，以下針對每個概念做進一步說明：

1. 以極大化（maximization）說明合作之優點：

- 對應句型：**"You don't waste resource you have, you use it; you don't break partnership you establish, you trust it". The combination of our resource can bring greater benefit to us.**

  在商場上當兩間公司要合作時，其著眼點就在於資源的極大化。當此都覺得有利可圖，成為夥伴的機率就高，反之則討論破局。**在本範例中，Jason 提到商場上對於資源以及夥伴的看法。強調這兩者對企業非常重要，故希望能與 MGN 公司合作創造更多利益。**

2. 以成本分攤（cost sharing）增加誘因：

- 對應句型：**Once we cooperate in the machining field, the cost of each machine can be reduced to 8,000 USD due to our expertise in programming.**

  承接上段有利可圖的論述。利益有時只的不是銷售額提高，而是成本降低。這樣的差異同樣可以為公司帶來利潤，因此已分攤成本的概念去商談合作案，是一個可行的策略。**在本範例中，Jason 提到自家公司的程式設計專業，可讓夥伴的機器成本下降，希望藉此說服 MGN 與我方合作。**

3. 以地域區隔（geological segmentation）發展最適策略：

- 對應句型：**Considering the transportation, people tend to buy the product with the similar quality at the place with shorter delivery time. The location of you company can make us utilize this strength.**

　　地理上的限制有時也是影響銷售的關鍵因素。若兩個產品的品質設計都相仿，但其中一個因為工廠或是公司位置具消費者所在區域較近，到貨時間較快，消費者可能就選擇購買該產品。**在本範例中，Jason 就是闡述了上述的這個概念，認為 MGN 公司的選址能讓這個優是徹底發揮。**

4. 以目標一致（goal congruence）確立進程：

- 對應句型：**Sharing the goal of generating more profit, we shall finalize the signing of the contract soon.**

　　當洽談合作一切幾乎塵埃落定時，最後後的臨門一腳就是強調我們彼此的利益是一致的。透過這樣的話術，可以再次強化共同獲利的概念，離簽約又更進一步。**在本範例中，Jason 就是運用這樣的手法，提醒對方若彼此合意，就可盡速進行簽約是宜。**

看《悲慘世界》（*Les Misérables*），學習如何尋求合作

篇章重點搶先看

1. 以《悲慘世界》（*Les Misérables*）尚萬強經典台詞學習如何尋求合作。
2. 以《悲慘世界》（*Les Misérables*）尚萬強的台詞 "*A dream you dream alone is only a dream. A dream you dream together is reality.*"「一個人的夢只是夢，一群人的夢卻會成真」。學習本單元核心句型：
   ★A N you... alone is only a N. A N you... together is a...「一個人…的…只是…。很多人一起…的…是…。」
3. 搭配學習本單元其他三大重點句型：
   a When the... of... is integrated from... to..., the... of... can be...（若將…從…到…加以整合…，…的…可以…。）
   b Though the... of... is... if we..., what we are looking for is...（如果我們…，…的…會…，但我們真正所期待的是…。）
   c With the... utilized, ...is 比較級 than that of the...（善用…，…的…會比其它…都…。）
4. 將四種句型放入實境對話練習，學習四大行銷概念：
   a 以漸進主義（Incrementalism）深化合作之必要。
   b 以水平／垂直整合（horizontal/vertical integration）提升資源效能。
   c 以低價傾銷（dumping）取得初期市佔。
   d 以綜效（synergy）重申合作效益。

影片背景介紹

本片的原型是法國文豪所著的同名小說。尚萬強是一名法國囚犯，因偷麵包而入獄，服刑期滿後得以假釋，但因破壞了規矩而遭警探賈維爾追捕。為了躲避追緝，尚萬強隱姓埋名且重新做人。經過努力，他成為一名市長，並認識了身世淒慘的女工傅安婷，她過世前將女兒託孤珂賽特給尚萬強。若將片中尚萬強說明萬眾一心威力的台詞，應用在商業領域上，其句構為我們學習邀請合作的好教材。

Les Misérables is adapted from the musical play based on the novel of the same name written by Victor Hugo. Jean Valjean is sentenced a nineteen-year of jail for stealing a loaf of bread. After released, he is still chased by Javert because he breaks some rules of the prison. To avoid being captured. Jean hides and tries to begin a new life. Few years later, Jean becomes a mayor and meets Fantine, the female worker who has a miserable life. Before Fantine's death, she asks Jean to take care of her daughter, Cosette. If we apply the words that Jean says about the power of sharing the a goal, the structure turns out to a good material for us to learn how to seek for cooperation from others.

看影片怎麼說、怎麼用

At the conference room of ABC Company.

（在 ABC 公司的會議室。）

Jason: Thank you all for coming today. Since the competition has become fiercer, I think we should find a solution through cooperation. (1) A goal you pursue alone is only a goal. A goal you pursue together is a vision. Once we share the same goal, we can survive from this challenge through **continuous** modification.

Jason：感謝各位今日前來。由於競爭日間激烈，我想這需要透過合作來找出解決方法。一個人所追求的目標叫目標，很多人一起追求的目標叫做願景。當我們目標一致，就可以透過持續的修正來克服難關。

Brown: Each of us is **specialized** in a different field, so I am wondering how to find the best **portfolio** of the resource we have.

Brown：我們都有各自專精的領域，所以我非常好奇要如何找出這些現有資源的最佳組合。

Jason: Some of us is in the upper stream of the chain; while some in the downstream, so the **vertical** integration is needed. (2) When the supplier **chain** is integrated from the producer to the retailer, the margin of the product can be better.

Jason：我們有些是供應鏈的上游，有些是下游，所已需要垂直整合。當供應鏈從生產者到零售商都加以整合，商品的利潤可以更好。

Andy: The idea is good. But the products we sell are not **lavish** goods, the profit per unit is just so so. As a result, the integration is not that attractive to me.

Andy：這想法很好，但我們所銷售的產品並非奢侈品，所以單位利潤還好。所已對我而言，這個整合吸引力不大。

Jason: You are right. We can earn little per unit, but we should view it at a bigger **picture**. (3) The profit is bad if we sell it at this low price, and what we are looking for is the volume when consumers find it necessary to buy it all the time.

Jason：沒錯。每單位的利潤真的不多，但我們要以更宏觀的視野看待這點。如果以此價格販售，利潤真的不好，而我們所真正期待的是當消費者覺得有必要經常購買時所帶來的銷量。

Andy: I am too **shallow**. What I see is the small margin in front of us, but what you see is the bigger in a larger perspective.

Andy：我太膚淺了。我只看到眼前的蠅頭小利，你看到是豐厚利潤。

Jason: We are partners. True partner will find the best for the rest. Now we have trucking, packing, manufacturing, and selling businesses, making this combination comprehensive. (4) With the abovementioned elements being utilized, the competiveness of our product is much higher than that of our competitors.

Jason：我們是夥伴，真正的夥伴會替其他夥伴找到最好的事物。我們現在有貨運、包裝、生產與銷售的專業，組合相當具全面性。善用上述支元素，我們產品會比同業更具競爭力。

Brown: It seems we finally share the same goal. We can start the detailed discussion of each part. How about the manufacturing goes first?

Brown：看來我們終於目標一致了，可以進行細部討論。就從製造的部分先開始好嗎？

Andy: Sure. Let me briefly tell you all the current status. Please take a look at the screen.

Andy：當然可以。讓我先告訴大家一下我這邊的近況。請看一下螢幕。

對話單字說分明

1. **continuous** *adj.* **持續的**

例：If you want to keep the competiveness, continuous improvement with time is needed. 如要保持競爭力，與時進步是必要的。

2. **specialized** *adj.* **專門的**

例：As the manufacturer which specialized in shoes, our product can give your feet the best support.

做為專門生產鞋款的公司，我們的產品能給您的雙腳最好的支撐。

3. **portfolio** *n.* **組合**

例：To utilizes each penny in the capital, we have to find the best portfolio for our investment.

為了善用每一分資金，我們要去找出投資的最佳組合。

4. **vertical** *adj.* **垂直的**

例：The vertical integration can prevent the exploitation from happening.

垂直整合可避免剝削。

5. **chain** *n.* **鏈條**

例：To have a better margin, we integrate our downstream with the supply chain. 為了要有更好的獲利，我們整合供應鏈的下游。

6. **lavish** *adj.* **奢侈的**

例：With the lavish decoration like diamond and ruby on it, the price of this phone is sky high.

由於上有像鑽石與紅寶石這樣的奢侈裝飾，這隻手機的價格可謂天價。

7. **picture** *n.* **狀況**

例：If you want to have some breakthroughs in sales, you need to see it with a bigger picture.

如果你想要在銷售上有所突破，就要以更寬廣的視野看待它。

8. **shallow** *adj.* **膚淺的**

例：Being shallow will make you lose many good opportunities in investing. 膚淺會讓你錯失許多投資良機。

重點句型分析

1. **A N you... alone is only a N, A N you... together is a...** 意思為「一個人…的…只是…。很多人一起…的…是…」，可用於說明單打獨鬥與合作之間的差異。

   例：A change you make alone is only a change. A change you make together is a revolution.

   一個人做出的改變只是改變。很多人一起做的改變教做革命。

2. **When the... of... is integrated from... to..., the... of... can be...** 意思為「若將…從…到…加以整合…，…的…可以…。」，可用於說明水平獲垂直整合所帶來之效益。

   例：When the supplier is integrated from the upper stream to the downstream, the exploitation can be reduced to the lower level.

   若能將供應商從上游至下游加以整合，當中的剝削就可以降至最低。

3. **Though the... of... is... if we..., what we are looking for is...** 意思為「如果我們…，…的…會…，但我們真正所期待的是…」，可用於說明所帶的後續效益為何。

   例：Though the profit of this product is not that good if we sell it at this price, what we are looking for is the volume when people get used to it.

   如果我們賣這個價格的話，此商品的利潤會不高。但我們真正所期待的是當消費者養成習慣後所帶來的銷量。

4. **With the... utilized, the... of...is 比較級 than that of the...** 意思為「善用…，…的…會比其它…都…」，可用於說明資源整合所可獲得成果為何。

   例：With the trucking business being utilized, the freight of our product is much lower compared to that our competitors.

   由於善用貨運資源，我們產品的運費比同業的都還更低廉。

本單元以某公司尋求與上下游廠商進行整合為場景，發展一段完整對話，其內容中一共提到四個行銷的常用概念，以下針對每個概念做進一步說明：

1. 以漸進主義（Incrementalism）深化合作之必要：

- 對應句型：**A goal you pursue alone is only a goal. A goal you pursue together is a vision. Once we share the same goal, we can survive from this challenge through continuous modification.**

  漸進主義指的是好的決策是需要一定時間的修正所得來，而修正所花費的時間可透過合作來縮短。著眼與此點，當企業遭逢困難時，尋求與其它公司合作，可加快度過難關。**在本範例中，Jason 提到一個人的目標叫目標，很多人一起的目標叫願景，就是利用此概念來吸引進一步合作。**

2. 以水平／垂直整合（horizontal/vertical integration ）提升資源效能：

- 對應句型：**Some of us is in the upper stream of the chain while some in the downstream, so the vertical integration is needed. When the supplier chains are integrated from the producer to the retailer, the margin of the product can be better.**

  由於供應鏈中的每個環節都需要獲得利潤，上游難免會對下游家已剝削，因此當消費者購買產品時，其價格已經被提高許多。若要改善此情況，則須進行垂直整合，當整個供應鏈目標一致，利潤共享，成本自然下降，售價也降低，產品在市場的競爭力相對提升。**在本範例中，Jason 提到由於夥伴中有人屬上游，有人位下游，透過垂直整合可讓大家一起獲得更多利潤。**

3. 以低價傾銷（dumping）取得初期市佔：

- 對應句型：**Though the profit is bad if we sell it at this low price, what we are looking for is the volume when consumers find it necessary to buy it all the time.**

  在競爭激烈的市場，為求先行搶得一定市佔率，許多公司會採取低價策略。即便這樣的策略可能無利可圖甚至會虧錢，但因為可以取的一定的銷售量，各公司還是願意執行。等到消費者習慣這類商品後，在將其售價調高，賺回之前所虧損或是少賺的部分。**在本範例中，Jason 就是根據此原理向 Andy 解釋為何當前的低利潤是具有未來性的。**

4. 以綜效（synergy）重申合作效益：

- 對應句型：**With the abovementioned elements being utilized, the competiveness of our product is much higher than that of our competitors.**

  正所謂團結力量大，當多間公司能夠整合資源彼此合作，找出彼此的最佳定位，其績效肯定比單打獨鬥好。而這也是綜效最吸引人的地方。**在本範例中，Jason 提到目前夥伴都各具專業，善用其特長，可讓整體組合充滿競爭力。**

看《男人百分百》（*What Women Want*），學習闡述合作真意

篇章重點搶先看

1. 以《男人百分百》（*What Women Want*）主角尼克經典台詞學習如何闡述合作真意。
2. 以《男人百分百》（*What Women Want*）主角尼克的台詞 "The key to communication is hearing what's not being said."「溝通的關鍵在於，聽出那些沒說出來的話」。學習本單元核心句型：

   ★The key to... is Ving what is not being...「…的關鍵在於…那些沒…的…。」
3. 搭配學習本單元其他三大重點句型：

   a When assuming..., we will/won't（當我們假設…，就會…。）

   b Integrating..., we conclude...（彙整…，所得出的推論…。）

   c Feeling..., we take the action of...（感覺…，我們採取…的行動…。）
4. 將四種句型放入實境對話練習，學習四大商業概念：

   a 以積極傾聽（proactive listening）發現需求。

   b 以 APCFB 模型中的 A 與 P 解釋行為訊息接收層面。

   c 以 APCFB 模型中的 C 解釋行為的資訊彙整層面。

   d 以 APCFB 模型中的 F 與 B 解釋行為的行動面。

影片背景介紹

尼克是一間廣告公司的經理，離婚後與女兒同住。尼克是典型的大男人主義性格，造成他與女兒無法好好相處。尼克在工作上十分努力，期待自己有朝一日成為創意總監。但凡事豈如人意，由於公司認為女性才是消費主力，團隊需要一名懂得女性心理的主管，於是選擇挖角達西。兩人在個性上大相逕庭，工作上常會針鋒相對，但達西認為尼克其實相當有魅力。達西一上任就要求所有同仁嘗試推銷女性產品，這讓尼克大傷腦筋，他在試用吹風機時意外觸電昏倒，醒來後發現自己可以聽聞女性心聲的特殊能力。這項能力讓尼克在工作上一帆風順，還改善了兩性關係。若將片中尼克探討溝通的台詞，應用在商業領域上，其句構也可用來做為闡述合作真意的良好教材。

Nick is a manager in an advertisement company. He lives with his daughter after the divorce. Nick is the guy with male chauvinism, making him hard to get along well with his daughter. Nick works hard in his job, hoping one day he could become the Creative Director. However, things don't go the way he expects. The company owner assumes females are the group with the purchase power, so they hunt a female manager named Darcy. One day, when testing the hair dryer, Nick faints due to the electric shock. When Nick awakes, he finds that he can hear women's mind. This ability helps him a lot in his job as well as the relationship with female colleagues. If we apply the word that Nick says about the true meaning of communication to the business, the structure turns out to be a good material for us to learn how to illustrate the true definition of cooperation.

看影片怎麼說、怎麼用

At the coffee shop near ABC Company.

（在 ABC 公司附近的咖啡廳。）

Paul: Ann and Lydia has a serious **quarrel** few hours ago, what happened?

Paul：幾個小時前 Ann 和 Lydia 吵得不可開交，發生什麼事了？

Jason: I was there when the conflict occurred, and I **settled** everything down through a **psychological** way. (1) The key to observation is noticing what is not being shown. I carefully listened what they are arguing and found the key point to make the two parties calm down.

Jason：衝突發生時我在場，而且我用心理學的方式來化解爭執。觀察的關鍵就是注意到沒表現出的行為。我仔細聆聽他們爭執的內容，從中發現關鍵點，好讓雙方冷靜。

Paul: You are insightful. If I were you, I might not be able to end the argument and even make it worse.

Paul：你觀察的真深入，如果換做是我，可能無法化解爭執，甚至可能把情況弄得更糟。

Jason: Why I can make it is the usage of APCFB model for analysis. This model is consisted of five elements: A for assumption, P for **perception**, C for conclusion, F for feelings, and B for behaviors. Now I re-illustrate the whole story and how I use this model. The conflict is **triggered** by the improper information convey. Ann was waiting for the reply from PHA Company for

Jason：我成功的原因在於使用 APCFB 模型做分析。這個模型有五大要素：A 代表假設、P 代表認知、C 代表結論、F 代表感覺、B 代表行為。現在就讓我重述整個情況，以及我是如何使用該模型。事件起因於不當的訊息傳達。Ann 正在等

the final confirmation of the purchase amount. Lydia received the call from PHA Company when Ann left her desk. Not knowing the emergent degree of this matter, Lydia informs Ann the exact number they reply near the time when they are about to get off work. Ann blamed Lydia for this, and they argued. If we apply the model to this situation, it can be used as follow. (2) When assuming the call is not that important, we will put it **aside**. That is how Ann's assumption affected her perception. (3) Integrating the information like that, we will not inform the person in charge immediately. That is why Lydia waited until the time to get off work to tell Lydia. (4) Feeling disrespected, we take the action of blaming. That how Ann felt influenced how she acted. The **fundamental** reason of this conflict is the gap of the perception, so I asked Lydia and Ann to find a solution for this to avoid repeating the same mistake. Lydia promised that she won't make a **judgment** without asking. Ann indicated that she will be more patient and careful. The conflict is finally settled down.

PHA 公司對於採購數量做最後確認。Lydia 在 Ann 離開座位時接到 PHA 公司來電。但因為不知道事情的緊急程度，到快下班才跟 Ann 講確切的數量。Ann 責備 Lydia，兩人開始爭吵。如果把此模型應用在此情況，方式如下。當我們覺得某通電話重要性不高，我們接完電話會擱置不理。這也是安的假設如何影響其認知。整合類似這類的訊息後，我們不會馬上去聯絡負責人。這也是 Lydia 拖到快下班才跟 Ann 講的原因。當我們覺得不受尊重時，我們會去罵人，這也是 Ann 的感受影響到其行為。此衝突的根本原因在於認知落差，因此我請 Ann 和 Lydia 為此種情況找到一個解決方法，以避免重蹈覆轍。Lydia 保證未來不會自作主張，Ann 也表示自己未來也會更有耐心與細心。衝突就這樣圓滿落幕。

Paul: I really learn a lesson today.

Paul：我今天真的獲益良多。

對話單字說分明

1. **quarrel** *n.* **爭執**

例：Emotional words are often the reason of a quarrel.
情緒性字眼常是導致爭執的原因。

2. **settle** *v.* **處理**

例：To settle down the conflict, we should find the cause first.
為了要化解衝突，要先去找出其發生原因。

3. **psychological** *adj.* **心理學的**

例：Through psychological analysis, we can interpret consumer behaviors in a scientific way.
透過心理分析，我們可以用科學的方式解讀消費者行為。

4. **perception** *n.* **認知**

例：The project fails due to our wrong perception in the durability of the parts. 專案失敗是因為我們對於零件耐用度的錯誤認知。

5. **trigger** *v.* **引發**

例：The cut-throat competition is triggered by the relaxation of restriction of foreign capital. 外資的放寬引發割喉競爭。

6. **aside** *adv.* **在旁邊**

例：If the task is not put in the priority, the chance is high to be put aside.
如果這工作沒在優先順序內，被擱置的機會很高。

7. **fundamental** *adj.* **根本的**

例：The fundamental reason of the drop in sales figure is financial recession. 銷售數字下滑的根本原因是經濟衰退。

8. **judgment** *n.* **判斷**

例：We face a great loss due to the wrong judgment we make in the real estate investment.
我們因為地產投資上的錯誤判斷而蒙受鉅額損失。

重點句型分析

1. **The key to... is Ving what is not being...** 意思為「…的關鍵在於…那些沒…的…」，可用於說明有效完成某事的關鍵因素為何。

   例：The key to service is noticing what is not being shown.
   服務的關鍵在於發現那些沒有被表現的需求。

2. **When assuming..., we will/won't...** 意思為「當我們假設…，就會…」，可用於說明假設如何影響認知。

   例：When assuming the formula is questionable, we will doubt the correctness of the financial report.
   當我們假設公式有問題時，就會對財務報表有所質疑。

3. **Integrating..., we conclude...** 意思為「彙整…，所得出的結論是…」，可用於說明再整合假設與認知的資訊過後，所得出的結論。

   例：Integrating the reference of the formula, we conclude that the depreciation shall be included.
   彙整關於公司的參考資料後，所得出的結論是折舊應被納入考慮。

4. **Feeling..., we take the action of...** 意思為「感覺…，我們採取…的行動」，可用於說明得出結論後，內心的感受為何，以及會採取怎樣的後續行動。

   例：Feeling upset, we take the action of blaming the Financial Advisor.
   覺得不高興，我們去責備理專。

本單元以處理公司內部衝突為場景，發展一段完整對話，其內容中一共提到四個組織行為的常用概念，以下針對每個概念做進一步說明：

1. 以積極傾聽（proactive listening）發現需求：

- 對應句型：**The key to observation is noticing what is not being shown. I carefully listened what they are arguing and found the key point to make the two parties to calm down.**

  在商場上不論是擔任上司還是下屬，認真傾聽都是非常重要的。懂得傾聽才能注意到話語之間的弦外之音，進行更有效的溝通。**在本範例中，Jason 表示他解決同事衝突的關鍵就是注意到對話中的細節，使雙方冷靜，避免不良溝通持續。**

2. 以 APCFB 模型中的 A 與 P 解釋訊息接收層面：

- 對應句型：**When assuming the call is not that important, we will put it aside. That is how Ann's assumption affected her perception.**

  APCFB 模型中的 A 與 P 分別代表假設（assumption）和認知（perception）。根據此模型的設定，當某人有某種假設時，其大腦會受到此假設影響，而出現某種認知。

3. 以 APCFB 模型中的 C 解釋行為的資訊彙整層面：

- 對應句型：**Integrating the information like that, we will not inform the person in charge immediately. That is why Lydia waited until the time to get off work to tell Lydia.**

  APCFB 模型中的 C 代表結論（assumption）。根據此模型的設定，當大腦綜合假設與認知的資訊後，就會形成結論。這個結論又在影響模型中的最後兩個環節。**在本範例中，整合上述訊息後，Lydia 得到的結論是並非急事，所以沒有馬上告知負責的 Ann。**

4. 以 APCFB 模型中的 F 與 B 解釋行為的行動面：

- 對應句型：**Feeling disrespected, we take the action of blaming. That is how Ann felt influenced how she acted.**

APCFB 模型中的 F 與 B 分別代感覺（feelings）和行為（behaviors）。根據此模型的設定，當大腦產生結論時，會連帶產生心理上的某種感覺，而這個感覺影響最後的行為。**在本範例中，Ann 認為 Lydia 的舉動是種不尊重對方的表現，因此責備她。**

MEMO

看《魔球》（*Moneyball*），學習如何帶領團隊

篇章重點搶先看

1. 以《魔球》（*Moneyball*）男主角比利經典台詞學習如何帶領團隊。
2. 以魔球男主角比利台詞 “Winning games is easy; winning hearts is not.” 「贏幾場球，得來容易；贏得大家的心，談何容易」。學習本單元核心句型：
   ★Ving N... is...; Ving N is not「…很…；…很不…。」
3. 搭配學習本單元其他三大重點句型：
   a Feeling confident in..., you can... without（對…有信心，你可以不用…就…。）
   b As long as the... can be Ved, I accept the... in...（只要能夠…，我接受在…上做任何…。）
   c If..., the... is waiting for you.（如果…，…在等著你。）
4. 將四種句型放入實境對話練習，學習四大商業概念：
   a 以同理心（empathy）取代權威。
   b 以賦予能力（empowerment ）提高員工熱忱。
   c 以目標管理（MBO）釋放執行權限。
   d 以獎勵制度（rewarding）提升團隊效能。

影片背景介紹

本片改編自同名書籍。故事敘述美國職棒大聯盟奧克蘭運動家隊總經理比利比恩如何帶領球隊創造連勝紀錄。若將片中比利關於如何帶領球隊的台詞應用在商業領域上，實為我們學如何表達帶人首重帶心的良好教材。

This movie is adapted from the book of the same name. The story is about how Billy Beane, the General Manager of Oakland Athletics have successive winnings. If we apply the words that Billy says about how to lead a team to the business field, they turn out to be good materials for us to learn how to lead a team well.

看影片怎麼說、怎麼用

At the conference room of ABC Company.

（在 ABC 公司的會議室。）

Jason: As the new leader of this team, today I would like to have some discussions concerning the ways I will **adopt** in leadership in the future. (1) Winning your submission is easy; winning your respect is not. I hope we can work in harmony all the time.

Jason：做為團隊的新主管，我想跟各位討論一下關於未來我會採用的領導方式。要讓各位屈服於我很容易，但要各位尊敬我不容易。我希望我們可以總是在工作上保持和諧。

Lisa: In the past, the **hierarchy** is obvious. The boss is the decision maker and we the executers. Does this mode continue?

Lisa：過去我們的階級觀念很明顯，老闆就是決策者，我們是執行者。這樣的模式會有所變動嗎？

Jason: I view my employees as my friends. True friends don't question each other. (2) Feeling confidence in your professional judgment, I think you can take the action without waiting for my **permission** if needed in the future. Being open and trusting the profession are the two pillars of my management.

Jason：把我的員工當作朋友。朋友不會相互質疑。我對各位的專業判斷有信心，如有在實務上有需要，你可以不請示我就直接執行。開放態度與專業至上是我管理上的兩大台柱。

Lisa: Though we enjoy more **authorization** in decision making, it also means we have to take more responsibility, right?

Lisa：雖然我們在決策上獲得較多權限，但這也代表需擔負更多責任對吧？

Jason: Right. Power and responsibility are the two sides of the one coin. When you are able to decide something, you should be responsible for your decision. Try to be **brave** to shoulder the responsibility because you can get the reward from the right decision you have made.

Jason：沒錯，權力與責任是一體兩面。當你由權決定某事、你就必須為這個決定負責。請勇於承擔責任，因為正確決定能讓你獲得獎賞。

Lisa: Indeed. But one thing I am still wondering now is the scope of the authorization. Under what kind of circumstance should we report it to you?

Lisa：的確是。但有個地方我還是有疑問，就是授權的範圍。何種情況下我們需要向您報告呢？

Jason: Unless the **seriousness** is above certain level or finding that you have no authorization in the problem you are facing, you can decide what to do for the rest

Jason：除非事態相當嚴重，或是你發現自己無權處理此事，其他的所有情況你都可以全權處理。只要能夠

situation on your own. (3) As long as the goal can be reached, I accept any changes made by the actions you take.

達成目標，我可以接受在方法上做改變。

Lisa: I see. About the rewarding, what kind of **mechanism** will be applied?

Lisa：了解了。在獎勵部分，會採用何種機制呢？

Jason: This mechanism will be divided into three parts: monthly, **successive**, and annul. (4) If you reach the monthly goal, the reward of 200 USD is waiting for you. If you reach the monthly goal for the successive months, the seasonal reward of 800 USD is waiting for you. If you reach all monthly goals in a year, the annul reward 5,000 USD is waiting for you. In other words, you earn another 10,600 USD, if you have a good performance every month.

Jason：這個機制可以分為三大部分：月獎金、連續獎金與年度獎金。如果你達到月目標，200 美金等著你。如果連續三個月達月目標，800 美金的季獎金再等著你。如果全年都達到月目標，5000 美金的年度獎金在等著你。換句話說，若你的績效良好，你就能得到10,600 元美金。

Lisa: It sounds so attractive. I should work ever harder from now on.

Lisa：還真吸引人。我要更認真工作了。

Lesson 31
Lesson 32
Lesson 33
Lesson 34
Lesson 35
Lesson 36

對話單字說分明

1. **adopt** *v.* 採用

   例：If you want to solve this problem, adapting the new method is crucial. 如要解決此問題，需要採用新方法。

2. **hierarchy** *n.* 階層

   例：With a clear hierarchy, each department has their own duties.
   階級分明，各部門各司其職。

3. **permission** *n.* **允許**

例：Accessing this data shall get the permission from the General Manager first. 存取此資料需要獲得總經理的許可。

4. **authorization** *n.* **授權**

例：Without your authorization, I can't start the plan.
沒有你的授權，我無法開始本計畫。

5. **brave** *adj.* **勇敢的**

例：Be brave to face the competition.
請勇敢面對競爭。

6. **seriousness** *n.* **嚴重性**

例：Do not underestimate the seriousness of the signal abnormality.
別低估訊號異常的嚴重性。

7. **mechanism** *n.* **機制**

例：This mechanism is developed to face the fiercer competition.
發展此機制是為了應付更激烈的競爭。

8. **successive** *adj.* **連續的**

例：If the sales figures can reach 10,000 in coming successive months, we will launch a special discount as the feedback to the consumers.
如果銷售數字連續三個月破 1 萬美金，我們會舉辦特惠回饋消費者。

重點句型分析

1. **Ving N... is...; Ving N is not...** 意思為「…很…；…很不…」，可用於說明做到某事的難易程度。

例：Remembering the general is easy; remembering the detail is not.
記住大概很容易，記住細節很不容易。

2. **Feeling confident in..., you can... without...** 意思為「對…有信心，你可以不用…就…。」，可用於說明上司對於下屬能力的信任

例：Feeling confident in your analysis, you can execute the project without asking me in advancc.
對你的分析有信心，你可以不先詢問我就直接執行專案。

3. **As long as the...can be Ved, I accept any......** 意思為「只要能夠…，我接受在…上做任何…」，可用於說明在某種前提下所能接受的改變範圍。
例：As long as the product can be shipped in time, I accept any extra charge in the freight.
只要貨品能夠準時出貨，我接受任何運費加價。

4. **If..., the...is waiting for you...** 意思為「如果…，…在等著你」，可用於說明達成目標後所可獲得的獎勵。
例：If you can reach the expected goal this money, the free employee trip is waiting for you.
如能達成本月預計目標，免費員工旅遊在等著你。

職場補給站

本單元以上司獎勵員工為場，發展一段完整對話，其內容中一共提到四個行銷的常用概念，以下針對每個概念做進一步說明：

1. 以同理心（empathy）取代權威：

- 對應句型：**Wining your submission is easy; winning your respect is not. Wining your submission is easy; winning your respect is not. I hope we can work in harmony all the time.**

在領導統御中，威權式管理雖能夠掌控團隊動向，但因為上司下屬的互動並不良好，容易產生摩擦。相反地，若主管能夠替下屬著想，整個團隊的工作氣氛可以更好。**在本範例中，Jason 表示帶人首重帶心，讓員工屈服很容易，但贏得員工尊敬並不容易。希望未來上下可以一心，工作愉快。**

Lesson 31
Lesson 32
Lesson 33
Lesson 34
Lesson 35
Lesson 36

2. 以賦予能力（empowerment ）提高員工熱忱：

- 對應句型：Feeling confidence in your professional judgment, you can take the action without asking me in advance if needed in the future.

  不同於權威式管理上對下的命令方式，成果導向管理對於激發員工對於工作的熱忱較有助益。在此模式下，員工會覺得自己的能力獲得重視，而更願意為公司付出。**在本範例中，Jason 提到他信任下屬的能力，所以授權他們可以依照自身專業判斷，執行必要動作，毋須請示。**

3. 以目標管理（MBO）釋放執行權限：

- 對應句型：Unless the seriousness is above certain level or finding that you have no authorization in the problem you are facing, you can decide what to for the rest situation on your own. As long as the goal can be reached, I accept any changes made by the actions you take.

  目標管理（Management by Objective）指的是上司告知某一目標後，下屬可自由決定實際執行方式，上司最後只針對成效加以評估，不問過程。在此模式下，下屬有極大的操作彈性，但也相對的必須對於市場有相當程度的了解，才能得心應手。**在本範例中，Jason 提到除非事態非常嚴重，或是該情況超過自身權限，其他所有狀況都與以全權授權，他只在意最後能否達成既定目標。**

4. 以獎勵制度(rewarding)提升團隊效能:

- 對應句型:**If you reach the monthly goal, the reward of 200 USD is waiting for you. If you reach the monthly goal for the successive months, the seasonal reward of 800 USD is waiting for you. If you reach all monthly goals in a year, the annul reward 5,000 USD is waiting for you.**

做為團隊的領導者,建立適當的獎勵制度是必要。透過這樣的機制,表現優良的員工可獲得薪水之外的獎賞做為其努力的回報。**在本範例中,Jason 表示公司的獎金制度共分為月獎金、連續獎金與年度獎金三種。月獎金是 200 美金,連續獎金是 800 美金,年度獎金是 5,000 美金。**

MEMO

Leader 021

36計生意英語溝通術：藏在電影裡的教戰策略

作　　者　邱佳翔
封面構成　高鍾琪
內頁構成　菩薩蠻數位文化有限公司

發 行 人　周瑞德
企劃編輯　饒美君
校　　對　陳欣慧、陳韋佑
印　　製　大亞彩色印刷製版股份有限公司
初　　版　2015 年 6 月
定　　價　新台幣 349 元
出　　版　力得文化
電　　話　(02) 2351-2007
傳　　真　(02) 2351-0887
地　　址　100 台北市中正區福州街 1 號 10 樓之 2
E-mail　best.books.service@gmail.com

港澳地區總經銷　泛華發行代理有限公司
地　　址　香港新界將軍澳工業邨駿昌街 7 號 2 樓
電　　話　(852) 2798-2323
傳　　真　(852) 2796-5471

國家圖書館出版品預行編目(CIP)資料

36計生意英語溝通術：藏在電影裡的教戰策略 / 邱佳翔著. -- 初版. -- 臺北市：力得文化, 2015.06
面；　公分. -- (Leader；21)
ISBN 978-986-91458-9-3(平裝)
1.商業英文 2.讀本

805.18　　104009244